DEMPRESS

ANASTASIYA SERADA

Let it all burn to ashes

ONE

PAGE.

A small ray of early morning light entered the room through the tightly curtained window and landed directly in Page's eyes, waking her up. She squinted against it and groaned. The room was still cool and fresh. The July sun had not yet heated up the air. Page stretched, and in the morning silence, she heard the crunch of clean bed linens like the sound of footsteps in the snow on a frosty but sunny day. The room was still asleep. An open book lay beside the bed. The floral pattern of the wallpaper was barely distinguishable in the almost total darkness.

Someone timidly knocked on the door. An elderly woman of short stature, with her gray hair in a bun and sun-kissed skin, stuck her head through the slightly open door. "Good morning, Princess," the woman whispered, her voice light and murmuring, sounding much younger than her seventy years.

"Still so early." Page sighed and pulled the blanket over her head.

Matilda, Page's lady's maid, entered with a smile on her face and went straight to the window, letting the gentle rays of sunshine into the room. Then, without hesitation, she pulled the blanket off Page in one quick movement.

"Okay, I'm getting up." Page frowned.

"The Princess of Wands should set an example for the whole Arcana, Sparkle. I think you need to show your father you're back to normal." Matilda's voice was a spiky staccato.

Matilda had called her Sparkle ever since she was Page's governess. The wands energy in Page's family manifested through their eyes—only instead of fiery eyes, like the rest of her family had, Page's were crystalline. It was one of the many ways she was different from everyone else.

"I'll show him." Page pouted with her lips. "I have a busy day, so I should get up anyway. Gaia's having her first big fashion show. I hope I'll finally get to meet and photograph the majors. Apart from Justice, of course. She can go to hell."

In a split second, Page's mood changed dramatically. Even though half a year had passed already since her return, she couldn't erase from her memory the years spent in Justice's dimension. And most importantly, what those years represented: her darkness, her inability to control wands energy.

A small flame lit up in her palm, and she quickly blew on it. "Stupid fire," Page muttered. "Don't tell my parents, please. They believe I've learned how to control my energy."

"You'll learn," Matilda said gently, staring at her palm. "So, who is coming to the show?"

"I think Sun and Star will come. And hopefully Empress. I heard she is so beautiful, people go speechless!" Page daydreamed, still sitting on the bed with her legs dangling, and unsuccessfully trying to unwind her long, curly hair, the color of a full moon.

"Haven't you heard?" Matilda bit her lip. "Sorry, I guess there's no way to receive news in Justice's dimension." Her voice dropped to a whisper, as if they might be overheard. "Empress has disappeared, and her dimension is empty. Maybe the deck has finally been reshuffled after so many years. It would mean big changes are coming. But only High Priestess knows for sure."

Page was silent for a while. Of course, she hadn't heard any news. Justice's dimension was a literal prison. All day long, Page had sat, the same as the other prisoners, in her snow-white room, staring at the walls, allowed to go out only once a day for a short walk. No visits, no news, no life. Page sighed heavily, pushing away the terrible memories.

"It's a pity. I've always liked Empress. Well, hopefully the rest of the majors will come." Page lay down again under the covers.

"Better without Devil. His demons are constantly spinning around him, looking for souls to tempt," her lady's maids whispered, her voice tinged with fear. "Now, quit chatting me up!" Matilda threw up her hands. "Come on!"

Page walked over to the bathtub made of amber and slowly sank into the hot water sprinkled with drops of peony oil. Her olive skin sent out small flames, making the water even hotter. She was the only one in the family, and in all minor courts, whose energy seeped through her whole body. No one else had real magic— not counting the majors, of course. They had magic according to their tarot card characteristics, ruling over minors as gods from their dimensions.

Matilda sat down next to Page's head and slowly combed her hair. The quiet sounds of nature reigned in the room. The quiet splashing of the water intertwined with the singing of the birds outside the open window.

"Serene." Page took a deep breath of already heated air and sank under the water.

<hr>

Page worked as a photographer for a fashion magazine owned by her mother, the Queen of Wands. Photography was one of the things Page had missed the most while she was in Justice's eleventh dimension.

She opened the drawers of a huge dresser and began to look for today's outfit: a short beige dress decorated with crystals in the form of flowers, with an open back, perfectly emphasizing her tiny waist, round hips, and smooth olive skin. Matilda already held a jewelry box open.

"Today, just this one." Page reached for the large diamond ring that her mother had given her last month on her twenty-fifth birthday. The royal families didn't live forever, but time passed much slower for them than for the rest of the minors. So, technically, Page was much older than her official age. It was frustrating that after all these years, she still had so little control over her fire.

The princess looked at herself in the mirror and smiled approvingly, then kissed Matilda and headed downstairs to the summer garden, where the royal family had breakfast together every morning.

"Good morning." Page sat down in the chair next to her brother.

The Prince of Wands looked disheveled. Most likely, he'd just returned from yet another party.

"You're late, as usual." The Queen of Wands raised an eyebrow and looked disapprovingly at her daughter.

"I believe I'm always on time, Mother," Page protested playfully and turned to their butler with a charming smile. "Coffee and peanut butter toast, please, Ricardo."

"Just a second." The butler disappeared into the kitchen.

"You won't eat anything normal?" The Queen of Wands raised her other eyebrow, and her eyes filled with fiery judgment. The queen was a striking woman with black hair, dressed in a long lava-red dress with a large cutout on her chest.

"Not this early." Page glanced around at the teeming table: several cakes with lots of cream, two baskets of bread, eggs, juice, chicken, turkey, a basket of fruits, and butter and jam. "Plus, I'm meeting Aqua and Gaia at the restaurant."

"Who are they?" The King of Wands appeared from behind a huge newspaper that had been covering his entire face.

"I've told you a million times: the Princess of Cups and the Princess of Pentacles. We were friends even before I got taken away." Page rolled her eyes.

"You must avoid going out too often. Rumors about you have already spread all over Arcana again," the king insisted. "Don't forget, Justice is still watching you."

"Yes, imprison me in this house, just like she did!" Rebellious fire flashed in her eyes.

Page took a deep breath, afraid that her body would catch fire. She couldn't have that—not now. She had to prove that she was a different person from the girl she'd been seven years ago. When Page had been taken, she was furious, spewing fire like the crater of an awakened volcano. But weeks and years had passed, and her energy calmed down. And not because she'd learned how to control it, as Justice and her parents thought. Life had become so pale and meaningless that indifference was the only emotion that filled Page's empty soul, drowning out even her fire.

"That's not what your father meant," the queen sang softly. "I also do not approve of friendship between Arcana. Much better to have friends from your own court."

"Friends aren't against the law. I'm not dating or marrying anyone outside our court," Page reasoned.

"I hope not. Violating a law that the major of the Blank Dimension proclaimed when he won the war would be a terrible idea, and I feel sorry for anyone who does so."

"What would happen?" Page looked out of the corner of her eye at her brother, who was clutching his glass so tightly, she could count all the veins on his hand. She knew that the Prince of Wands and Aqua liked each other, and despite the fact that such relationships were forbidden, they were secretly dating.

"Why would you even ask something like this? Save us, Sun!" the Queen of Wands pleaded, opening her fan, decorated with flames. She began fanning herself with it as if she were running out of air.

"Just wondering. You know my opinion about the laws, Mother." Page shrugged.

"If the majors find out about the violation of one of the main laws, then Justice herself would descend from her eleventh dimension to decide the fate of the criminal."

"Just like she did with me." Page's voice echoed through the garden.

"You're back home with us, daughter. It's time to forget this tragic incident," the Queen of Wands said hesitantly.

Deathly silence descended on the summer garden, and Page sighed sadly. "I have to go." She kissed her mother and brother before heading out the door.

"Don't forget to control your fire! And try not to stand out," the King of Wands ordered, staring at Page. "You could dye your hair black to be like the rest of us, as I've insisted many times."

Page's moon-colored hair had been a source of contention with her father ever since she came back from Justice's dimension. He wanted her to blend in. But all Page wanted was to control her energy. Her eyes and hair had nothing to do with it. She knew there was no point in answering, and instead she hurried out of the garden.

"Don't forget to stop by the High Priestess's shop!" the Queen of Wands shouted after her.

"La Papesse just wants to spy on us to keep us under control!" Page yelled without turning around.

High Priestess, also known as La Papesse, was the major of the second dimension. She had a special connection to the tarot universe, to its shuffling, to its sacred knowledge and veiled secrets.

As a gift and to provide guidance to the royal families, High Priestess had opened a tarot shop in Minor Arcana. Page was required to have a reading every week —another "benefit" of her dark past. The rest of the minors had to come only once a month. The driver parked on the opposite side of the street, and Page carefully crossed the road and opened the door. The air in the room was thick with spices—notes of wild berries, musk, and mystery. The racks were filled with vials of potions, amulets, and relics for sale. They even sold animal parts for witchcraft. Since childhood, Page had always been a little afraid of this place.

"Good morning, Agatha!" Page's voice sounded like a bell ringing in the middle of a thick forest.

When Page didn't get a response, she headed to the far corner, where Agatha, the right hand of La Papesse, usually did readings. The fortune teller was sitting at the table, shuffling her sacred cards. The small deck was a representation of the universe itself. High Priestess used this deck to interpret and predict what was going to happen in the big deck: the tarot universe.

Agatha looked almost like High Priestess herself in the portrait hanging on the wall behind her, wearing a long blue robe and a cross on her chest. Page pulled back the chair carefully, trying not to make any noise. Agatha shuffled the sacred deck for a long time before she laid it out on the table.

"Pick a card, and hand it to me without looking," Agatha said, extremely serious.

"I know the drill." Page stared at the deck for a while and then finally chose a card right from the middle. "What is it today? Seven of Pentacles? You see, I'm very busy at work. Or maybe Three of Cups? We're having some kind of party tonight."

"The Fool. Major arcana," the fortune teller said in a mystical voice and looked Page straight in the eyes for the first time since she'd arrived. Her level gaze made Page uncomfortable, and she cleared her throat, clasping her hands in front of her.

"I've never drawn a major arcana card before. What does it mean?"

"The journey to your destiny has begun." The reader's voice seemed distant, and she no longer looked at Page.

"Okaaaay…" Page frowned. So much for hoping that her journey had actually finished when Justice finally allowed her to go back home to the Wands Arcana.

Instead of explaining, Agatha collected the cards and looked at the bottom of the deck. Page knew that the last card in the spread was just as important as the one she chose, but Agatha had never shown her the last card.

"It's not supposed to be clear. Come back tomorrow. Good day." Agatha got up and went into the next room.

Tomorrow? Soon they'll tell me to come three times a day! Page was outraged by the fact that she was still under Justice's close watch. Page was sure it was Justice who had told Agatha she needed more readings than the rest of the minors.

Page waited a couple of seconds before picking up the tarot deck and flipping it over. Her blood froze immediately. A creature with bat wings and ram horns looked Page straight in the eyes. It was the fifteenth card of the major arcana: Devil. He was one of the most feared majors, because he was mystery and sin itself, and he rarely descended to the Minor Arcana from his dimension. He was wrapped in a fog of enigma. Placing the card carefully back, Page nervously headed toward the exit, wondering what such a card meant for her. *Demons… That's the last thing I need.*

TWO

BAPHOMET.

Baphomet woke up to a foreign smell penetrating every cell of his skin and twisted his face in displeasure. He opened his raven eyes, faded in loneliness, and looked around the huge hotel suite. It felt empty and soulless. The scent was coming from a naked girl who was still sleeping next to him. It was like this every time. Spending a night with some girl was one thing, but waking up next to them immersed his soul in the unbearable hopelessness of his immortal existence. And their smell… His body refused to accept the scent of any girl he had been with. Strength, his customary paramour, was tolerable, but only because her immortal energy slightly overpowered her true animal-like aroma.

Baphomet got dressed automatically, and in a few minutes, he was already flying in his chariot, overtaking the sunrise.

His devoted servant was waiting for him at the entrance of the dark castle. "Master, welcome back." Oliver bowed with a sad smile. "Breakfast?"

"After I take a shower." Baphomet hurried upstairs. "You can set the table."

Baphomet slowly sipped his coffee as usual, looking at the portraits of the demons on the wall. They were his only company. Centuries had passed, and the Wheel of Fortune had turned countless times, shuffling the tarot universe, but his life remained the same, filled only with punishment, addictions, and damned souls.

"Master, do you wish to look at the invitations?" Oliver had placed at least twenty envelopes on a small tray.

"No." Baphomet didn't even look.

There had been a time, though it was long ago, when Baphomet believed that the deck held something more for him than just his duty as the major Devil. He had been naive enough to hope he could find someone with whom he would want to start a family, maybe have children one day. But ultimately, he'd realized that the deck was cruel. Baphomet could spend time with a woman only while using his magical ashes to block her scent for a bit, let alone leaving together. And after Abyss, the major of the Blank Dimension, had won the war and imposed the law about children, he'd finally accepted that he was destined to remain truly alone forever.

"If I may, Master." Oliver carefully handed him one of the envelopes. "This one is not a dinner. It's a fashion show by an aspiring and promising designer. Lots of majors will be there, including Chariot and Lover."

"Hmm..." Devil glanced at the invitation for a moment. "No."

"Master..." Oliver hesitated. "I took the liberty of asking the fortune teller to do a reading." The man lowered his eyes. "Agatha insisted you must go."

"Did she, now?" Baphomet hid his smile. "All right, Oliver, but only this time."

Oliver seemed to be the only one who had never lost hope. He constantly tried to insist on Baphomet attending some events, hoping his master's lonely destiny could change.

"Yes, my Lord." Oliver beamed.

Baphomet drove his matte-black car to the event, still not sure why he had agreed to go. Lately, he'd left his dimension less and less, preferring to avoid everyone. Life had lost its flavor. His relationship with Strength had long strained him more than it pleased him. It could never be more than sex. Months could pass without him seeing her, and he wouldn't even notice. But Strength had been ready to accept any terms. It had worked for a while, considering his lonely reality, but now, more and more often, he thought about ending it.

Devil arrived at the fashion show last, cursing Oliver in his mind as he entered the hall. Everyone, as usual, froze, magnetized by his presence. Baphomet slowly examined the hall, noticing his fellow majors.

Suddenly, he heard a wordless singing, like a luring siren call from the depths of the ocean. He saw the minor girl immediately, flaming with chaos, alluring and so inexplicably perfect in her white translucent dress that reminded him of a shadow of a forbidden spell. Baphomet tilted his head, trying to sense the mystery girl. The more he studied her, the more he thought she might be a beautiful demon in disguise that he hadn't claimed. Yet she couldn't be more different from anyone he had ever met. Her hair was like a river of moonlight, and her starry eyes dwarfed the reality around him. Somehow, she wasn't magnetized like other minors. She looked at him without any fear.

He wanted her this very second, wanted to tame this demon so badly, a desire so strong that he had never felt anything of the like before. Wanting to see the true form of this enchanted perfection, he spread his invisible ashes out toward her. He waited impatiently, like a spider in a web. Finally, the ashes touched her glowing skin. But the girl didn't change. She just … coughed.

His mouth almost fell open in shock. There had never been a being who could sense his ashes, let alone inhale them. He used the ashes in every spell, enveloping his subjects and subjugating their element. But no one could *inhale* his true nature—all the light and darkness of his soul, his memories and desires. They were affected by his smoky veil, unable to see and love the real him behind the Devil.

Like a moth to a flame, Baphomet moved toward her. He felt smitten, overtaken with desperate desire bigger than this universe.

"Breathe." Devil dove into her mysterious eyes, where he saw the northern lights that shed brightness on his dark soul. He called his ashes away.

CHAPTER
THREE
PAGE.

P age stood next to the huge old mansion that Gaia had rented for the fashion show in the neutral zone. The population of Minor Arcana was not allowed to cross the borders into different courts, which is why Emperor, one of the majors, considered as powerful and rich as Sun himself, had created a neutral zone where all four courts could meet. It had many cafes, restaurants, offices, and theaters, and even a stadium.

Many photographers from other agencies had already arrived. Page was supposed to photograph the front row guests and the collection itself for her mother's magazine, *Celebrities*. It was the first big event that Page had attended since her release. The eleventh dimension where she had been imprisoned for the last seven years was far from fun.

I wonder what majors will descend tonight. Maybe Emperor and Star. It's rumored that they're dating. Or Chariot. Matilda said that he loves constant movement and often comes down to the neutral zone, Page thought to herself, not noticing the late hour.

Fool, the very first and oldest of the majors, never appeared. He had not been seen for several hundred years. Rumor had it that he was always wandering around his dimension with another crazy idea, not thinking about anything other than his own path. Hermit and Hanged Man didn't really have any interest in minors. But there were also "serious" majors, those who did not want anything to do with minors, unless it came to their direct duty of judgment and punishment: Justice, Judgment, Hight Priest, and Death. Page deliberately tried not to think about Devil—not after she'd seen his card in her reading earlier today. She knew that all the unimaginable vices that destroyed everything human in people were his doing. Devil just had to send his faithful demons to tempt the souls.

The hall was still empty, and Page decided to go backstage and find her friend. On her way, she ran into Aqua.

"Page! Gaia is looking for you," Aqua said as she stepped into the hall, likely coming from the prep area. She was stunning, with large sea-colored eyes and sandy hair. Page often thought that she could have been one of the angels from Lovers' paradise, and not just because of her external beauty. The Princess of Cups had a good heart, too. She had supported Page like no one else when she'd come back home after so many years, always finding time to see her.

"I was just on my way to see her now." Page gave her friend a quick hug, about to step past her, when Aqua blushed slightly.

"Is your brother coming?"

"He knows you're here, so he wouldn't miss it for the world, even though he hates things like this."

"Today, at my tarot reading, I pulled the Tower,"

Aqua whispered so quietly that Page had to read her lips. "I got scared."

"Cards can't know everything," Page reassured her, thinking about the Devil card staring right into her soul that morning. "Do you want me to talk to my brother?"

"No, I don't want to impose my paranoia on him." Aqua shook her head. "You should go. Gaia is in a state."

Aqua wasn't wrong. Turmoil was evident when Page entered the staging area. Gaia was hemming the gown on one of the models, holding a needle and thread in her mouth while people ran back and forth all around them.

"Page!" Gaia's voice sounded higher than usual, with a note of anguish.

"Deep breaths, Gaia. The dresses look absolutely gorgeous," Page assured the talented princess.

Page looked around and smiled. Gaia had listened to her advice and made dresses in different colors. Her last show with only green dresses had almost left Page color-blind. In this collection, each court could find its own color. Ever since the minors had been created, each court was associated with a color according to their energy. Cups Arcana, the element of water, wore all shades of blue; Pentacles, the element of earth, wore green; Wands, the element of fire, wore red; and Swords, the element of air, wore white. Page understood the roots of this tradition, but refused to wear only one color for her entire life. After all, there were no documents stating that it was against the law.

"I hope so. Many majors confirmed at the last minute!" Gaia reported proudly, straightening her long mint-green dress.

"I told you! You know, I can't believe I'm finally

going to meet some other majors, apart from Justice." Page practically jumped up and down in excitement, and small flames lit up on her skin.

"You look so beautiful tonight. I love that dress."

Page thanked her, smoothing her hands over her gown. Her dress was a translucent white with an open back and dropped shoulders, embroidered with white flowers in several places. The fabric wrapped and emphasized every curve of her body. Matilda had arranged her long, thick hair to cascade down her back, all the way to her hips, like a moonlit waterfall. Page had completed the look with a small diamond bracelet and round diamond earrings, and dab of peony oil rubbed into her skin. She truly felt like a princess.

"I have a favor to ask." Gaia folded her hands in prayer, interrupting Page's thoughts. "I was hoping that you would agree to close the show in one of my dresses."

"Gaia, I'm so much shorter than all the girls you've hired," Page reasoned, looking at an extremely tall model standing beside them. "I'll look ridiculous."

"I made this dress especially for you. It'll fit you perfectly. It looks like it's on fire," Gaia insisted.

Page didn't know what to say, but what she knew for sure was that her father would not like it. Ever since she was a child, she had understood that she was different, and not in a good way. And after Page broke the law because of her uncontrollable flame, her father had become obsessed with the idea of making her normal, frightened by the thought that she might be taken away again.

"Please," Gaia pleaded. "Please."

Page sighed. "Okay, I can't say no to my friend on

her big night. But you're buying me breakfast until the end of the month."

"Agreed." Gaia smiled, and they shook hands as if they'd just made an important deal.

"Good luck." Page headed into the hall.

Many guests had already arrived and were taking their seats. Page spotted the Queen of Wands on the opposite side of the room. Her mother's eyes darkened when she saw her.

"Not the biggest fan of my translucent dress, I guess," Page muttered to herself and waved to the queen with a big smile.

At that moment, Page noticed Emperor entering the room, holding Star's arm. They took front row seats. She couldn't help but notice how different they were. His girlfriend looked soaring, shining, and gentle, like stardust. Emperor, by contrast, was solid and strong, and his face seemed serious and expressionless. Taking a deep breath, Page walked toward them.

"Good evening. Do you mind if I take a picture of you for *Celebrities* magazine?" Page's voice sounded unnatural and too formal, even to herself.

"Of course not." Star smiled, shining, and moved closer to her companion.

"Fine," Emperor reluctantly agreed, his voice extremely sharp and low.

Page quickly snapped a few photos before the unshakable major could change his mind. "Thank you." She bowed and turned to hurry away.

"You look unforgettable," Star's crystal voice called before Page could take a step.

"Thank you," Page replied, and a small tongue of flame rose from her palm.

Dammit! Page cursed and quickly turned around to

see if people had noticed. Justice said that as long as she could control her energy and didn't hurt anyone with her fire, she could stay home. And Page planned to never go back to that hated dimension.

Walking away, she noticed Lover and Chariot seated together. There was something childlike about Chariot's sun-kissed, freckled face. He held a glass of champagne in each hand and drank from both at the same time. As Page got closer, Chariot fixed his eyes on her and smiled.

"Am I wrong, or have the photographers gotten so much hotter?" Chariot asked his beautiful airy friend, staring at Page.

She could feel the heat creeping up her neck at the compliment.

"Are you from the Cups Arcana, judging by your hair?" Lover spoke for the first time, and his voice sounded like an echo in paradise.

"No, the eyes are different," Chariot said, still staring at Page, clearly confused.

"Princess of Wands." Page cleared her throat and bowed. "Pleasure to meet you. Smile for the camera!" She took a few pictures.

"Your flash almost blinded me!" Chariot opened and closed his golden eyes a few times, as if he truly could not see.

"Sorry." She couldn't help but laugh. "Just doing my job."

"All right." He gazed at Page with his restless eyes. "But I expect to see you at the after-party."

"Maybe," she answered, not sure whether she would actually be attending.

Her thirst for life and adventure had grown even stronger after the years of being imprisoned. She dreamed of living a full and amazing life, like a butterfly finally growing wings, ready to see the world.

The show was about to start, and Page moved to the end of the runway to get the best view of the collection. She was adjusting the camera lens for wider shots when everyone suddenly stared at the entrance, and dead silence descended on the room. It felt like time had stopped.

A tall, muscular man with curly raven hair entered. He wore a black suit and a black silk shirt, unbuttoned at the top. An inverted pentagram hung against his chest. Page glanced up to his full lips and then at his ash-colored eyes, where smoky flames flared from time to time, like the remnants of a wildfire. The man looked like a mesmerizing demon from the land of the damned, and she wanted to be forsaken along with him. It seemed he had plunged everyone into a trance; no one in the hall moved or even blinked. When his gaze met Page's, a hot wave passed through her body.

The man tilted his head as if he were studying her. He licked his hot lips slowly, like a predator tasting his juicy prey. Page smelled an intense ashy aroma and began coughing as if she'd inhaled too much smoke. Everyone was looking at her now, but she couldn't tear her gaze away from him. He moved toward his chair deliberately, never taking his magnetic eyes off Page for a second. When he stopped beside her, she felt as if invisible wings were hovering over her.

"Breathe." His voice was mesmerizing, hazy and full of tempting demons.

Page finally managed to take a breath, under-standing dawning on her. Of course: it was Devil. She hadn't expected him to be like this: handsome, danger-ously alluring, embodying all sins to perfection. He lingered next to her for a few more seconds, his eyes not leaving hers before taking his seat beside Chariot. Page's gaze unwillingly followed him, only to meet his bottomless eyes again as he sat down and turned to find her. She felt dizzy, even poisoned. He didn't even try to maintain decency, his sinful eyes not leaving her once, not even when the show had started. She was unable to focus on her work, feeling the searing weight of Devil's gaze on her. Only Gaia, who was waving from behind the stage, brought Page back to reality. Page snuck backstage.

"I've been waving to you forever!" Gaia scolded, her face red.

"I'm sorry." Page stumbled. "I lost track of time."

"Let's get you ready quickly." Gaia was already pulling off Page's dress.

"Did you see that Devil himself came to your show?" Page began to tremble, recalling the ashen flame in his eyes as he looked at her, and the heat on her skin in response.

"It's incredible!" Her friend sounded pleased.

"Not sure. He looks like sin in the flesh," Page whispered, mostly talking to herself.

"Don't exaggerate. I think he looks handsome."

Page didn't know how to respond. The heat and desire that Devil raised in her with his presence had not gone away, but she didn't intend to discuss it right now.

"Ready," Gaia reported, satisfied. "Here's a mirror."

Page turned to look at herself. The tight cherry-red dress with an open back was held in place only by a few lines of diamonds straps, creating a beautiful contrast with her hair and eyes. Page looked like a blood moon wrapped in the silvery rays of the stars.

"Come on." Gaia practically pushed her onto the stage.

Page took a deep breath and started to walk. She could feel Devil's piercing gaze light a fire in her, but she forced herself not to look at him with all the power she had left.

"Damn!" Chariot screamed enthusiastically, and a slight smile touched Page's face.

She posed for a few seconds for the photographers, then turned around to go back. Her eyes found Devil. She couldn't help it. He sat in his chair like a lord of shadows, staring at her and slowly sipping his champagne. Her eyes were riveted to his sensual mouth, and she licked her lips as a wave of lust nearly drowned her. Devil smiled, his smoky eyes blazing as they darted over her body—first her thighs, then her breasts, and then her lips. Feeling as though she were going to burst into flames, Page passed by and disappeared backstage. It took a few minutes to calm down her fire at least a little. Gaia bowed to a wave of applause, and the official part was over. Page changed back to her normal dress and went out to join her family and friends.

"Gaia, an incredible collection!" Aqua said admiringly and hugged her.

"Sister, you were the star of the show. Unforgettable exit." The Prince of Wands smiled approvingly at Page.

"We will discuss this at home," the King of Wands snapped with anger. "It's time to greet the majors." He looked at Page quickly. "Act normal."

Other royal families were already standing by Emperor and Star. Chariot and Lover also approached them. Only Devil was still sitting in his chair, never taking his ashen eyes off Page as she walked toward the majors.

"Greetings." The King of Wands bowed.

"King of Wands." Emperor sounded upbeat. "You seem to be the only one who still follows the traditions." The major glanced at the other royal families standing nearby, implying that none of them had bowed.

"You have met my son before," the King of Wands said to them. "Allow me to introduce my daughter, Page, Princess of Wands."

Page bowed. Devil quickly got up from his seat and walked right up to her, pushing Chariot and Lover aside. "It's a pleasure to meet you." Devil took Page's hand and brought it to his burning yet icy lips, gently kissing her skin. It felt like the fire had ignited her skin, and a volcano grew at the place of his touch. Page couldn't control her flame, and her body caught fire under the gentle and passionate kiss of this major. To her surprise, Devil stared at her flames like she was a goddess, not an outcast. Clearing her throat, she tried to pull herself together and utter at least a word.

"The pleasure is mine." The words came out too sensual, and even alluring.

Devil's hand clenched into a fist, but he smiled at the same time, continuing to look deep into her eyes, completely ignoring everyone else.

"I positively can't remember when I've heard your voice, Baphomet." Chariot broke the silence, but Devil didn't even turn in his direction.

"Peonies," he whispered, intending the words just for Page.

Her eyes widened at the word, and Devil moved even closer. At this distance, Page was able to breathe him in—the mix of ashes, flame, and the taste of tar. She felt like his smell penetrated every cell of her body, which demanded to be even closer to the source of her agony.

"Princess of Pentacles, amazing show. I might order a gown from you, for the majors' gala." Star almost shouted the words to Gaia, breaking the uncomfortable silence.

"I have to go." Baphomet paused and whispered, "But I will see you later."

Page couldn't help the disappointment that filled her. Ignoring everyone else, she watched Devil leave, wishing he would stay with her all evening. People fearfully stared at the major as he headed to the exit.

"We're going to my penthouse for the after-party. You all should join us." Chariot stepped forward.

"I'm not sure that's a good idea," the King of Wands snapped.

"Dear, going home with us so early is not fair to the kids, and it's boring on top of that. Let them join the majors," the Queen of Wands sang.

"You think so, but Page…"

"Please, Father," Page begged and stepped closer, whispering a lie. "I released the wave on purpose, to scare Devil away."

"Fine, but no fire incidents," the king whispered back at her, still frowning.

"Thanks!" Page jumped on the spot.

"Great. I'm glad to see everyone." Chariot moved to the exit, accompanied by three princesses.

A thrill went through Page. Her first big public event, and now her first after-party. Perhaps her life after the tragic incident could be even more amazing than she had hoped.

FOUR

BAPHOMET.

Baphomet sat in the car, trying to come to his senses. When he'd touched Page's gentle hand, sinful madness had consumed his being. She'd felt like a part of him. He'd had an urge to taste her lips that very second, but instead he was constantly clenching his fist, trying to resist the pull. And when she'd spoken, he'd finally tasted her smell. It was that of obscure seduction, blossoming with peonies and fire under a moonlit night sky. It was the only scent he wanted to breathe in for the rest of his existence. Sweet storms danced in his awakening soul.

"Fuck. I'm going to kiss Oliver's old face." He smiled at the thought of how his servant had insisted on tonight's show, probably changing Baphomet's fate forever.

He sensed the movement of the Wheel of Fortune shuffling the deck, and the promise of unworldly happiness filled his dried-up soul. Not only was his siren's scent actually pleasing, but she could also inhale him. She'd be able to know the real him without being magnetized and affected. A true union—the one he had always dreamed of.

"Peonies?" Baphomet repeated his words and cursed himself. "You could've said something more alluring." He remembered her scent again and felt drunk with images of the vivid pleasures they could share.

With a sigh, he realized he had to find Strength. He had to break up with her right away. They had an open relationship, but Devil didn't want that with Page. He needed her to be only his. Even the thought of someone else coming between them made his demons wake up, ready for slaughter.

<hr>

Baphomet drove to the end of the neutral zone, where his chariot was waiting for him, then flew up to the eighth dimension and waited for the gates guarded by two enormous lions to open. He hadn't visited Strength here for over a hundred years. They saw each other very little these days, mostly for official events. Standing here now, waiting, Baphomet regretted that he had not ended it earlier.

Strength's servant, Leo, showed up at the gate instead of the major herself. Devil breathed wickedly.

"Major Devil." Leo bowed to the ground. "What a rare and wonderful occasion to see you here."

"Where is Strength?" Baphomet didn't want to waste any time.

"The major is visiting Magician for a long weekend. I am afraid it is impossible to contact her."

"Tell Strength that I need to see her as soon as she's back." Devil returned to his chariot.

Magician—or Magus, as other majors called him—

was definitely planning something. He'd been avoiding everyone for quite a while. But Baphomet couldn't think about it now. He wanted—no, *needed* to see Page. She'd claimed his body and soul with one glance. Yes, officially he hadn't broken up with Strength yet, but that didn't mean he couldn't try to get to know his siren better in the meantime.

Just to get to know each other, he lied to himself, knowing very well that he wouldn't be able to control his desire around her. She was fucking perfection. Her every inch sent his sinful imagination to wander in a forbidden land.

Baphomet went straight to Chariot's penthouse, knowing very well that the major loved to invite everyone for after-parties. Devil hoped that Page would be there. He didn't even want to think that he would not see her again tonight. Baphomet unbuttoned his shirt a little, hot from the sweet agony of anticipation.

When you see her, hold yourself together, or she'll think you're a maniac, he commanded himself before knocking on the door.

FIVE

PAGE.

Page found herself sitting in a huge limousine with leather seats right next to Chariot, with Gaia on his other side. Aqua and Lover sat opposite them.

"Driver—champagne!" Chariot shouted.

"Chariot, you don't know the name of your driver?" Page laughed.

"I have too many drivers. I simply can't remember them all. And friends call me Triumph. Lover is Amador." He opened a bottle of champagne, and everyone raised their glasses.

"To Gaia and her success," Aqua said proudly.

"Cheers!" Triumph drank his champagne in one sip and refilled his glass again.

"Do you work?" Amador's voice sounded gentle and curious as he looked at the Princess of Cups.

"Yes, in a shelter for homeless animals. Well, it's hard to call it work, since I don't get paid. It's more like volunteering."

"Amazing." Amador studied Aqua with near admiration.

"Are you dating anyone?" Triumph quickly changed the subject of the conversation.

Page glanced at her girlfriend, hoping Aqua would not talk openly about her relationship with the Prince of Wands. Page loved her friend and didn't want Aqua to repeat her own fate. Relationships between different courts were forbidden, and if someone heard about it, Aqua would be taken away, just like Page had been.

"No." Aqua lowered her eyes.

"What about you, Page? We definitely saw one candidate today." Triumph raised his eyebrows suggestively as he turned to face Page, forcing Gaia to look at his back.

"No idea what you're talking about." Page felt heat creeping up her neck in embarrassment.

"And you?" Gaia cleared her throat, forcing the major to turn back to her.

"No, and not for a long time now," Triumph said. "Since Mort broke my heart." His voice sounded different, and for a moment, there was silence in the car.

"I'm free too," Amador reported to Aqua.

Triumph's penthouse was located in the tallest building of the neutral zone—so high that Page's ears began to click as they went up in the elevator. As they entered Triumph's apartment, Page saw an actual DJ playing music in the corner, and waiters were serving fancy snacks on small silver trays. Her brother was already there, standing next to Star. She walked toward them.

"Are you alone?" Page smiled at Star.

"Emperor is not a fan of such evenings." Star looked a little downcast.

"Excuse me." The Prince of Wands quickly moved toward Aqua as she headed to the bar.

"So, you're a photographer." Star turned to Page, studying her face.

"Yes, you should check out your photos in the next *Celebrities* issue."

"I will." The major smiled. "What do you think of our friend?"

"Triumph? I like him. He seems real."

"No." Star looked into Page's eyes knowingly. "Of Baphomet."

"Oh…" Page blushed from head to toe. "I don't even know what to say."

"Alluring?"

"Uh-huh." She pretended to sip her champagne as a knock sounded through the apartment, barely audible over the music.

"Someone get the door!" Triumph shouted from behind the bar, where he was preparing glasses for a champagne tower.

"I will!" Page said, jumping at the chance to leave before the conversation became even more uncomfortable.

Trying not to spill the champagne in her very full glass, Page went to the door and opened it. Devil stood in front of her, wearing the same suit as before, but his shirt was unbuttoned a bit lower than she remembered. Page involuntarily slid her eyes over his body while he stood there, slightly smiling. She had the feeling he enjoyed her devouring gaze.

"I thought you weren't coming." Page tried to sound casual and indifferent, but the words turned out to be too quiet.

Tilting his head, Devil moved closer, his eclipsing

energy entering Page's body, penetrating even the most hidden parts of her soul. "Pardon?" He smiled again, and fire flared in his ashen eyes.

"I thought you weren't coming to the after-party!" she almost screamed this time.

"Yes, I don't usually go to such events."

"Why tonight?" Page immediately regretted the question and bit her lip.

"The company seemed interesting." His gleaming ashy eyes focused on her mouth, and again Page noticed that Devil had clenched his hand into a fist.

"I can't believe my eyes!" Triumph flew up to them. "Welcome. You haven't been to this apartment, have you?" The major tapped Devil on the shoulder.

"No." Baphomet looked at Triumph only for a second before going back to Page.

Page slowly turned to slip away. She didn't want to leave, but felt that his darkness was slowly creeping closer to her soul, driving her mad with desire. She needed to get away before she was consumed.

"Are you leaving?" Baphomet sounded disappointed.

"No, just need more champagne." Page looked down at her full glass.

Luckily, Aqua and the Prince of Wands stood nearby. Page made her way over to them, squeezing past dancing people. Unable to help herself, she tried to hear the conversation between the majors.

"Came for her?" Triumph sounded intrigued.

"I haven't come yet," Baphomet replied, still watching Page. She flushed at his arrogance.

"Typical Baphomet." The major laughed. "Let's get something to drink. But I should warn you, I don't think her father likes you. You know the temperament of the Wand family."

"And he likes you?" Devil looked surprised.

"I know of my reputation with women. But I can fix it. On the other hand, the fact that you are the Devil is irreparable. By the way, how is Strength?"

They moved away before Page could hear the rest. With a shrug, she joined the other princesses as they danced in the middle of the room, ignoring the staring crowd. Page could clearly feel Devil's shadow on her. She scanned the space. He sat alone at the bar and studied her with his head titled. His inky curls touched his shoulder, and Page was seized with the desire to feel his silky hair and breathe in his night scent.

"Page, come here!" Triumph waved to her from behind the bar. "Time to make a champagne tower!"

Page walked toward Triumph with a smile. She had to squeeze right next to Baphomet and accidentally touched his thigh with her hip. They both seemed to catch fire in an instant, like two matches, and Page felt his burning, harsh hand on her wrist. The heat within her stomach became even stronger, and she unsuccessfully tried to force herself to move away. It was insanity, but she felt as if their energies were intertwined. She wanted to dissolve into him. Luckily, Triumph pulled her to the bar.

"So, we're going for a ten-tier champagne tower. Let's start with the base. Make sure your glasses sit snug. Understood?" Triumph said, drinking champagne straight from the bottle. "Amador, mark the time! Page and I are going for a new record," he sang playfully.

On Amador's count, Page and Triumph quickly lined up even squares of glasses, which were promptly handed to them by the bartender. Soon Page forgot about everything else and completely focused on the tower, trying not to drop the glasses.

When the tower became too high, they both climbed onto bar stools and continued to work in unison. Triumph looked at Page struggling to balance on the chair and laughed sincerely. He had the talent of creating light and playful energy around him.

There was no way to reach the last two layers, and Triumph decided to lift Page up in his arms. To put it mildly, the idea was questionable. The chair was already unstable, and the sight of Triumph standing on it with Page in his arms was not for the faint of heart. She gently reached for the top with the last glass.

"The last glass, number three eighty-three!" Amador reported to the audience.

"Let's open the champagne. We need seventy-seven bottles. Make it rain!" Triumph tried to turn to the bartender as he shook the bottle in his hand.

"No!" Page laughed out loud and couldn't stop as champagne splashed her body.

"Stop laughing at once! Otherwise, we'll fall!" Triumph tried his best to sound serious, but he was laughing too.

"I can't!" Page began slowly pouring champagne down the tower. It was beautiful, liquid was overflowing into the glasses below, filling each coupe like an inner-most desire filling the soul of a dreamer.

When the glasses were filled, everyone clapped. Triumph slowly put Page down and quickly kissed her cheek with his cold champagne lips. "Well done, part-ner." He raised her hand up as if they'd just set a world record in something extremely important.

Page caught Devil's hungry, piercing gaze on her body. Looking down, she realized she was completely drenched. The champagne had literally soaked her dress, making it somehow even more transparent than it had been before. Page hurried to the bathroom, and as soon as she closed the door, she heard a knock.

"Busy," she said, looking for a hair dryer.

"Open up." Baphomet's voice sounded gentle and enticing at the same time.

Page opened the door slightly and poked her head out. "I'm sure there's another bathroom in this enormous penthouse." She tried to sound annoyed, but without much success.

"No doubt." Devil smiled. "I'm afraid your dress cannot be saved." He cleared his throat. "I can offer my jacket."

"Thank you." Page eagerly studied his body while Baphomet removed his jacket. She touched his strong chest with her gaze, then moved her eyes to his burning lips, unable to look away. The major caught her gaze and smiled, clearly satisfied with her reaction. She blushed, and quickly grabbing the jacket, she closed the door. Page took off her dress, put the jacket on, pulled up the sleeves, and tied the waist with a black ribbon she had found in one of the bathroom's cabinets. She slowly opened the door. Baphomet was still standing in the same place, waiting for her. His gaze flickered over her high-heeled sandals, her tanned legs, her waist, and then her face. Finally, their eyes met.

"My clothes have never looked so good." He sounded defeated. "Can I give you a ride home?"

"I need to tell my brother." Page felt a sweet, inexplicable anticipation. *Stay away from him*, a voice in her head warned, but Page had already followed the major.

It turned out that both the Prince of Wands and Aqua had already left. Gaia was talking to Triumph and Amador on the balcony, and Page decided not to disturb them. She went to the exit, where Baphomet was waiting for her. She tugged at the jacket from behind. It barely covered her hips.

"After you." Devil waved his hand as the elevator opened, and Page entered first, cursing her short outfit. "I parked the car nearby."

"Do you drive your own car?" she asked abruptly, unable to concentrate as Baphomet huddled closer.

"It gives me much more privacy." His eyes lit up like lightning in the night sky.

A matte black car was parked across the street. Baphomet opened the door for Page. She was trying to hold the jacket in place as she sat down.

The major drove extremely fast, but his concentration was not on the road, his dark eyes constantly darting to Page. She burned at his look, his smell, her closeness to his perfectly sculpted body.

"You're not going to look at the road at all?" Page managed to put some words together.

"I'm a very good driver." Baphomet smirked and held his gaze on her burning lips.

"Can you open a window? It's so hot tonight." She looked away.

Devil smiled and lowered her window almost completely. The wind played with Page's hair, and she kept having to brush it out of her face.

"I can't think of anyone with blonde hair in the Wands bloodline, not to mention hair as white as yours." Devil stared.

"Yes, I'm the only one," Page whispered, holding her breath as his hand gently touched her flying hair.

"A masterpiece, truly." Baphomet's eyes flickered over her body.

She felt happy. Someone, for once, liked her *otherness*. Page licked her lips, literally burning under his touch.

Devil's hand slowly walked over the jacket and for a second touched her bare leg.

"Almost there!" she shouted. The major smiled. "I must admit, I did not expect Devil to smile this much."

He smiled again. "This is a rare occurrence. And call me Baphomet," he replied so tenderly that Page's heartbeat quickened.

"We've arrived."

Page saw that the major was about to get out of the car, so she quickly opened the door. She felt as if Baphomet were slowly taking possession of her soul. Reminding herself of who he actually was, Page jumped out of the car.

"Thanks for the ride and the jacket. See you." Page slammed the door and made her way to the entrance of the house. She couldn't stay away from him. It was pure madness. But the worry that Devil could transform her own darkness into a much darker shade made her shiver.

"Any time. Good night, Princess of Wands." Baphomet's voice sounded like a deadly spell on a dark, moonlit night.

SIX

BAPHOMET.

Baphomet had hardly slept the night before, trying in vain to settle his ashes that raged at every sinful thought of his siren. He didn't touch his breakfast, thinking about Page instead. The night spent next to her reminded him of a sweet mirage. Her quiet, erotic scent had pulled his lost soul to her like a black hole inevitably pulls everything in.

Baphomet had been trying to breathe Page's scent into every molecule of his ashen blood all evening. If just being next to her drove him crazy, he dared not imagine what it would feel like to taste her sacred body, and maybe one day her blood. The thought set him on fire hellaciously. His vampire bat side was thirsty. He'd tried Strength's blood once, but it was so bad that he had abandoned the idea of tasting any blood ever again. But Page seemed so raw and real, like a wildflower that somehow grew in the middle of a burnt forest glade. This siren had caught Baphomet in her depths, and he wished to be held there forever.

The thought that for the first time it could be more than just sex made him smile. He wanted to study her mystery—why she could inhale his ashes, why she looked so different from her family, how she was able to release her fire into the world. Baphomet wanted to know every inch of her skin, her soul.

Devil impatiently waited for Oliver. He'd sent him to find out a little bit more about the Princess of Wands, and more importantly, about her plans for the weekend. He could not and did not intend to stand aside. She would be his.

"Master." Oliver approached, slightly out of breath.

"Finally. What took you so long?" Baphomet looked at his old servant and added, "Tell me."

"You suspected correctly. You haven't met the Princess of Wands before because she was imprisoned by Justice. Also, her father seems very strict," Oliver added, slightly hesitantly. "Lots of minors think she's cursed. They're even afraid of her. But it seems the princess does not let those rumors get to her. She even refuses to dye her hair, as her father has ordered."

That's my girl, Devil thought to himself, and a faint smile touched his lips. "I will need to speak to Justice. What did Page do to be sentenced to the eleventh dimension? And what about the weekend?" Baphomet asked impatiently. Even a casual conversation about her with Oliver stirred his soul.

"Lady Page has decided to spend the weekend on the beach with her friends, including Chariot and Lover." His servant cleared his throat. "May I add that major Chariot even kissed her while they were getting in the car…"

"Again? It's becoming a habit!" Baphomet squeezed

through his teeth, remembering yesterday's kiss. Even the thought of someone else touching his siren clouded him with rage.

"Master, you did not let me finish. The kiss was very chaste."

"I doubt that, knowing Triumph."

"I don't think the princess is interested, if I may." Oliver lowered his head slightly. "Why don't you simply woo the girl, let her see how charming you are?"

"Charming?" Baphomet raised his eyebrows.

"Something tells me that the Princess of Wands does not want to reach for Triumph's light. When I watched them, she reminded me…" Oliver stumbled on his words.

"Yes?" Devil prodded, his impatience rising.

"Of you, Master. She is shrouded in a haze of darkness."

Baphomet kept quiet for a few seconds, mulling that over. Yesterday, he'd sensed the darkness too, but also a beaming light that had shone through it. Whatever Page was, it was something different—something the deck had never created before.

"Get ready, Oliver. I intend to spend the weekend in my summer house." His bottomless eyes sparkled with dark ashes.

"I will leave right away!" the servant sang.

"Oliver!" Baphomet called after him. "Make it … romantic."

"Will do, Master." The man couldn't help but smile, his old, freckled face lighting up.

SEVEN

PAGE.

The next morning, Page was not eager to go downstairs. Her parents had been informed that she'd left the party with Baphomet.

"Good morning." Page sank into her chair almost soundlessly.

"I heard Devil gave you a ride yesterday!" her father bellowed. The King of Wands had clearly gotten up on the wrong side of the bed that morning. "I'm surprised he came to the after-party at all."

"Why are you looking at me like that? I didn't invite him," Page responded defensively.

"You don't stand out enough? Justice can take you back at any time!" the king shouted. "On top of everything, you had to leave with Baphomet!"

The king quickly stood up, blazing with anger, and grasped Page's arm tightly. She didn't move, even though her arm began to ache. The Prince of Wands jumped up to defend her, but at their father's withering look of rage, he sat back down.

"Let her go … please," the Queen of Wands whispered with trepidation.

The king furiously looked at everyone present once again and then left the garden, muttering something under his breath.

"But your father is right. Devil is not the best company for a young girl like you. He is the embodiment of temptation, of sin and deceit. It's scary to even think about all the stories we've heard about him and other girls. But I can't blame him for yesterday, given what kind of dress you wore. I can't believe Matilda let you out of the house!"

If Page could cry, she would have sobbed, but only the Cups Arcana could cry. Apparently, she'd left Justice's prison just to end up in another one: her own house, with a father who was obsessed with the idea that she should hide for the rest of her life. Page felt that her body was about to catch fire and quickly rose from her chair, running toward the exit.

"You're always on his side! I'm not hungry." Page left before the queen could notice her fire.

***

Page was looking forward to her reading. She hoped to get some answers about Baphomet. Without knowing it, he'd taken possession of all her thoughts and desires, like a demon over the soul of a sinner. As she opened the oracle's door, she met Agatha face to face. It seemed the reader had already been waiting for her.

"Hello, Page." The fortune teller scanned her from head to toe as if seeing her for the first time.

"Wow, that's a first." Page raised her eyebrows in surprise that the woman had actually greeted her.

"I've already shuffled the deck." Agatha sat down at

the table and laid out the cards in front of Page as usual. "Choose a card."

Page picked the card that "looked" at her.

"The Magician, upside down," the woman uttered thoughtfully.

Deep down, even realizing it was just her fantasy, Page had hoped to get the Devil card again, along with the Two of Cups, or the Lovers card, even.

"And what does it mean?" Page asked, a bit disappointed.

"This means you need to be careful. Don't let anyone manipulate you," Agatha advised.

She immediately thought of Baphomet. *That's stupid. I'll probably never see him again,* she thought to herself, and the needle of disappointment pricked her.

Page quickly stopped by her house. Aqua and Gaia had sent her a message that morning that they were having a beach weekend. Page had work to do, editing the photos from the fashion show, but she figured she'd be able to work while getting some sun. She packed a small suitcase for the weekend. She wore a white skirt and matching crop top for the trip. An hour later, she was sitting in a limousine with Aqua and Gaia, as well as Triumph and Amador, ready for an adventure.

"Triumph, move over a little. You're almost sitting on my lap." Page tried to push the major away, but he was too big, and his body resembled a stone block.

"Stop complaining." Triumph rolled his eyes, but moved.

"It's so hot." Aqua waved her fan and drank water nonstop.

Page opened the window and watched the scenery fly by. Her skin glowed in the sun, her curly hair growing messier the closer they got to the water.

"How was your night, Page?" Triumph narrowed his eyes. "Desires fulfilled?"

"I have no idea what you mean." Page grimaced.

"Passion. It's delicious." The major sat in the seat as if it were his famous chariot.

"My parents gave me a moral lecture this morning." Page lowered her eyes.

"Baphomet isn't so bad." Amador came to Devil's defense. "At some point, he should be lucky enough to meet his true love. Plus, I've never seen him like this before. Something was different yesterday."

"You're a hopeless romantic." Triumph laughed. "Considering how quickly one girl replaces another, he clearly doesn't waste time in the search for his soulmate."

Page blushed, and her heartbeat quickened. Maybe he was just playing with her as well. But yesterday, he'd seemed so genuine. *Well, Devil can be deceiving,* she reminded herself. "And how many girls are we talking about?" She felt stupid for asking, but couldn't resist.

"New one every week, roughly," Triumph reported casually.

"And this is considering that he has…" Amador didn't finish the sentence, catching Triumph's look. "Doesn't matter. Just be careful."

"I wasn't planning on anything happening." Page lowered her eyes.

"Rest assured that he's already planned everything for the two of you." Triumph took Page's head in his hands and kissed her forehead.

"That's how my dad kisses me. How old are you, exactly?" Page playfully narrowed her eyes.

Everyone laughed.

"Old enough, but I assure you, my body and my heart are forever young."

"I would also like to be immortal," Gaia whispered bitterly.

"Don't worry, the royals live very long," Amador assured her.

"But not forever. Things happen unpredictably, like they did with my family." Gaia lowered her eyes.

"I'm sorry, Gaia." Page sighed.

No one said anything else. Page knew that Gaia had lost her whole family when she was a teenager. They'd gotten into a car accident, and Gaia, the only one who'd managed to get out of the burning car, had watched in horror as her whole family died. The loss left a deep scar Page imagined would never heal.

"Air conditioner!" Aqua literally ran up to the reception when they finally arrived.

"Cold drinks?" A beautiful girl brought cocktails on a small tray, and Triumph scanned her, clearly undressing the girl in his mind.

"Great idea." He took two glasses at once.

"We'll stay with Princess of Cups in the same room," Page notified the receptionist.

"But then I won't be able to visit you at night, princess." Triumph embraced Page and twirled her around.

"I don't know how I'll survive a night without you." Page laughed, rolling her eyes.

The beach club was a hotel with restaurants and an incredibly beautiful white sand beach. Her friends had reserved a big cabana. While everyone was hanging out at the bar, Page worked on her computer. She wanted to sort out the photos from the fashion show as quickly as possible. She lay on her stomach in a purple swimsuit that highlighted her olive skin tone, zooming in on Baphomet's photos. Suddenly, someone blocked the sun, and she heard a voice speak, soaked in tart honey.

EIGHT

BAPHOMET.

Baphomet sensed his siren even before he saw her. Her smell got into his veins, intoxicating his thoughts with desire.

"For Sun's sake, hold yourself together," Devil cursed at himself.

Page was lying on her stomach in a purple bikini, working on her computer. His mind flew to the thought of all the ways he could taste her, the images in his head making him shiver.

"Working even on the weekend?" Baphomet sang, eagerly studying her body.

"The press never rests. By the way, you're very photogenic." Page smiled, and Baphomet saw happiness behind her starry eyes. It gave him hope that she wanted to see him.

"I don't like being photographed, but I'll make an exception for you," the major said seductively, thinking that he'd never made any exceptions for anyone before.

"What a generous Devil you are!" Page teased, and he caught a little hellish flame in her eyes he desperately wanted to feed. "I didn't think you spent your weekends on the beach with ordinary people."

"I don't, but this weekend is different. You know you're anything but ordinary." Baphomet tilted his head.

She doesn't know how special she is. Even if her father is trying kill her fire, I will help fire it up so high that it will be visible in the Blank Dimension. Baphomet made a silent promise.

He noticed that Page was studying him, and he glowed under her gaze, hoping she wouldn't notice how hungry he was for her. He desperately wanted to tear her apart.

"Aren't you hot in all black in this heat?" she finally said.

"There are very few things that can warm me up, and even fewer that can fire me up." Baphomet smiled and slowly licked his lips. "The sun is very strong today. You should be careful, don't get burned," he said, getting closer.

"I never burn." Page was about to roll over, but in a split second, he was next to her, placing his icy hand on her waist.

"Let me help," Baphomet whispered the words like an enchantment.

She was so tiny, so perfectly fitting into his enormous, beastly hands. Her lips parted, and for a second, Devil thought he wouldn't be able to control himself. Her silky skin demanded to be kissed. Baphomet reached for the sunscreen and rubbed it into her back, lowering his hand slowly. Her fire, mixed with a heavenly floral scent, flooded him, and he couldn't stop. Baphomet had never thought he could be in heaven, but here he was. His wings were about to come out, electrified by passion, and he silently growled, keeping them in place.

"It's not…" She struggled to get the words out.

Devil wished she wouldn't speak. Her hazy voice penetrated all his armor, and he was about to lose any self-control he still had left.

"Necessary. Your skin is too delicate." Baphomet had to interrupt her, otherwise he wouldn't be able to resist the urge to taste her.

Page closed her eyes, and he imagined how she'd close them like that right before he would bring her to euphoria, lighting up the sky. Baphomet felt that she was slowly surrendering to the foggy labyrinth of his wicked darkness. He smiled at the thought that his siren was hungry for him as well.

"Well, well, well. I can't leave my date for even a second before Baphomet himself decides to court her. I bet this is your first visit to the beach in a millennium," Triumph playfully challenged Baphomet as he approached with the rest of the group.

Devil didn't even answer, overpowered with the desire to throw annoying Triumph, with a flap of his wings, into another dimension.

"Triumph, leave Page alone. Let's go swimming, it's impossible to stay in the sun," Gaia complained and walked to the sea. Page looked at her with gratitude.

"Fine." Triumph rolled his eyes.

"Good to see you, Baphomet." Amador shook Devil's hand.

"I'll join you soon!" Page yelled after her friends.

"Interesting company." Baphomet smiled for a second, looking after them, and then turned back to Page, devouring her with his eyes.

"Oh, yes. I'm guessing you don't want to swim." She

rose to her knees and pulled her hair into a bun. Page moved with a natural grace, unlike other girls, who watched their every move around him.

"No, I don't want to scare people," the major lied. He simply didn't trust that he could control himself around her.

"I'm afraid to disappoint you, but you're not that scary."

"You don't think so?" Baphomet smiled.

Fuck, here we go again. Stop smiling like a fool, he cursed to himself.

"You know, I could get used to your smile." Page dove into his ashy eyes with hers, her lips parting, and Devil wasn't ready for it. Her gaze found a way inside the most hidden place of his long-dead soul, and everything inside bloomed, as if dry soil had finally been saturated with life-giving water.

"I hope so," Baphomet finally confessed and smiled even more. "I have to take care of some things, but I hope to see you tonight."

"I hope so too," Page replied shyly and lowered her reddened face.

"Sweet," Devil thought out loud and licked his lips, tasting her passion in the air between them.

Page ran to the water, but turned to look at him one more time. "Until the evening!" She waved her hand.

The wind was playing with her hair, and her scent reached him, straining all his muscles with desire. He watched Page get in the water.

Fucking Triumph, you try my patience. Baphomet watched in anger as the golden major took Page in his arms. *I will seriously burn your hands off*.

NINE

PAGE.

Page ran to the water and then turned for a second to look at Devil one more time. She didn't want him to leave, either the beach or her life. She still had the taste of the grapes in her mouth after Baphomet's touch. Page felt so alive next to him, a feeling she'd completely forgotten after her imprisonment.

She was not paying attention, and a large wave crashed over her head.

"Page, be careful!" Triumph swam up to her at the speed of light and grabbed her in his arms before a new wave covered them both. To her surprise, the major didn't move even a millimeter under the weight of the water.

"I need to keep an eye on you." Triumph was still holding Page in his arms.

"I didn't realize you were so strong," she said, her eyes wide.

"I'm full of surprises." The major broke into a smile, his sun-kissed face shining with happiness.

"There are some beautiful shells over here!" Aqua said. "They're too deep for me to get to, though."

"Let me," Amador volunteered.

"Wait." Triumph stopped him. "Let's see who finds more shells. I'll collect for Page, and you for Aqua."

"And for Gaia?" Page looked at him reproachfully.

"Okay, I'll collect for Page and Gaia, and Amador for the Princess of Cups."

Amador and Triumph both took a deep breath and disappeared under the water. Ten minutes later, they were still nowhere to be seen.

"Do you think they're okay?" Aqua began to worry.

"They're immortal majors. They'll be more than fine," Gaia assured her, continuing to float amongst the waves.

"Gaia is probably right." Page tried to cheer Aqua and herself up, though worry niggled at the back of her mind.

Twenty minutes later, the two majors finally swam ashore.

"You're crazy!" Aqua screamed. "I was so worried!"

"Sorry." Amador lowered his eyes.

"I see Aqua has already tamed you." Triumph clapped his hand on Amador's shoulder. "Let's see who won."

"Someone loves competition too much." Page narrowed her eyes on Triumph.

"It's in my blood. It's the way I was created," he explained proudly.

The majors poured onto the sand a huge number of shells of all possible colors and sizes. They shone under the sun like a lost treasure.

"How beautiful!" Aqua jumped up and down with

happiness. "I'll take them home to decorate my bathroom!"

"I'm glad you like them." Amador looked at her gently.

"So, twenty-one for Page, and twenty for Gaia. How many do you have?" Triumph was determined to win.

"Twenty," Amador declared, clearly pleased with himself.

"We have our winner!" Page concluded. "Oh, wait!" She quickly ran to the cabana and returned with her camera. "We need to ask someone to take our picture, so we can remember today," she explained.

As if from thin air, a middle-aged man appeared in front of them, covered in smoke. He was dressed modern, but his snakelike belt looked as though it had been forged in another era. The nails on his hands reminded Page of sharp raven claws.

"I'll be happy to help," the man said in a hissing voice. "Triumph, Amador, glad to see you."

"I can't say the same, Magus," Triumph squeezed out through his teeth.

Magician laughed. His voice sounded terrifying, like the hiss of a snake with venomous fangs.

"Sit closer." Magus snatched the camera out of Page's hands. "Ready?"

"Triumph, don't frown." Page looked at her friend and hugged him. "Thank you," she said to Magician once he had snapped a few photos. She walked over to him and took the camera back.

"Princess of Wands, if I am not mistaken." He examined Page's face, and she could swear she felt the snake crawling through her hair.

Not knowing what to say, Page settled on "Hi."

"Moon-colored hair?" Magus whispered, his eyes

moving quickly as he looked at her as if he were reading a book. "For the first time in your family, if I recall correctly."

At her nod, he turned to Amador. "And you, Amador, found yourself the Princess of Cups. Her energy is similar to yours," Magus sang to the airy major.

"That's none of your business," Amador boomed.

"As welcoming as always. No respect for an elder major," Magician scoffed. "I have to go. Bye for now." The major of the first dimension vanished as quickly as he had appeared.

Page's mouth dropped open. "Can you do that too?" She'd no idea that the majors were capable of just disappearing, and she wondered what else they could do. She only knew Justice, and the only things she'd seen in that dimension were her cell and barred windows.

"No, only the oldest Arcana: Fool, High Priestess, and Magician. They were created first, and for the longest time, only their three dimensions existed," Triumph explained.

"I take it you don't like him," Aqua said to Amador.

"I've never been close to him, but after his card turned upside down, he became simply unbearable."

"How long has his card been in the reversed position?" Page asked. She couldn't help but remember Agatha's words earlier that morning. Maybe Magus wanted something from Page. It was too much of a coincidence to see him after the reading.

I don't have anything of value. Page brushed the heavy thoughts away.

Amador spoke, bringing her back to the conversation. "For a long time now. That means that all the qualities of the Magician are now in an inverted position. He used to be the seeker of true potential. But after the deck created the rest of the majors, he changed. I think he doesn't like to share the power. Before, with only Fool and High Priestess, he was the true ruler."

The friends went to their rooms to rest a bit from the sun and get ready for the evening. Page was lying in the bathtub playing with bubbles while Aqua leafed through a magazine.

"What's your brother doing this weekend?" Aqua asked, but didn't take her eyes off the magazine.

"I think he went sailing with our father."

Page fell silent. After she'd returned home, she had dreamed of going on a boat with her father. But the king didn't allow it, afraid her energy might get out and put them in danger.

"I wonder if he misses me," Aqua whispered. "I feel the prince is distant these days." She lowered her bottomless blue eyes.

"Of course he does. I'm sure you'll find a way to meet as soon as we get back to town." Page hesitated for a second. "Do you like Amador?"

"I'm not going to lie. I like him, and it's nice to be around him." Aqua blushed.

"Well, of course, he's head over heels in love with you!" Page threw foam at Aqua, which landed on her leg. "Poor Amador!"

"Look who's talking! I can't even count how many times Triumph has already kissed you during this trip." Aqua pursed her lips in a kiss, copying the major.

"He's just flirting. It's meaningless." Page took a breath and went under the water for a few seconds.

"What did Baphomet tell you? If you want to talk about it…" Aqua added quietly.

"That he hopes to see me this evening." Page felt the

excitement in the lower part of her stomach, as if she had not eaten anything for a week.

"I like him, apart from the rumors that he's a womanizer. But again, rumors aren't always true."

"I hope not. Honestly, I don't understand why I'm so drawn to him." Page's face grew rosy. It was unpleasant even to think that she might be just another temporary fling for him.

"I saw it in both of you." Aqua paused. "Be careful, that's all."

TEN

BAPHOMET.

Baphomet returned to his dimension, and taking his raw form, entered the labyrinth. Flapping his strong wings, Devil watched Iblis, his faithful demon, melt a metal wall that blocked his way.

"Not everything can be taken by force." Baphomet smirked.

Iblis sniffed the air. "You smell nice, Boss."

"Shut up," Baphomet cut him off, afraid he might smile like an idiot even at the innocent memory of his siren. "What did you find out?"

Iblis had been trying to locate Magician for a long time, which was almost impossible because of Magus's vanishing power, plus he rarely left his dimension. Devil suspected that Magus was conspiring with Abyss. Still, he couldn't understand what exactly they had planned. Baphomet had long believed that it was time to put an end to the tyranny of the major of the Blank Dimension, even more so now, after he'd met Page. The dream of having children with her captured his soul.

"Not much," Iblis said, obviously angry at himself. "But at least I finally spotted him at the beach. I don't understand when Magus became so powerful. His magic armor is almost untouchable."

"So, you saw nothing at all?" Baphomet started to lose his patience.

"Don't be rash, Boss." Iblis lowered his head.

Baphomet had a temper. His demons were used to being punished for even a tiny mistake. But today, he didn't feel like fighting.

My siren calmed me down. The realization came to him immediately. He wasn't sure if that was a good thing, but he couldn't help himself and smiled. His life could be different, after all. He could have Page, and one day maybe even children with her. Although, according to Abyss's law, the majors weren't allowed to have children. Baphomet growled, getting angry at the thought.

"And?" He stared at Iblis.

"Ooh, I was waiting for punishment." He looked at his master in surprise. "I only got a few fragments of his memory. He was the last who saw Empress. After that, total darkness."

"That's all?" Baphomet fired off. "And you call yourself a memory demon? Oliver could find out more over a cup of tea!"

Iblis laughed, and Baphomet turned to him, flapping his wings.

"Sorry, Boss."

"I guess I need to sort this out for myself," Baphomet said, mostly to himself. "Find Magus again, and set up a meeting with me. Mention Empress. He'll want to find out what we know."

Iblis had been able to read Magician's memories before, but apparently his armor had become stronger. This new power had to come from somewhere. Either

Magus had taken Empress's energy, or somehow, Abyss had given it to him.

Devil left Iblis, still thinking about Magician. If he was working with Abyss, then Baphomet could find the answers he needed using the major of the first dimension.

Baphomet's thoughts quickly moved to Page. He was going crazy remembering her gentle, silky skin under his touch. He had to taste Page tonight. Otherwise, he might explode from the unreleased desire that had possessed his soul. He remembered her getting into the water, and the thought of Triumph next to Page made him growl.

Baphomet, you are turning into a jealous idiot.

After making sure Oliver had prepared everything in the summer house, Baphomet headed for the rooftop. The night air was blooming with a burnt magical peony scent. His invisible ashes rose, electrified by Page's closeness, and swirled his energy in a promising, blissful dance.

Devil couldn't control his reaction to this beautiful woman. It was the first time this had ever happened to him. He loved sex and had had many women, but it felt different with Page. Not only was his body craving this perfect siren, but so was his long-lost soul.

CHAPTER

ELEVEN

PAGE.

Triumph had booked a table on the rooftop. Page wore a short iris-colored dress with strappy shoulders and an open back all the way to her hips. Her hair had grown even bigger; it always went crazy with the humidity. She had gently massaged the peony oil into her skin before they left.

When the girls entered, Gaia was already spinning on the dance floor with some stranger. The majors waved to the princesses.

"Six shots of tequila." Triumph smiled dazzlingly at the waitress.

"I can't drink tequila! It's too strong," Aqua protested.

"Just one shot to warm up." He didn't take a no for an answer.

"The extra shot is for you, am I correct?" Page teased.

"I'm afraid to disappoint you, but this time it's for Gaia. She insisted on shots. Who knows how much she's already had?" Triumph looked at the Princess of Pentacles dancing with a stranger.

"She needs to be looked after," Page whispered with a smile as Gaia approached.

"To us!" The friends took the shots in one gulp.

Gaia, with slightly drunken eyes, jealously looked at Triumph as he was courting a pretty waitress before throwing a displeased glance at the girl and approaching the major.

"Triumph, let's dance!" She pulled him by the hand.

"Okay, but only one dance," the major agreed. "I reserve the bachata for Page."

The rooftop was packed with people. It was likely that the whole city had decided to escape the summer heat on the beach. The night was so hot, it seemed that the air didn't move at all. Page touched her hair, which was out of control.

"Do I look like a poodle?" she plaintively asked Aqua and Amador sitting across from her.

"Don't talk nonsense, you look amazing." Aqua smiled and turned to Amador for support. "Doesn't she?"

"It's not just your appearance, it's your zest," the major quickly agreed. "No wonder Baphomet likes you. He loves everything that's outside of the usual framework, like himself. You're similar in some way."

"Do you know him well?" Page tried to sound casual.

"Well enough, but he's closest to High Priestess and Sun."

Triumph returned to the table out of breath and immediately plopped down on the couch next to Page.

"I suggest not giving any more shots to Gaia. Otherwise, we'll have to carry her back."

"This task falls on your strong shoulders, Triumph." Page laughed and looked around.

Baphomet had promised to come, and she was hoping he would. Page felt different with him. An unknown part of her soul had woken from a liturgic dream in his presence, and this part made her soar above the ground.

"Looking for Baphomet?" Triumph intercepted her glance.

"Not at all." Page blushed. "Wanna dance?"

"I love the bachata!" Aqua also stood up as the song began and led Amador along.

Triumph and Page swirled to the rhythm of the music. Now she could see Triumph's face like never before, his blue eyes framed in a shining yellow ring. His delicate light skin was covered with freckles, and his curly golden hair playfully fell to his shoulders. The major looked a little holy.

"I like it when you look at me this way." Triumph smiled, quirking the corners of his lips.

"You look like a saint. Only the halo above your head is missing."

"I doubt that." Triumph laughed. "In the war with the major Abyss, I was far from being a saint."

Page didn't answer. She had read about the Millennium War with the major of the Blank card. His dimension was ever-growing, an all-consuming black hole. The other majors had no chance of defeating him. Inevitably, they lost the war, and now, all the majors and minors had to comply with Abyss's laws.

"Why did he let you continue to exist?" Page asked quietly.

"We're immortal, remember?" He smirked. "Plus, his dimension is emptiness. He needs us all to keep the balance, like two magnetic poles."

"And the stupid laws?" Page paused. "Like the

minors not being allowed to marry between different Arcana?"

"I think he's afraid that the deck will be shuffled unpredictably. That's why the majors aren't allowed to have children. Someone more powerful than Abyss may appear, and he won't have it."

"It's a sign of weakness. Coward." Page's anger flared up.

"I'm surprised you care so much." Triumph stared into her eyes.

"I suppose you know I was imprisoned by Justice," she stuttered. "They probably expected me to become obedient. Justice is all about accepting responsibilities and consequences. But I only started to hate the laws even more."

"Your punishment was unfair?" Triumph whispered.

"Every stupid law that Abyss has proclaimed is unfair." Page stopped herself, afraid of the heat growing inside. "Let's not talk about it tonight."

"Sure." He smiled gently. "I fought side by side with Baphomet. He's a real warrior. But he's promiscuous with women." The major winked at Page, and again she saw something childish in this strong man.

"It's your common trait, I guess." Page narrowed her eyes.

"What a sharp tongue you have!" Triumph laughed, throwing back his golden head.

Page straightened suddenly. She didn't see Baphomet, but she clearly felt his gaze on her. His presence eclipsed everything around, or at least it did for Page. Triumph deftly turned her to the last chords, gently holding her by the waist.

"Thank you for the dance." The major bowed, and they returned to the table.

Baphomet stood near the bar, his ebony hair in a bun, emphasizing the perfect lines of his face. Triumph caught Page's gaze.

"Don't worry, Page. I know we're just friends." The major smiled softly.

Page smiled back and kissed his cheek, glad he understood. She saw Baphomet moving toward them, leaving a trace of blurry shadow behind him.

"Baphomet, twice in one day! To what do we owe this pleasure?" Triumph was already filling his glass with champagne.

"You owe Page, of course," he replied in an echoing voice. "Amador, Princess of Cups." The major tilted his head in greeting to each of them. "Princess of Wands." He lightly touched Page's hand before kissing it.

"Baphomet." She bowed, laughing at his formality, but also secretly thrilled by it. She held her hand close, feeling it tingle from his icy-hot kiss. Baphomet smiled back, pushing a strand of her white hair from her face as he moved closer.

"Laughing at Devil?" Baphomet whispered seductively and glared playfully at Page. "I should punish you."

"If you must." Page grinned, a spark of desire shooting through her.

"Tequila?" Amador interrupted, bringing shots almost to their faces.

"Hmm." Baphomet looked at Page as she smiled gently. "Why not?"

"Wait—where's Gaia?" Page scanned the dance floor.

"I think she left with that stranger from her Arcana." Amador smiled.

"At least someone will have a passionate tequila night," Triumph said approvingly.

Page didn't finish her drink. She hadn't eaten much today and didn't want to lose her head too soon.

"A dance?" Baphomet looked at her with heavy, blazing eyes.

What am I doing? Trying to pick up more demons? she thought to herself while Baphomet patiently waited for her answer. But Page quickly convinced herself that one night wouldn't change anything. After all, she deserved to finally have some fun in her life.

"How can I say no to Devil himself?" Page bit her burning lips.

He picked Page up in his arms and carried her to the dance floor, everyone staring at them. Page laughed and tried to straighten her dress. She felt as light as a feather in his arms. When they started to dance, Baphomet put his hand on Page's back so low that for a second, she thought he was going to reach under her dress. His hand was rough, the skin on both palms burned. She loved his cheeky touch, and a wave of desire washed over her.

CHAPTER

TWELVE

BAPHOMET.

Page felt so small in his big hands, like a fragile crystal glass in which promise of sweet madness burned.

"What happened to your palms?" She tilted her head back to look into his eyes.

"Cost of the profession. Devil is not Sun or Chariot. I was created full of demons and temptations. The same demons that I send to the people of the Minor Arcana first have to pass through my soul. This is a reminder of one of them." Baphomet stared at her, looking for fear or disgust.

"I like your hands. Very manly," she answered without a hint of fear or contempt.

The major smiled and whirled her even faster. "I've been thinking about you all day. Couldn't concentrate on anything," he whispered. Baphomet pulled Page closer to his solid body, eagerly devouring the heat of her energy. He wanted to be left alone with her, wanted to leave sweet imprints on her skin with his kisses.

"I thought about you too." Page's voice sounded gentle, like the slow, flickering flame of a candle.

65

Before the dance, he'd sensed that his siren was fighting her attraction to him. Now he tried to hide his smile, realizing he was slowly winning.

"I'm sure Triumph helped you distract yourself." Baphomet cleared his throat, trying to hide his jealousy.

"Are you jealous?" Page smiled, teasing.

"No," he lied.

Yes. And it's a miracle that Triumph's hands are still in place, Baphomet thought.

"Why did you decide to become a photographer?" He continued to dive into her eyes, trying to see everything that her soul was hiding.

"I always liked it, and I missed it so much when…" Page paused. "I guess it's my passion." She timidly lowered her eyes.

Baphomet knew she was thinking about Justice, but decided not to rush her. It seemed she wasn't ready to talk about it with him yet. "Interesting." He smiled gently, hoping one day Page would share with him all her dreams and fears.

When the song ended, he lifted her up again.

"Put me down!" she said, laughing out loud.

"I must return the lady safe and sound." Devil carried her to the table.

Page tried to adjust her dress as soon as she was back on the ground, but Baphomet couldn't wait. It was becoming torture. He grabbed her waist and moved Page closer to him. "Shall we leave?" He couldn't resist and gently touched her lips—lips that burnt so blissfully with the promise of showing him pleasures he didn't dare dream of.

"Yes." Page dug her fingers into his shirt as she whispered.

Devilish fire raged in his eyes, and Baphomet quickly turned to the rest of the group. "It was nice seeing everyone." He bowed.

"Are you stealing the princess from us already?" Triumph looked directly into Devil's eyes. "Take care of her."

"I will, don't worry." Baphomet took Page's hand, and their fingers intertwined.

They walked to the car without saying a word. Baphomet couldn't take his eyes off her, couldn't believe it wasn't all just a wonderful mirage that would disappear as quickly as it had appeared on his path.

"Where are we going?" Page couldn't find a comfortable position and was crossing one leg over the other in turns.

"I want to show you my summer house," he sang, never taking his gaze off her.

"You have a house on the beach?" Page opened her eyes wide in surprise, and their bright light pierced his darkness.

"Yes, I love water, despite the fact that I was born from the ashes of fire." He smiled tenderly.

Devil smirked, remembering his promise to never bring any woman to this house—the same promise he'd made to himself about his house in the fifteenth dimension. And there he was, not only inviting Page willingly, but also hoping she would live together with him there one day.

Devil parked at the pier, and they walked to a small black motorboat.

"Let me help you take off your shoes." Baphomet slowly dropped to one knee. He held his breath as his fingers slid down her thighs toward her feet, leaving trails of ashes in their wake. He slowly unfastened the clasps on her shoes and smiled with satisfaction when he heard her deep breathing. He wasn't the only one affected here. He felt like a thief who had finally taken possession of a priceless treasure.

CHAPTER

THIRTEEN

PAGE.

Baphomet easily jumped into the boat and offered his hand to Page. Soon they were speeding forward. The fresh, salty wind blew her hair and clothes, taking her breath away, just like Devil did. She was sitting so close to Baphomet that her thighs touched his body, and she saw a blazing flame in his eyes.

"You are an inexplicable mystery." He studied her face over and over, as if trying to find demons hidden deep inside.

Page's skin was covered with goosebumps at the thought that they would be alone in his house. Sweet obsession spread through her fiery veins. She knew she should be careful, but Devil's forbidden darkness was pulling her deep, and she was ready to dive in despite all the warnings.

Page saw an island in front of them. Someone with a lantern stood on the pier.

"Good evening, Master." An old man with gray hair and wrinkled skin bowed.

"Oliver, this is Lady Page. Page, this is Oliver."

"Nice to meet you." Page smiled.

"Nice to meet you, Lady Page." The man bowed, almost touching the ground. "Master, I've arranged everything as you requested. If you would like, I could take you there."

"That won't be necessary." Baphomet took the lantern. "Good night, Oliver. Don't wait for us."

"As you please, Master." The old man silently withdrew.

Devil took Page's hand and led her along, lighting the way.

"I want to show you something," he whispered, squeezing her hand a little tighter.

Page tried to breathe deeply as sweet excitement took over her body. After a couple of minutes, Baphomet put out the lantern and Page realized that they had practically crossed the small island to the other side. They entered a small cave, where she saw a hidden lagoon.

"Look." Devil's ashy eyes sparkled in the night, and Page felt drawn to them like a moth to a flame.

The water was filled with millions of luminous blue moving dots. She had never seen anything like it before. It looked like magic.

"It's beautiful. Are they alive?"

"Yes. I thought we could take a swim. They're harmless, and the water is as warm as hell's pit today." The sapphire glow of the water illuminated Baphomet's face.

No one had ever looked at her this way, with pure devotion. Or at least, that's what she saw in his eyes.

"I didn't bring my bathing suit." Page flushed.

"Not a problem. Oliver took care of everything."

A fire was burning not far from the water, and a large blanket was spread out some distance away. Page saw big towels and a short, almost transparent white nightgown.

"You can change. I'll check the fire." Baphomet cleared his throat.

Page picked up the nightgown, a small, delicate piece of fabric that was unlikely to cover anything. She put it on, not taking her eyes off Devil. He was straightening the burning logs with his bare hands and didn't look at her.

"Ready," she whispered, and the major turned to her and froze, hypnotized.

Eyes wide, Page looked down to see that her breasts were almost visible through the thin fabric. The nightie was made for someone with smaller hips, so it barely covered her body. Baphomet clenched his hands into fists and growled almost soundlessly. Page slowly went into the water and swam a little further. It was warm and her body lit up, looking as though it were covered in blue diamonds. Devil was still standing on the bank, watching her, mesmerized.

"Are you just going to stand there?" Page gently ran her hands over the glowing water.

"You are a siren." He slowly entered and swam up to Page, so close that she felt his breath on her lips. "Capturing Devil himself and luring him into your depths," Baphomet whispered and gently pulled Page to his body with one arm.

She couldn't breathe, couldn't think. Devil's touch burned her skin, and she desperately needed more. His other hand slid down her hair, then her neck, and settled on her breast, which was now completely visible under the wet fabric. Her nipples became hard, and she tilted her head slightly, unconsciously getting closer to his alluring lips.

"I'm going insane," Page whispered.

"I went insane the moment I saw you at the show." Baphomet pulled her even closer. He kissed her hungrily, as if it were the only thing he dreamed of, sending scorching arrows through her veins. Page wrapped her arms and legs around him, his body so hard and so inviting. Baphomet squeezed her thighs, and Page moaned, driven close to madness, feeling his hard flesh against her. Their tongues were exploring each other passionately, deeply. Page began to move, unable to contain her intoxicating desire. Devil let out a deep, low sound like the roar of a hungry beast, encouraging Page to wrap herself around him even tighter. Flames erupted from her skin, illuminating in a blue glow that shifted into white fire.

"Fucking perfection," Baphomet sang into her ear.

He didn't even move away from her flame, watching it with admiration. Page had never been with a man before. All the candidates had quickly disappeared after seeing her fire. And she was happy they had. Now, she couldn't imagine being with anyone but him.

Baphomet held Page with one arm while the fingers of his other hand gently touched her clit. She buried her face in his neck and bit into the skin.

"Fuck. I've never wanted anyone as I want you," the major groaned.

Page dug her long nails into his back as Devil continued to press on her center. His hard flesh was so close to her core that Page trembled. His lips found her nipples and she threw her head back in pleasure, wanting more of him.

"I want to taste you." Baphomet looked into her eyes almost demanding.

"Please," Page begged.

Devil slowly carried her to the shore and gently lowered her onto the blanket. He knelt over Page and studied her body through the wet nightgown.

"You are a promise of salvation," Baphomet sang, and she believed him.

He spread her legs, kissing them as he moved up, closer and closer to where she wanted him. His touch was silky and sinful. The major lingered on her inner thigh, and Page arched her back, torn with pleasure and anticipation. Finally, his tongue pressed against her center. Page's moans intertwined with his animalistic growls. It was the most beautiful, forbidden, midnight song ever composed, dipped in primal desire.

"So wet." Devil sounded thirsty as he reached up to her breast while the other held her hips. His tongue moved deeper and deeper into her pulsing core. Page began to move against his mouth and arched her back even more under his kisses.

"I burn," she whispered breathlessly.

Baphomet growled and slightly quickened the pace. She felt like she was floating in the air, filled with hypnotic spells. The wave of pleasure grew, and Page forgot everything around her. She could only feel their flaming bodies. She froze for a second as the arrow of bliss exploded at her center, and millions of fires of pleasure flew through every cell of her being. Page moaned loudly, her legs shaking around his head.

Baphomet was still kissing her slowly, and after a while, when her moans became almost silent, he looked at her. Wet hair was stuck to Page's face, which had grown red with delight like rose petals after a summer rain. Her lips seemed even fuller now. Devil rose up and kissed her gently.

"I won't be able to stop if we continue." Baphomet found her ear and kissed the lobe.

Page closed her eyes in pleasure. "Then don't stop," she whispered, touching his skin with her lips and her breath.

"Let's go to the house." Baphomet sounded drunk.

The major covered Page with the towel and picked her up. She looked at him, surprised.

"I'm faster." He smiled and kissed her again.

Page wrapped her arms around his neck and buried her face in his fire-scented hair. A few minutes later, they had reached the house. As soon as they stepped in, Page saw two big staircases going up and coming together at the top. Devil practically flew up the stairs and opened the door to his room. The large window was open, and Page could hear the sounds of the surf. The room was dark, only a couple of candles burning down on the table, illuminating the space. Page noticed a large book-case and a big bed right next to the window. Baphomet gently lowered her onto it. He helped her take off the wet nightgown and then took off his own towel. Page stared at his powerful body and licked her lips, which tasted of grapes soaked in tar. Devil smiled and slowly approached her, leaning over her on his hands, and kissed her stomach, then her breasts. Page grabbed his head in her hands and pulled him to her lips. She opened her legs wide, unable to wait any longer. Devil snarled, squeezing her so hard that Page felt like she was being torn to pieces by a wild creature. She lowered her hand, and as she touched his hardened flesh, Devil hissed.

"I want to claim you," Baphomet growled.

Page groaned in pleasure and anticipation, but to

her surprise, Devil moved away from her slightly and froze. He quickly covered Page and himself with a sheet.

"Get the fuck out, La Papesse!" Baphomet yelled.

High Priestess appeared out of thin air, just as Magician had earlier today at the beach. Page pulled the cover even tighter. The major was an older woman. Lit by candlelight, she looked like a ghost that haunted wicked souls.

"Hopefully I didn't interrupt anything important," La Papesse said dismissively in a soft voice.

Devil's face was contorted with anger, and Page thought he might pounce on his uninvited guest. "You've got to be kidding me! I said get the fuck out!" Baphomet could hardly control himself, and for some reason, Page wanted to laugh at seeing his frustration.

She giggled. Devil and High Priestess looked at her in bewilderment.

"I am so sorry." She held a hand to her mouth to hide the smile. "Just ignore me."

A smile also touched Baphomet's face as he looked at Page.

"Glad to finally meet you, Princess of Wands." High Priestess bowed and slowly examined her.

"You still here?" Devil blurted out, but not with rage anymore.

"You are a darling, as always." La Papesse drawled every word, speaking with an accent Page had never heard.

"We're busy. You can't join in, sorry." Baphomet showed the major the door.

Page laughed at his words.

"Get ready." High Priestess turned away and added, "And for Sun's sake, wear something."

Baphomet practically growled in response. "Wait in the kitchen."

"You wish. I'll wait outside the door. And there's no point in the Princess of Wands waiting for you. I'll stay here all night."

When High Priestess left, Baphomet turned to Page and gently touched her hair.

"I'm sorry, I think she's lost it. Will I see you tomorrow?" His eyes sank into her heart.

Page lifted her eyes, still heavy with desire, and got closer to Devil until her mouth brushed against his ear. "I hope you'll make it up to me tomorrow … repeatedly." Page seductively bit his earlobe.

"Rest assured, siren," Baphomet growled, grabbing her by the hips and pressing her tight to his body.

"I'm waiting!" High Priestess shouted from behind the door.

"How do I get back?" Page comfortably lay down on the bed filled with his invisible, inviting scent.

"La Papesse will transfer you. She should at least do something useful." Baphomet was getting ready, but didn't take his eyes off Page. "You look like a fragrant flower."

Page blushed slightly. She was still naked, covered only with a delicate silk sheet. "I have nothing to wear." The princess pouted her lips.

Baphomet smiled and took a black shirt out of his closet. "Here." His eyes glittered as he watched Page get dressed. "I love seeing you wear my clothes, even though I prefer you naked." Devil pulled her closer and slipped his hands under the shirt, touching her silky hips.

"I'm coming in." La Papesse knocked on the door.

"Buzzkill." Baphomet rolled his eyes as they

emerged from the room. "Send Page back to the hotel." He looked at High Priestess.

"I wonder what happened to her clothes." La Papesse paused, her eyebrow raised, and Page blushed.

"Curiosity kills the cat," he snapped.

"All right. See you again soon, Princess of Wands, under more civilized circumstances."

Page felt her skin burn anew as Baphomet approached and kissed her gently, ignoring High Priestess. "Good night. 'Til tomorrow." He leaned closer to her and whispered, "You lured me in, siren."

Smoke stroked her body, and in a split second, Page was in her bed next to the peacefully sleeping Princess of Cups.

FOURTEEN

BAPHOMET.

Baphomet's heart sank when Page disappeared. He felt like he'd known this siren for many lifetimes in many dimensions, even though they had just met. He decided that he would find her first thing tomorrow morning, so they could spend the whole day together without leaving his room. Baphomet poured himself a drink and looked accusingly at La Papesse. Page's light was still flaming in the depths of his eyes.

"Stop glowering at me." The major of the second dimension met his eyes.

"Go to hell. I hate you right now." Devil sipped his drink. "What's so urgent?"

"Here's the thing." High Priestess paused. "It's actually about your Page."

"What's wrong?" Baphomet tensed at the thought that she might be in danger, especially now that she was out of his sight and protection.

"She's a bad fit for you. Find yourself another princess, or a few, if you must," La Papesse said, her voice full of steel.

"You've lost it, I swear." The major's eyes danced with ashes. "Not a chance. I want no one but Page."

"Since when do you want only one girl?" His friend smirked.

"Since the moment I saw her. I want Page to be mine, in every meaning of the word," Baphomet confessed, mostly to himself. "And since when do I need to report to you?"

"Since the deck has been reshuffled," High Priestess said. "Your Page is the future Empress. I can't risk losing her. The existence of the whole universe depends on it."

"Seriously, are you on something?" Baphomet snapped. "We have Empress. And she's immortal, wherever she is."

"I know. I can't explain how it's possible, but the Princess of Wands is the future Empress," La Papesse insisted. "The Wheel of Fortune is about to make a full turn. I can feel it. The deck is shuffling, and her card will be drawn, along with the Empress."

Baphomet remembered the flames exiting Page's body and opened his mouth in shock. *Fuck, maybe La Papesse is right.*

"Let's say you're right. It doesn't change anything. I want to be with Page."

"My sinful friend, you know the deck has a bad sense of humor. I hear you, even though it's ridiculous to hear something so romantic from Devil," La Papesse said guiltily. "She is the future Empress, the purest major in the deck. And you... Well, you are the Devil."

"She doesn't mind my darkness," Baphomet interjected.

"Your darkness will corrupt her, and you can't help it. Don't doubt my connection to the deck. If she doesn't manifest all four energies on time, she'll die." High

Priestess nudged closer to Baphomet, staring into his eyes. "She's already got very little time, but if you insist, I'm afraid she is destined to find certain death."

"How much time?" Devil's voice echoed with emptiness. He'd just found Page, and the deck was taking her away already.

"Until the full blood moon."

"And after that? Can we be together?" Baphomet asked with hope.

"Who knows? It's never happened before." High Priestess didn't sound optimistic.

"Then I need to talk to Page and explain everything," the major decided. "Dammit, we'll have to wait."

"You don't understand. You can't be next to her. And the future Empress can't know what is happening until the very last moment. The transition should happen naturally. It can't be forced," La Papesse explained.

"I'm sick of your prophecies!" he snapped. "What do you suggest?" Baphomet wanted to tear everything apart in this universe that always seemed to be against him.

"Don't see her again. I hope you haven't corrupted her energy yet with your darkness," High Priestess continued. "Let the princess become who she's destined to be," the major concluded.

"The Empress… It can't be true," Devil thought out loud. "I need to look into this myself."

"Fine, but promise it'll be the last time you see her. With Devil next to her, the princess's chances of living are close to nothing," High Priestess foretold.

FIFTEEN

PAGE.

Aqua woke up first and immediately opened the window to let in the sunlight, allowing the harmony of morning to fill the room. Page slowly stretched in bed, feeling sweet euphoria flooding through her blossoming body.

"What time is it?" Page yawned.

"Seven a.m.," Aqua sang. "I signed us up for a yoga class."

"You want to kill me!" Page pulled the blanket over her head.

While Aqua smoothly flowed from the pose of cobra to the pose of downward dog, Page sat by the empty pool and looked at the sea's surface. To her surprise, she saw Triumph and Amador getting ready for surfing. Page walked over to the majors barefoot. The sand was still cold. Her hair and delicate creamy dress billowed like a sail in the sea. She felt reborn, greedily breathing in the winds of change.

Triumph spotted her first. "I didn't expect to see you up so early." He smiled, putting on a surf suit.

"It's Aqua's fault." Page closed her eyes against the sun.

"I told you staying in my room was a much better idea." The major playfully touched her nose.

"Next time, I might seriously consider your offer." Page gestured for Triumph to turn around and helped him zip up the suit.

"How was your evening?" Amador approached them, carrying a surfboard.

"Don't ask." Page rolled her eyes. "You said High Priestess and Baphomet were close, but her showing up in his bedroom in the middle of the night when he wasn't alone is too close, if you ask me."

Triumph burst into laughter. "What did she do?"

"Just appeared out of nowhere, interrupting us." Page could hardly contain her laugher either.

"Wait, I'm imagining in detail what exactly she interrupted…" Triumph raised his eyes to the sky.

"Triumph, stop it." Page pushed his shoulder.

"She probably had a good reason," Amador said knowingly as always. "Did she tell you anything?"

"That she was glad to meet me, and hoped to see me…" Page paused. "Under different circumstances."

"That's not like her. High Priestess never comes into direct contact with the minors. She prefers to send Agatha," Amador concluded.

"Agreed. Maybe I'll visit her and find out what she wants from you," Triumph decided.

"I doubt she wants anything from me. I'm just the Princess of Wands." Page shrugged.

"I wouldn't be so sure," Triumph thought out loud. "First Magus, now La Papesse."

Page watched the majors break through the waves on their surfboards, opting to watch from the beach. In the morning stillness, their bodies seemed like an extension of the ocean. She didn't even notice when Aqua sat down next to her.

"Beautiful," Aqua whispered almost silently. "How was your night?" She narrowed her eyes playfully.

"Sooooo good." Page blushed, and her fingers caught fire. She quickly buried her hands in the sand, impatiently waiting for the flames to die. "Ugh, I can't be mad, I can't be happy—just great!" Page snapped, looking at her undying fire. She hated how all of her emotions erupted through flame. Yesterday, with Baphomet, it had felt different. But now, Page looked around again, afraid someone would notice.

"You'll get there," Aqua said, her voice gentle like a stream. "So, Baphomet. I'm waiting for the spicy details!"

Page laughed and told Aqua about her night, finishing with High Priestess's visit.

"Do you think she came to talk about you?" Aqua asked once Page had finished her story.

"I doubt she cares who Baphomet spends his time with. Have you seen Gaia?" Page was a little worried. Gaia had been acting a bit strange this weekend, constantly drinking. Page had never seen her spend a night with a stranger before.

"I was going to knock on her door, but I suspect she's not alone." Aqua smiled slightly.

"I think we should ask High Priestess to assist in this matter. Seems like it's her specialty."

They both giggled.

After a couple of hours, the whole company went down to the pool. The sun shone so brightly that the only escape was to lie in the shade or take a dip in the water.

"Hangover, Triumph?" Gaia walked towards her friends with a margarita in her hand. "Welcome to the club."

"Perhaps I drank too much yesterday. I thought surfing would help, but it was all in vain." The major put an ice cube to his forehead.

"What happened to your two companions from last night?" Aqua narrowed her eyes.

"Ah?" Triumph pretended he had no clue what she was talking about.

"The stunning girl and the man that went up to the room with you. I'm pretty sure they work at reception," she insisted.

"They left in a hurry. I like to fall asleep alone if the company isn't quite right, if you must know." The major obviously didn't enjoy this little interrogation.

Indicating that the conversation was over, Triumph comfortably lounged on the chair, watching his friends play cards.

"Let me order you a coffee." Page turned to the waiter.

"I've already ordered champagne," Triumph protested.

"Triumph, it's ten in the morning! Let's at least change it to a mimosa." Page laughed.

"By the way, according to Madame Astrid, a meteor shower is expected tonight. It can be seen from another part of the beach." Aqua almost jumped up and down with enthusiasm.

"Who is Madame Astrid?" Amador asked.

"Just the most popular astrologer!" Aqua obviously couldn't believe her ears.

"Got it, my bad." Amador smiled.

"So, I talked to the concierge. We can rent open Jeeps and go at sunset to watch the stars fall. It's on the other side of the island," Aqua reported.

"I'm in if Triumph comes," Gaia blurted out, then bit her lip.

"Will Baphomet join us?" Triumph looked at Page.

"Maybe. I'll send him a note. I don't know what his plans are." She hesitated. Page was hoping he wouldn't forget his promise to see her today. Baphomet raised a fire of desire in her, but she also needed him to calm it down.

"Fine, I'm in." Triumph moved closer, resting his head on Page's legs. She gently ran her fingers through his sunny hair and began to braid it. Triumph closed his eyes in pleasure, and in a second, he fell asleep quietly.

Aqua clapped her hands. "Wonderful, I'm going to arrange transportation." With that, she took her beach bag and headed inside, Amador following her like an adoring puppy.

CHAPTER

SIXTEEN

BAPHOMET.

Baphomet finally fell asleep with the first rays of light. He believed La Papesse. In the long millennia of their friendship, she had never let him down; her visions always came true. But for some reason, this time, Devil felt like it was a mistake to follow her advice. The idea that he would continue to live his normal life while his siren became the Empress without even knowing it seemed like a death sentence. He didn't even want to think about the blood moon and what would happen if Page didn't manifest all four energies of the Empress. Devil decided to see Page again today to look closer, even though deep down, he knew the answer. He'd seen her flaming body yesterday, shining like the first star in the night sky.

It would be so hard to walk away from this magnetic creature who had taken possession of his wicked soul. But Baphomet hoped that after the full moon, he could win Page back. He knew that he wouldn't be able to be with any other woman; it seemed simply impossible. Page burned the memories of everyone else but her to ashes. Devil pondered this while sitting at the table, eating grapes.

"Get ready, Oliver. We're leaving later tonight." Baphomet sounded angry.

"Already?" the old man asked, surprised. "I have just received a letter from the Princess of Wands." Oliver paused. "The bell boy from the hotel is waiting outside to bring her a response."

The major quickly read the letter written in neat handwriting. The paper was slightly wet. Most likely, Page had been with her friends at the pool when she'd written it.

Baphomet quickly got ready and headed to the hotel. It was time to let Page go. A wave of despair covered him with renewed vigor.

Devil entered the lobby and immediately saw Page standing by the window.

Amador noticed him first. "Baphomet! So nice to see you again. Last century, you rarely graced us with your presence."

"Hi, all." Devil's eyes darted to Page, peacefully watching the ocean. "How're you, siren?" He gently hugged Page's waist. She smelled like an intoxicating potion mixed specially for him.

"Hi." Page blushed and wrapped her arms around him too.

They stood silently looking at each other. He sent his ashes around her, hoping to see if Page was indeed becoming the Empress. But without even knowing it, she breathed the ashes in. Devil couldn't read her like he did others.

"I am getting used to your handsome face, Baphomet," Triumph greeted him loudly as he came out of the elevator.

"He's as handsome as hell is hot." Page tossed her head a little.

Baphomet impatiently moved her closer and buried his face in her hair. He wanted to savor every moment next to his siren. "My sheets smell like you: fire and peonies. I woke up daydreaming about you," Baphomet whispered into the princess's ear.

"Me too, but I didn't have the privilege of being alone in the room to find release myself," Page teased him.

Devil tightened his grasp around her body. "Don't tempt me," he growled.

"All over each other already." Triumph rolled his eyes.

"Since when did you become a morality check?" Aqua came down with a picnic basket.

Three parked open Jeeps were already waiting for them on the beach. Baphomet took his shoes off, and throwing Page over his shoulder, he carried the girl to the car. He wished to carry her like this to his dimension, protecting her from all the danger in the world.

The Jeeps rushed forward. The sun was already beginning to go down, staining the sky and water in a reddish-purple glow. Page stood up, raising her hands and facing the piercing wind. Her hair billowed like a sail in the open sea. "Freedom!" she screamed.

Devil looked at her and laughed duskily. She was life. A day spent with her was worth more than a whole lonely immortal existence.

"Do you want to drive?" The major straightened her rebel hair with one hand.

"I don't know how to drive! My parents always forbade me to try anything." Page grew quiet. "Plus, I didn't have a chance to do anything until recently."

Should I ask her about Justice? Baphomet looked at her hesitating. *Maybe it's too painful.*

"Justice took me." Page seemed to read his mind. "I am the only minor whose energy exits into the world. My flame is uncontrollable. Or maybe I just suck at controlling it."

"What did you do?" Baphomet whispered.

He felt the pain in her eyes as if it were his own. "I was in a club. Some guy attempted to do something bad to me. I wanted to stop him." She paused. "I was so angry and scared, my whole body caught fire. I burnt him—terribly. No one even tried to listen to me."

"Who was it?" Baphomet growled. He was determined to hunt the guy down and finish him off.

"It doesn't matter, it's in the past now." Page lowered her eyes. "Don't do anything, please."

"I'm sorry," Baphomet whispered gently, touching her face.

"If I had killed him, they would've sent me to your dimension." She looked away. "Justice is cruel."

Baphomet wanted to erase her painful memories. She'd lived through a lot, but she still stayed so pure, so hungry for life.

"Come on, I'll teach you to drive. It's easy." He looked at her encouragingly.

Devil stopped the Jeep, and Page sat between his legs. He wrapped her waist with his hands, and his face touched the girl's cheek. "So..." The major was breathing heavily. "Here's the brake, right pedal is the gas. This is the steering wheel. The good news is that the beach has nowhere to crash."

"Understood," Page whispered and turned her face to meet his lips.

"Careful, I am very weak around you." Baphomet squeezed her waist in his strong hands.

Page pushed down on the gas, and they rushed forward. Their car quickly caught up with the rest of the group.

"Bravo, Page!" Aqua screamed.

"Now you can come to my racing club, Princess of Wands!" Triumph smiled.

Baphomet noticed Page looking at the ocean. The sun was almost gone below the horizon, gently wrapped in seawater. She slowed down and then stopped the car, separating from the group. There was not a soul on the deserted beach.

"I want to photograph the sunset." Page moved to the hood of the car and took a few pictures.

Baphomet watched her, and his heart sank at the thought that he had to let her go. He moved closer, wishing the sun would never go down. Page was still sitting on the hood, and when the major approached, she spread her legs widely. Baphomet pressed his body against hers. His tenacious hands touched her hips, and Page moaned—the most perfect sound in the whole universe. He was obsessed. Her holy body answered to his every touch.

"You're bursting with life. Places in my heart untouched for centuries have awakened for you." Baphomet moved her even closer, unable to stay away.

Page tilted her head, and their lips merged in a hungry kiss. Devil slowly went down, kissing her neck, then lifted her top and eagerly sucked her nipples, playing with them for a while until Page's body strained with the dark magic running through the maze of her heart.

"Fuck." Baphomet squeezed her in his rough palms. "What delicate skin you have."

His fingers found her core and slowly entered. Page threw her head back, and her lips opened with the thrill.

"I can come just by looking at you." Devil watched her like a demon hungry for a soul.

The major accelerated the pace, and Page put her hands on the hood, opening her hips even more. She moved into the rhythm of his fingers, like an obedient instrument in the hands of a virtuoso musician. "So good." She burned for him.

Baphomet cursed again. It was too hot. "Fuck."

Picking her up, he carried Page to the seat of the car. He went down and eagerly pressed his mouth to her center. Page grabbed his shirt, grasping for support. He knew she was already close to delicious madness and worked her to euphoria, whipped up by her cries.

"Baphomet," Page whispered breathlessly. She covered her mouth with her hand and bit her fingers, unable to last any longer. Baphomet watched her as if possessed. Large white flames rose from her body, filling the air with her smoky peony scent. Devil rose up to meet her rosy lips, and Page hugged him tightly, looking at the sun on the horizon. At least for now, he was part of her tale, and it felt like a blessing.

She slowly lowered a hand to touch his flesh, moving up and down, first gentle and slow, and then faster and faster.

"Page," Baphomet growled.

But she didn't stop. She went down, hungry for him. Page took him all the way into her throat, moving deeply, almost choking with pleasure. It was fucking perfect. He couldn't hold back, growling, pulling her hair tight. "Fuck," Baphomet cursed, shaking the reality around them before his release.

Page rose and sat comfortably on his lap. They were completely dissolved in each other.

"Seriously, I might go insane from my desire for you." Baphomet looked into her shimmering eyes, and a cloud of sadness shadowed him. He couldn't imagine how he would be able to let her go…

They sat hugging each other silently, watching the sunset. Two cars were approaching, and Page quickly straightened her clothes.

"Page, we thought you were lost!" Aqua shouted.

"Just wanted to photograph the sunset." She playfully looked at Baphomet.

"You drive." He handed Page the keys and went to the passenger's seat.

Page drove excitedly without taking her eyes off the beach.

"What are you doing?" She looked at Baphomet as he snapped a photo of her with her own camera.

"We must capture this historical moment." He laughed, throwing his raven hair back. "You are the most serious driver in this universe."

This innocent moment was everything. It was so simple, but at the same time so special. Baphomet had finally connected his soul with someone.

"Laugh again, and I will drive straight into the sea." Page frowned.

"Yes, just like this! Don't move!" Baphomet photographed her again.

When they had reached the other side of the island, it was already dark. At first rarely, and then more frequently, the stars began to fall.

"Make a wish!" Page raised her eyes to the sky quickly, making a wish.

Baphomet didn't care about the stars. He didn't want to take his eyes off Page for a second.

"You don't have a wish?" she whispered gently, touching his lips with hers.

You're my wish, he thought.

"I've already made a wish, but I'm afraid it's not destined to come true," Devil said in a forlorn voice.

"Who knows? Dreams tend to come true." Page moved even closer and buried her face in his hair.

Baphomet squeezed his hand into a fist. The evening was almost over, and with every second, his heart sank deeper and deeper into darkness.

"Who's hungry?" Aqua took out some raw meat.

"Aqua, I love you. I'm glad you brought meat and not marshmallows." Triumph kissed the princess, helping her with the food.

Baphomet envied her friends; they would stay in her life, unlike him. Hight Priestess was right: only the majors could manipulate the energy as Page did. The minors didn't have real power. The energy flowed inside them, but it would never come out.

* * *

Baphomet drove the car without taking his eyes off the gently sleeping princess. Even in a dream, her face shone mysteriously like a lunar eclipse.

"Did I fall asleep?" Page's hazy voice, without any resistance, penetrated his very heart.

"Like a baby. I carried you into the car." Baphomet tried to sound distant; his siren must believe he was no longer interested.

"You…" Page paused. She probably felt that something was wrong. "Will you come up?"

The major was trying to gather his will. He silently parked outside and turned to face her. Page's beautiful eyes were full of devotion and temptation.

"Page." Baphomet clenched his hand into a fist, fighting his helplessness. "I'm afraid we can't see each other anymore."

Devil looked at her, feeling doomed. His siren was hurting, and he was the reason. All he wanted to do at that moment was fold her into his arms forever and return the light to her extinct eyes, showering her with a million burning kisses. But instead, he had to let her go.

"I really like you, but I think you're safer without me," Baphomet added, his eyes drowned in black ashes. It was done, and there was no going back.

At that moment, the flame erupted from her hands, her chest, from her whole body, setting the car on fire.

"I'm so stupid!" she screamed, raising her fire even higher.

Baphomet was lost for a moment just staring at her. Page looked like a she-Devil in the middle of the pit of hell. Her eyes darted back to him. Baphomet finally came to his senses and sent out the ashes. They collided with the white fire, slowly putting it out.

"Go to hell." Page slammed the door and quickly headed to the hotel.

"I'm sorry," Baphomet whispered to himself, and his voice was quiet, like the dying flame of a bonfire.

Devil spent the next day in a terrible state, lashing out at everyone around him, including poor Oliver. The feeling that he had made a huge mistake did not leave him.

"Master," Oliver whispered.

"I said I want to be alone!" Baphomet growled.

"A letter for you." Oliver bowed his head, handing him an envelope. "I assume it's from the major Strength, judging by the press."

Baphomet had completely forgotten about his current girlfriend and angrily opened the envelope.

My Devil, Leo said that you're looking for me. I miss you. Let's meet today in the neutral zone. I'll let you know exactly where later. Forever yours, Strength.

Baphomet tore up the letter. "Time to end this," he muttered under his breath and went straight to the chariot.

SEVENTEEN

PAGE.

Page returned home that night without even saying goodbye to her friends. She woke up before the sun rose, feeling like a fallen angel whose wings had been ruthlessly cut off. She should never have trusted Baphomet. After all, he was the Devil for a reason. But the prospect of being accepted and loved for who she was, even if her fire was a mess, had clouded all the warning signs. She still cared for him, wanted him. But it didn't matter anymore; she would never let him manipulate her again.

Page thought of the incident in the car with horror. She had never erupted in such a flame. It was a disaster. She had to do something about her fire before it was too late.

Page quickly put some clothes on and went outside. While everybody was still asleep, she could train freely. She stood in the garden while it was still half dark outside. She took a breath and deliberately thought about Baphomet, about Justice, about her father, and the flame rose higher and higher. Soon it illuminated everything around her. She smiled. At least she'd managed to start the fire on her own. The problem was that she couldn't put it out. Page shook her hands, trying in vain to kill the fire. It wasn't the brightest idea; the flames grew and reached a tree, setting it on fire.

"No, no, no!" Page begged helplessly.

Matilda ran outside, ready with a huge bucket of water, pouring it on the burning tree.

"Thank Sun, Matilda." Page took a deep breath, and the fire finally died in her palms. "My parents will notice. Tell Ricardo to cut down the tree."

"And what am I supposed to tell your father about what happened to the poor tree?" Matilda threw her hands up.

"Tell him we needed wood." Page turned to go back to her room.

"It's summer!" Matilda shouted.

Page got ready and went to the office. She needed to take her mind off Baphomet, off fire, and off Justice. Work should help. To keep her sanity during her imprisonment, Page had often thought of photography. Now, she wanted to create something no one ever had before. That was when she got the idea of a new tarot deck. But first, she needed approval from her mother.

The Queen of Wands was already waiting for Page when she walked in.

"How was your weekend, dear?" The queen stood in her huge office, dressed in a magnificent garnet dress, and carefully leafed through the pictures for tomorrow's issue. "Oh, even a photo of Baphomet!" She clapped her hands. "A wonderful shot, and he's so handsome here!"

"Ordinary," Page muttered.

"If you say so." The Queen of Wands stared at her daughter.

"Mother, do you have a moment to discuss my new idea?"

"New idea?" The queen smiled approvingly. "What is it?"

"For centuries, we've had the one and only tarot deck, which High Priestess created based on the prototype of our universe. It's really boring. Not to mention, no one can use it but La Papesse and Agatha. What if I make photos for each card of the real population, the majors, and the noble part of the Arcana to create a modern tarot deck?" Page looked at her mother, trying to read the reaction on her face. "We can post a new card each week or month in our magazine, explaining the card's meaning, elements, and reversed positions."

"Actually…" The Queen of Wands paused, touching her chin. "It's not a bad idea. But it might be hard. We would have to recreate some scenes, not to mention you have to convince the majors to pose."

"Some of the majors might be difficult to convince. But I can count on Triumph and Amador, and probably Star." Page jumped in excitement.

"Who?"

"I mean Chariot and Lover." Page giggled.

"You are definitely a breath of fresh air for this magazine. And we need it; our ratings are terrible." She paused. "Go ahead. We'll call it the Modern Tarot Deck by the Princess of Wands."

"Thank you, Mother." Page beamed.

"You should start with the major arcana cards, to drive the media and people's attention to your project."

Page went back to her office to start immediately.

The tarot deck had seventy-eight cards, plus the unknown Blank card, of course. This card was Page's favorite. It didn't give an answer, so it was your choice to decide your destiny. Page liked that idea. All the minors' card scenes, except for the Wands Arcana, would need to be recreated at the studio. She couldn't enter the courts of the Cups, Swords, or Pentacles. It would be expensive, but possible. Page decided not to waste time and secured the first card.

She had a hard time finding the place Aqua had chosen for lunch. It was a café that looked like a railway station eatery in the middle of nowhere.

"Why exactly are we meeting in this Sun-forgotten café with plastic cups?" Triumph looked disgusted.

"Not everyone is as rich as you are," Aqua teased.

"Aqua is leading a new project for rescuing dogs, and we decided to help by saving money on our expensive restaurants," Page explained.

"How much do you need? I'll give you everything just to get out of here." Triumph frowned, sniffing a cup as Page and Aqua laughed.

"Thank you, but that's not how it works, Triumph. But your money will be more than welcome at the charity event." Aqua kissed him.

"You are amazing, Aqua," Amador said as the friends stared at him. "I mean, I support the animals and stuff."

After a small pause, everyone laughed.

"Page, what happened with Baphomet?" Gaia asked, and dead silence hung in the air.

"Gaia, I don't want to talk about Baphomet anymore. He broke up with me without even really starting anything. Moving on." Page forced a smile.

Except her heart hadn't moved on. She still thought

about his perfect darkness enveloping her body in her moment of bliss.

I just need time and distractions, she decided.

"Actually, I also have a project." Page clasped her hands.

"Don't tell me we need to give up champagne to save money for it?" Triumph begged.

"I am not that cruel, my friend." Page smiled.

"'My friend'. I like how that sounds." The major grabbed and kissed her hand.

"I'm going to create a new tarot deck, a modern version. I was wondering if you could be my first model." Page looked at Amador.

"Me?" He seemed lost.

"Everyone is obsessed with you. You're Lovers. Everyone wants love." Page looked at him pleadingly.

"Come on, help Page out before she changes her mind about champagne." Triumph tapped Amador on the shoulder.

"I guess... Fine, I'm in," the major agreed without much enthusiasm.

With a laugh, Page kissed him.

"What about my kiss? I practically convinced him!" Triumph protested.

She got closer and kissed him too. "What would I do without your help?" She smiled and sat beside him.

"Do you want to photograph me in my raw form?" Amador obviously wasn't convinced.

"That's the idea for a modern deck. I want it to be different than the old tarot deck, so people can relate and understand the meaning of the card more easily. Actually…" Page cleared her throat. "I might ask you to be naked."

Triumph started to laugh.

"You're not helping!" Page looked at him furiously.

"I can't." Triumph burst out laughing.

"It will be tasteful, I promise." Page looked at Amador, her gaze begging.

"Shut up, Triumph." Amador rolled his eyes.

"We can start tomorrow. It will be amazing. Do you mind if I pick a model for you myself?"

"Is she going to be naked too?" Amador raised his brows.

"We'll leave the panties on. I'll edit them out," Page explained.

Triumph laughed again, and Page threw an empty cup at him.

"Maybe Aqua." Amador paused. "Or Gaia could model with me. So it's more comfortable."

"Ooh, I'm sure it will be very *comfortable*." Triumph emphasized the last word.

"Girls?" Page stared at her girlfriends.

"I can do it," Aqua said, surprising everyone. "I think it's revolutionary. It might inspire people."

Amador looked like he was over the moon.

"You'll look like two pieces that have come together. A perfect masculine and feminine match!" Page almost yelled in excitement. "I have to prepare for the shoot. I'll see you tomorrow."

"Can I come … to help?" Triumph asked.

"Just don't bring champagne!" Page shouted, exiting the café.

Page worked in the studio all day, until everything was ready for the shoot. She wanted to show Lovers' card as a raw union of masculine and feminine energy, but also as a volcano of passion pierced with true love and closure. A set designer prepared the scene, with a volcano crater representing the depth of passion and love. During the shoot, her mother would help "set fire" behind Amador and Aqua.

The next day, Page arrived at the studio.

"Here are my models!" she greeted Aqua and Amador as they entered the room. "How are you both feeling?"

"A little nervous." Aqua said, carefully studying the space.

"Don't worry, the set will be closed. It's just us and my mother." Page smiled, hoping to put her friend at ease.

"And me." Triumph entered with a big smile. "Can't leave my friends on an important day."

"No comments about the nudity, please." Page looked at him seriously.

"Champagne, anyone?" His driver entered, bringing in a case of bottles.

Page rolled her eyes, smiling.

Aqua and Amador looked amazing together. Page couldn't help but wonder what it would be like if they were a couple, especially now that her brother was giving less and less attention to her girlfriend. Plus, everyone could see that Amador was in love with Aqua.

"Amador, you sit here, and Aqua will sit on top of you. Like this…" Page showed them what she wanted, helping them get into position. "Your legs separated. Yes, exactly."

"Free porn." Triumph smirked, drinking champagne next to Page.

"Shh." Page continued, "Put your hands around him, and let Amador kiss your neck… Yes, that's the shot. Mother!" she yelled to the Queen of Wands, who was working on her computer. "We need fire!" Turning back to her friends, she said, "You look amazing!" Then she fetched her camera and began snapping photos.

It took a few hours to get different varieties of the picture, but by the end of the shoot, Page had plenty of photos to choose from.

"Longest foreplay ever, huh, Amador?" Triumph teased.

"I've had longer." Amador smirked.

"Let's get some coffee. And everyone is invited to the club this weekend to celebrate," Page said, beaming.

Her first shoot for the new tarot deck had been a definite success—in more ways than one, judging from the looks Amador was giving Aqua.

"We do deserve it." Triumph nodded.

"You didn't do anything apart from drink!" Page playfully tried to hit him, but the major was too fast for her, ducking away with a laugh.

They said their goodbyes to her mother and went to a small, cozy bakery not far from the office. The window was full of all sorts of sweets.

When the desserts were bought, Aqua asked to exchange an eclair for Amador's lemon meringue pie.

"Lemon meringue pie is his favorite," Triumph let Aqua know. "He must really like you if he's willing to part with it."

"Triumph." Amador gave him an angry look.

Suddenly, Aqua's eyes widened, and she leaned slightly toward Page. "Page, don't look back," she whispered.

Of course, everyone turned around the second the words were out of her mouth. At a table next to the entrance sat Baphomet and a gorgeous woman with lion's hair. Her skin was so light that Page could count all the freckles on her face. She couldn't hear anything for a second except her quickened heartbeat. It felt like her soul had exploded and the pieces fell, piercing her from the inside. Of course, Page recognized the woman: it was Strength. She was constantly in magazines, giving interviews. Page took a slow, deep breath, afraid she might burst into tears, which was odd, given that only the Cups Arcana could cry.

"Is that Strength with Baphomet?" Aqua asked quietly.

"Yes, they…" Triumph faltered and looked at Page. "They've been dating for a very long time. Amador and I didn't tell you. We thought Baphomet himself would explain. They have some kind of open relationship." The major guiltily lowered his eyes.

"He missed that little detail." Page turned involuntarily and met Devil's eyes.

A fiery wave of anger erupted from her palms, and Page abruptly turned back, afraid she might burn the café to ashes. Some people stared at her, but Page quickly doused the flame with some water from a glass.

"I'm sorry, Page," Aqua whispered.

"I'm okay, Aqua." A small tear rolled down her cheek, and Page quickly caught it with her hand.

What the hell?! Page screamed internally. She looked down at her palms, seeing the remnants of black water there. Her head was going to explode. Whatever was happening to her, it had to stop.

Aqua dropped her fork. "Page, was that a tear?"

"There must have been something in my eye." Page tried to smile awkwardly. She was terrified, not knowing how to react.

"Page, how is that possible?" Aqua wasn't dropping

this. "Triumph, Amador, how is this possible? Page is from the Wands Arcana; she doesn't hold water." Aqua looked from Page to the majors, her expression demanding answers.

"I don't know, Aqua." Triumph stared intently at Page. "Have you ever cried before?"

She shook her head. *No, no, no,* Page begged soundlessly. *I can't cry water!*

"Allow me." Triumph touched Page's hand with his finger and tasted the tear she'd caught. "Black, but salty —real tears."

Maybe I'm truly broken, Page confessed to herself.

"Page, do you feel sick? Tell me honestly." Aqua began to worry.

"Aqua, I'm fine. How's your lemon meringue pie?" Page tried to change the subject. She didn't want to talk about one of the many ways she was different. But it wasn't necessary, because at that moment, the whole café turned toward Baphomet's table. His date threw a napkin at him and angrily left, calling him a bastard. Page didn't turn around; she was determined to ignore him and everything connected to him. She had enough on her plate without Baphomet.

"He's coming over here," Aqua reported in a whisper.

"Baphomet." Triumph came to the rescue. "I wouldn't have taken you for a sweet tooth."

"Hello, Page." Devil tilted his head slightly.

Page raised her red eyes at him, ready to burst into tears at any moment. "Hello," she squeezed out formally.

Baphomet kept quiet for a moment, studying her eyes so intently that it seemed like he was trying to see into her soul.

"How was your date?" Triumph broke the silence.

"Strength did not take the news of our breakup as well as I had hoped." Devil stepped a little closer to Page. "I tried to talk to her before the weekend, but she was visiting Magician at his dimension. I'm not on the best terms with him."

Pathetic excuse, Page angrily thought to herself.

An uncomfortable pause hung in the air. Page bit her lip, trying to hold back more tears. Baphomet tilted his head and touched her chin, trying to look into her eyes again. "Page, are you crying?" Devil seemed hurt.

He lifted her face, and their eyes met.

"Don't touch me!" Page blurted out, her eyes covered in black tears. She quickly got up and left the restaurant, just wanting to be away from Baphomet, and from everyone's stares.

EIGHTEEN

BAPHOMET.

Strength chose a small bakery as their meeting place. Baphomet thought it was odd, given the fact that she fanatically followed her diet. But he did not give it much thought. He just wanted to end this as quickly as possible.

As soon as Baphomet entered the café, the light aroma of blooming peonies made his breath catch. His siren was sitting at the far table, talking casually to her friends. Baphomet glared at Strength. Of course her spies had reported how they'd spent the weekend, and she'd decided to show Page that they were still together.

"Is something wrong?" Strength smiled mischievously.

"We need to talk," Baphomet replied dismissively. "It's over. I don't want to see you anymore."

"Is it because of her?!" she almost screamed, turning with a look of hatred toward Page.

His siren turned around, and Baphomet met her eyes, burning with pain. A strong, magnificent wave of anger erupted from Page's palms.

Of course she's mad. She probably hates you, he thought helplessly.

"It's none of your business. I've never promised a real relationship." Baphomet managed to squeeze out at least some explanation. But all he wanted at that moment was to get closer to Page and calm her down.

"Your Page is a joke, a freak, if you ask me." Strength showed her lion's teeth.

"Don't you dare even say her name." Baphomet clenched his hand into a fist. "We're done here."

Strength stood with a huff and threw a napkin in his face.

"A napkin? Seriously?" Baphomet smirked. It felt so good to finally end this meaningless relationship. Even if he could never be with Page, he would prefer to stay alone forever than ever touch another woman but her.

"You're a cheating bastard!" Strength yelled, exiting the bakery.

Everyone was looking at Devil, but he couldn't care less. He inhaled the air and tasted crystallized salt on the peony's petals. Baphomet grew worried. Something was happening to his precious siren, and he needed to find out what.

He slowly got up and went to Page's table. When he approached, she didn't even look at him. Baphomet tilted his head slightly, the need to look into Page's bottomless eyes all-consuming. Her gaze was full of pain, fire, and rage. Page was crying.

The realization hit him in the heart. She was indeed becoming the Empress...

"Don't touch me!" Page blurted out and left the restaurant.

She hates me. Devil repeated these words like a mantra as he drove to a place where he'd always managed to forget everything. It had been a very long time since he'd last crossed the threshold of a gambling club to actually play and not to collect souls. It was his addiction. In the past, he'd spend months here without leaving at all. The last time he'd gambled, it had gotten so bad that High Priestess and Sun had to come and practically drag him home, locking him up in his own labyrinth. As he approached the door, Baphomet realized that he was making a mistake, that this poisonous habit would drag him down again. But he didn't care; he just wanted to be numb.

"May I get struck by the tarot card Tower if I'm lying! It's the best surprise I've ever had!" The manager bowed, letting Devil in. "It's been … well, forever!"

"Hello, Capio. I need to get faded." Baphomet sat at the poker table, inhaling cigar smoke.

"Say no more. Drinks, high rollers, girls, cigars!" The manager practically flew in excitement.

Days and nights blended into one numb trance. Devil didn't really realize how long he had been here, but he knew it wasn't enough. Everything in the club was as he remembered, except for the fact that all the women Capio brought didn't interest Baphomet at all. In the old days, he would stop gambling once in a while to spend time in a private room with a few girls. The manager probably thought that he hadn't brought him the right women, so each day he brought new company, hoping to please Baphomet.

"Major Devil, I think you remember Margo and her

friends. You pleasantly spent time together at one of Chariot's parties." Capio beamed.

Devil put his cards aside for a second and glanced at the girls. He probably had spent the night with them, but he couldn't remember. The girls quickly surrounded Baphomet, with the blonde taking the initiative and sitting next to him. He couldn't have cared less and continued to play, lighting a cigar and inhaling its tart aroma.

Then a foreign smell got mixed with the nicotine fog. It was a gentle peony scent. He quickly turned toward the intoxicating perfume and saw his siren. She sat next to Amador in a satin bra perfectly enveloping her breasts, and a short skirt that looked like a second skin on her olive body. She was raw seduction. Baphomet noticed how a few men were looking at her hungrily, and jealousy took hold of him. He wished to blind every man who dared to look at her.

What the fuck? Amador thinks he can bring Page here? This trashy place is not for someone as divine as her. Devil cursed, losing his sanity.

CHAPTER
NINETEEN

PAGE.

For the next few days, Page worked from home and didn't go out at all. Tears frequently took over, splashing out all the accumulated emotions over the years of being unable to cry. But the surprises didn't end there. When Page walked through the summer garden and touched the flowers, drops of black water poured out of her fingers.

She didn't tell her parents anything. Her father most definitely would lock her up if he knew that not only could she not control her fire, but now she could not control the stupid black water either. She tried and tried, failing every time. It seemed to decide on its own when to start and when to stop.

Page knew her father loved her, but he had become obsessed with the idea of keeping her away from another imprisonment, without even realizing that he was doing the very same thing Justice had done to her: taking away her freedom.

The black Cups energy wouldn't go away, and Page decided to ask her friends to help. She couldn't continue to train in the house. It wasn't safe, and her parents could see. She wanted to go somewhere remote to train, but needed someone to be there in case something went wrong.

The week passed by, and Page was glad to get out of the house at last. She chose a satin bra top that accentuated her ample breasts and a short skirt that matched the top, with two small slits on the sides. She added a choker and large, round earrings.

Page was already at the door when her parents called after her from the garden.

"Daughter, you look like a dream in the flesh!" The Queen of Wands kissed Page on the cheek. "And you smell like the rarest flower in this world."

"Thank you, Mother." Page blushed a little.

"Who are you going with tonight?" the King of Wands asked, sounding a bit stern.

"Lover, Chariot, Aqua, and Gaia," Page reported.

"Good." The king almost smiled. "Does that mean Baphomet is old news? We don't need more problems than we're already dealing with."

"Don't kill the mood with your questions." The Queen of Wands neatly straightened her daughter's hair and kissed Page again. "Have fun."

Page took a deep, refreshing breath of warm night air as soon as she closed the door behind her. Triumph was already waiting outside in his limousine. When Page got into the car, he didn't utter a word, just stared at her.

"You look…" He cleared his throat. "Breathtaking."

"Thank you, Triumph." Page smiled. "You also look stunning tonight."

The major smoothed his golden hair and smiled

tenderly. "Champagne?" He had already filled the glasses.

When they got to the club, it was packed. Loud music and the search for something more filled the air. Triumph moved to the rhythm, waving sparklers brought by waitresses with several bottles of champagne.

"Page, I'm also waiting for my naked photo shoot, preferably with you as a partner." Triumph danced, swinging the sparklers around.

"I'm afraid it's going to be hard to arrange, given your card description," Page tried to shout over the music.

"You could lie naked on one of my sphinxes. I think a black sphinx would be better to create a contrast with your moon-like hair."

"Obviously." Page laughed. "Where is Aqua?"

"I have no idea. She disappeared somewhere," Amador said, craning his neck to look for the Princess of Cups in the crowd.

"I'll go look for her!" Page yelled again and made her way through the people on the dance floor.

Her friend wasn't there, so Page headed to the terrace. She thought that Aqua had probably needed some fresh air. As soon as Page stepped outside, she saw Aqua standing at the far corner of the terrace. The Prince of Wands was squeezing her hand, and it looked like Aqua was trying to free herself.

"Since when is it okay to take nude photos? And especially with this annoying major. He ogles you all the time!" the prince screamed furiously.

"It's an art project. We just took pictures, nothing more!" Aqua almost cried.

"Mother showed me these 'just' pictures." He

squeezed her hand even tighter, and Aqua yelped in pain.

"And since when do I have to justify myself to you?" Then she noticed her friend. "Page!"

The Prince of Wands turned toward Page. "And here comes the main matchmaker!" he said sarcastically.

"Shut up, brother. Let Aqua go, you're hurting her." Page noticed that her brother was a little drunk.

The Prince of Wands had always been like this: partying, getting into fights, constantly changing girlfriends. Page believed that he did all of these things on purpose, trying to get their parents' attention. They were always focused on Page because of her weird fire, letting her brother do whatever he wanted.

"You'd better go." Page stared at him.

"Don't worry, dear sister, I was already leaving. You're free as the wind, Aqua." The Prince of Wands turned abruptly and walked away.

Page stepped closer and gently hugged Aqua as the girl burst into tears.

"Don't pay attention to him. He's just drunk. I'm sure tomorrow he's going to regret his words." She gently wiped away Aqua's tears.

"His jealousy has no limits recently. The other day, he wasn't happy with my outfit! He thought my dress was too revealing." Aqua broke down in tears even more.

"I know that he's my brother, but he has no right to behave like that. Not to mention hurting you." Page kissed Aqua's red hand.

"Have you decided to take turns crying now?" Triumph said, joining them on the terrace. "What are the tears about?"

"My brother broke up with Aqua. He's jealous of Amador," Page reported.

"Idiot." Triumph gave Aqua a gentle look.

"I think I should clean myself up. See you at the table." Aqua quickly left to go to the restroom.

"Poor girl. Let's go give the news to Amador." Triumph took Page's hand and led the way inside.

Gaia and Amador sat alone at the table, watching the crowd of dancing people without speaking.

"Gaia, how's your collection selling?" Page leaned toward her friend.

"I can't hear you. Loud music." Gaia looked away dismissively.

It seemed like Gaia was avoiding her. Obviously, she was mad at her for something, but Page couldn't think of any reason why.

Triumph interrupted Page's thoughts. "Who wants to dance?"

"Me!" Gaia quickly got up from the sofa and took his arm.

"Okay." Triumph followed her to the dance floor. "Next dance is yours, Page."

"Obviously," Gaia muttered.

Is she jealous of me because she likes Triumph? The realization hit Page.

"You play?" Amador turned to Page. "The club has a gambling area."

"Not really my thing." She sipped her champagne, still looking at Triumph and Gaia. Gaia couldn't be serious. Triumph and Page were just friends. She was sure everybody knew it.

"Come on. Keep me company." Amador got up.

"Okay, but not for too long. Aqua will be back soon." Page filled her glass before leaving the table.

"Deal." Amador headed toward the end of the room.

The gambling part of the club was dark and quiet, the air filled with cigar smoke. Page could barely see anything in the midst of the nicotine fog. Amador took her hand so they wouldn't lose each other in the crowd and led her to a half-empty blackjack table. They sat down, and the dealer started the game. Page slowly sipped her champagne, studying people at the other tables.

"Twenty-one," the dealer concluded.

"It's my lucky night!" Amador said excitedly.

"Well done, Amador." Page raised her glass.

During the next round, several people sat down at their table. Obviously, Amador, as a major, was getting attention. Still, a few of the men were eyeing her, and Page moved her chair a bit closer to Amador, making sure everyone knew they had come together. The last thing she wanted right now was a man's attention.

"This seat is taken." Page heard Baphomet's tart voice close behind her, and goose bumps covered her spine.

The major touched the stranger seated next to her, and the man quickly withdrew with fear and horror in his eyes. Devil didn't look his best. His raven hair was disheveled, the buttons on his crumpled shirt half undone.

"Oh, Amador, Princess of Wands, what a surprise." Baphomet's voice wrapped Page's body in a dark lucid dream.

A few gorgeous girls surrounded Devil, trying to regain his attention. They'd obviously come with him. Seeing them fawn over him made the fire inside Page rage, and she tried hard not to let it out.

"Baphomet." Amador looked him up and down. "I thought you didn't gamble anymore." The major paused. "When did you get here?"

"Not too long ago. I came right after we saw each other at the bakery." One of the girls tried to put her hand on Devil's shoulder, but he gave her a menacing look.

"That was almost a week ago." Amador tilted his head slightly.

"As I said, not too long ago." Devil casually glanced at his cards and then stared at Page, ignoring his company. His eyes moved slowly, studying her round hips, then her waist, settling on her breasts. Baphomet swallowed and clenched his hand. "How are you, Princess of Wands?" Now he devoted his gaze to her lips.

"Not as good as you," Page blurted out, unable to contain her anger.

He has the nerve to speak to me after breaking my heart? After lying about Strength? Look at him—brought five girls for me to see. Not that I'm counting. Jealousy pierced Page's heart.

One of the girls, noticing Baphomet's interest, glared at her and moved even closer to the major. "Darling, should we go somewhere more private? This table is boring." The girl drew her fingers along his neck, almost touching Devil's ear.

"Leave me," Baphomet boomed, his voice laced with anger, and waved his hand without raising his eyes.

The girls left in a hurry, looking at Page with hatred.

"How will you manage without your entourage?" Page smirked.

"I'm tired of them." Baphomet glared at her.

"I'm not surprised. You get tired quickly." Page's eyes burned.

"I've lost my taste for girls." Devil looked at Page and licked his lips.

"I hardly believe it." She turned away to face Amador, who watched them quietly with a faint smile.

Baphomet rose from his chair and moved closer to Page. "Believe me," he whispered with a voice shrouded in bitter honey.

"I won't make that mistake again." She tilted her head slightly, and their lips almost touched.

Stop it, Page. He was just having fun with other girls. Have some self-respect, she lectured herself, still staring into his eyes.

Devil inhaled her deeply. Everyone was looking at them, including the dealer, who had stopped the game. The space was quiet, and Page could hear his manic breathing.

"For whom are you such a siren tonight?" Baphomet demanded.

"None of your business." Page got up to leave, but Devil grabbed her by the waist. She held her breath, unable to move, lured into the web of his burning touch. Her body was betraying her, but she hadn't forgotten how easily he'd broken up with her.

He's playing with you. She tried to fight her reaction to his alluring darkness.

"I have to go." Page managed to escape from his grasp and hurried away.

TWENTY

BAPHOMET.

Baphomet finally found the strength to pull himself out of the gambling club and returned to his dimension. He decided to watch over Page from afar. Seeing her was too dangerous; he couldn't control himself next to this magnificent future Empress. The incident at the gambling club had made that clear.

"Master!" Oliver cried with relief. "I thought something bad had happened!"

"Well, most definitely nothing good can happen to the Devil," he muttered. "Iblis is here?"

"Yes. The idiot still thinks he can trick his way out of the labyrinth." Oliver rolled his eyes.

Baphomet spread his black wings, and hovering above the endless maze, he spotted Iblis. He quickly flew down and landed in front of him.

Iblis turned to him. "Long time no see, Boss."

"Don't tell me you've missed me." Baphomet smirked.

"I wouldn't go that far." The smile touched Iblis's face. "Magus has agreed to meet."

Baphomet got excited. In the last century, Magus had practically disappeared, rarely leaving his dimension. And when he did leave, he used his famous magic to move from place to place. It was impossible to track him down.

"Finally!"

"He is ready to meet somewhere neutral," Iblis added.

Magician had never met in his own castle. Practically no one knew where the entrance to his dimension was.

"Bring him to the high cliff." Baphomet flew up. "I'll be waiting."

Devil landed on the deserted cliff at the far end of the neutral zone, waiting for Magus to arrive. He stood at the edge, breathing in the salty air and looking at the restless water.

"Devil," Magician sang unnaturally behind him. "I thought you were avoiding me."

Baphomet slowly turned around and studied him. He hadn't really planned to talk to Magus; he just needed to get close enough so his invisible ashes could envelop him. Devil hoped Magus's magic armor would give way, and he could learn his plans.

Baphomet was the only major who had ashes as his element. His magic could do a lot of things, but most importantly, his ashes could pick up memories. Magician and Empress were the only majors in the deck who had control of all four elements at once, so breaking Magus's shield wasn't that easy; too many elements raged in him. But Baphomet had done it before, and he hoped today would be no different.

"I bet you're undressing me in your mind." Magus

broke the silence with the stupid joke. "I don't have all day."

"Me neither." Baphomet moved closer, releasing his ashes. They slowly approached Magus, but couldn't enter and bounced back.

Tricky bastard. He's gotten stronger. Baphomet breathed wickedly. Magus had probably been hiding all this time, until he'd gained enough power to be untouchable even by Baphomet's ashes. Nothing could have resisted Devil's foggy veil before—not even Magician's power. But Baphomet didn't plan to give up, sending another wave, larger and stronger. He enveloped Magus completely and sensed how a few ashes squeeze past his armor. Hiding a smile, he closed his eyes and inhaled the visions. A few ashes could pick up very little memories, but he hoped it would be enough to learn something useful.

Devil swiped through the visions from Magus's memories. *No… No…* He turned through slide after slide in his mind. *Gotcha!*

He dove into the memory. The old Empress was chained up in some kind of cave, a huge, nasty snake slowly sucking the energy out of her. Baphomet now could be certain that Magus had gained the new power by taking Empress's magic. He was the one who'd captured her. Magus could drain her forever, growing his strength with her immortal elements. If Magician continued like this, he would soon become the strongest major of them all.

"As you can see, my magic shield is unbreakable." Magus smugly smirked.

"I wonder, where did you get such a power?" Baphomet moved closer and tilted his head. "Of course, it has nothing to do with Empress being chained up in a cave."

Magus's tiny eyes widened. He obviously hadn't expected Baphomet to see through anything.

"That would be against the rules. I respect Abyss too much to break his law," Magus lied through his teeth.

"Undoubtedly," Baphomet answered, turning around.

His attention shifted to a group of people walking on the beach. Baphomet's heart sank at the smell of burnt peonies swaying on the invisible waves. Page was walking toward the water like a vivid mirage in the desert. He didn't even notice that Magus was watching her too.

"She has the power anyone would envy," Magician hissed.

Baphomet turned to him with furious eyes, and taking his raw form, he immediately wrapped his tail around Magus's neck. "Don't even think about it. You'll never touch her," Devil growled. "Or you'll be locked in one of my labyrinths forever."

"Crazy monster." Magician spoke with hatred, grasping for air. "Let me go!"

Baphomet loosened his grip.

"I'll get even with you," Magus threatened, evaporating.

Devil quietly watched his siren with her friends. He couldn't believe his eyes when he saw what she could do with her elements. Her power was much stronger than the power of the old Empress.

"She's not bad. And pretty." Iblis joined Baphomet, looking at Page.

"Do you have a death wish?" Devil growled, turning Iblis around by the shoulders.

"All right, all right." The demon walked away, suppressing a laugh.

Devil took another look at Page and turned away, following Iblis. He felt like he was leaving a part of himself with her. But time was of the essence.

"How many remote caves do you know of? And I mean super hidden," he asked Iblis, still inhaling Page's scent in the air.

"Maybe five," Iblis thought out loud. "No, probably four that no one should know about."

"Where?" Baphomet tensed.

"I can show you," he suggested.

"You expect me to fly, carrying you in my arms?" Baphomet raised his eyebrow. "Tell me where."

If Devil knew the major of the first dimension at all, then Magus would try to move Empress soon. He couldn't take a chance that Baphomet might have seen something else in his head. It meant Devil had to act fast. Otherwise, he could lose the Empress's trail forever.

Baphomet flew to a few caves before he finally found the right one. It was hidden in the midst of inaccessible and unassailable rocks. Devil was on the lookout, surrounded by the thick darkness of the cave. In total silence, he heard the hissing of a snake.

"Fuck you, Magus. I hate snakes!" Baphomet cursed.

He saw two huge yellowish eyes with slitted pupils staring at him. Devil took his raw form, shrouded in a cloud of ashes, and flew close to the enormous monster, raising his flaming torch. The unnaturally huge snake was slowly getting closer, hissing at him. In the next second, the serpent opened its enormous mouth, showing venomous fangs, and lunged forward with impossible speed. Baphomet managed to burn the snake's skin around its eyes. The creature hissed again. The serpent stood no chance. Baphomet was one of the most powerful majors. Flying up, Devil threw the snake back with one flap of his hematite wings. He flew closer, and wrapping his tail around the monster's throat, he slowly suffocated it. It managed to bite his arm. Baphomet looked at the snake with raging eyes and plunged his fangs into its throat, tearing the artery. Blood as dark as wolfberry gushed out. The serpent fell to the ground. Devil only glanced at it before moving deeper into the cave.

TWENTY-ONE

PAGE.

Page walked on the windy beach, absorbed in her thoughts, leaving her friends a little behind. She couldn't understand why the deck was so cruel to her. First, uncontrollable white fire, and now also the black water. Page was starting to believe that she had probably been broken from the moment she was born. She was constantly training to get control of her fire energy, but all in vain. Now she had to deal with the water too.

And why black? she couldn't help but wonder. *Maybe because it's the color of my soul.*

Even if the man who'd attacked her was bad, she'd still hurt him. And the worst part was that she hadn't felt guilty even for a second. Not then, after spending years in the eleventh dimension, and not now. Before, she had believed that the system was broken. Abyss's laws went against anything sensible. But now Page thought that she might be broken as well.

"We can make the firewater show here!" Triumph playfully called after Page. "There isn't a soul in this place."

Page turned and smiled. Triumph could lift her mood even at the worst times.

"Did we miss anything?" Aqua yelled, approaching, holding Amador's hand.

"Finally! It's about time!" Triumph glanced at their entwined hands and tapped Amador on the shoulder.

Page winked at Aqua. She was happy for her. Aqua deserved love more than anyone. And Amador seemed like a perfect match, madly in love with the Princess of Cups.

Gaia didn't say anything about the new couple and turned to Triumph. "I still don't understand why we're here."

"Page needs to practice controlling her energy. We're babysitting," Triumph explained.

"I don't know what to do with the stupid water." Page pouted.

Gaia widened her eyes. "You hold water too?"

"Apparently," Page confessed. "Dammit."

"Some of us don't get anything, and you get *two* energies!" Gaia said, and Page sensed anger in her voice. It seemed odd to Page. Gaia knew very well how much she'd suffered because of her fire.

"Hold your horses, Gaia." Triumph stared at her.

Amador moved closer to Page and took her shoulders in his hands. "Stand here, look at the water, and just relax. Then imagine things."

"Amador, you'll be an amazing father," Triumph teased. "Come on, Page. Give us a few drops or something."

"You can do it," Aqua whispered encouragingly.

Nothing was happening, no matter how hard Page tried. Time passed, but she just stood there, trying.

"It's not like we're in a rush." Triumph couldn't hold

his tongue. "But I was expecting something a little more exciting."

"Shh!" Aqua silenced him.

Page took a deep breath, staring at the ocean, merging her eyes with its endlessness. She raised her hands slowly, and the water followed her movement, rising higher and higher. She felt excitement, thrill. She couldn't believe she was capable of such things. Her body caught fire, flaming stronger and stronger while the water wall rose to the sky. Page followed it with her eyes. For the first time in her life, she didn't feel helplessness; she felt power. Standing there in flames, she looked like a burning phoenix.

"Holy shit!" Triumph yelled in excitement.

She stared at the water she controlled for quite a while. After some time, Page wanted to stop the energies, but she didn't know how.

"I can't make it stop!" She turned to her friends.

"I don't know about you, but I'll take a nap." Triumph lay down on the sand. "We can be here all night."

His playful mood affected Page, and she laughed. At that moment, the water wall loudly fell back, and the flames slowly died on her skin.

"Oh, my Sun, thank you, Triumph!" Page turned to him. "I thought it would never end."

"I'm ready to make you laugh at any time." He got up and kissed her.

Amador was standing with Aqua in his embrace. "I won't lie. I'm impressed." He spoke gently, as usual.

"Page, you're a miracle!" Aqua ran up and hugged her friend.

"I think that's an overstatement." Page laughed.

"But thanks, it's nice to think that maybe one day, I'll control things in my life."

Gaia stood silently. She seemed to be lost in her own thoughts. Page didn't understand why she'd reacted so strangely to her energies.

"I didn't realize you held such a power," Gaia finally muttered.

"We'll make Page a pro. You wait and see." Triumph twirled Page around and carried her toward the car. Page was laughing, feeling truly happy.

"I don't like this creepy, deserted place," Amador said, walking behind them with Aqua. "We should find another place to train next time."

Page looked up at the high cliff, and for a second, she noted the tart smell in the air. She narrowed her eyes, but didn't see anyone.

Great. This is just what I need: a hallucination. She pursed her lips.

Of course, her hallucination was of Baphomet. Despite how he'd treated her, she still thought about him —sometimes with rage and anger, remembering his rejection of her, or his date with Strength, and sometimes with tenderness, thinking of how he'd kissed her, how her body had responded to his every sinful touch. Page closed her eyes, trying to get rid of these thoughts and the taste of grapes in her mouth.

TWENTY-TWO

PAGE.

age spent an hour trying to fill up the bathtub with her water. She was satisfied when it was done, looking at the full bathtub that reminded her of a dark portal to another dimension. She snorted, noticing that her body was still flaming. She hadn't figured out yet how to separate the two elements.

"Sparkle!" Matilda ran into the room, out of breath. Her eyes froze on the bathtub. "Oh, Sun, what happened to the water?"

"The bathtub was dirty." Page giggled.

"Impossible! I cleaned it myself. Doesn't matter." She glowed. "You have guests. The majors!"

"They can come up." Page suppressed a smile.

The woman ran downstairs, arranging her messy hair in a hurry. Page sat on the bed in a black silk dressing gown, waiting for the majors. Amador and Triumph had never visited her house before, and she couldn't help but wonder what they wanted.

"Princess of Wands, majors Chariot and Lover are here to see you," Matilda officially reported and bowed.

"Thank you, Matilda." Page laughed, looking at her

servant, who didn't take her eyes off Triumph. "Matilda likes you."

"She has good taste." He looked at the woman with a smile.

Poor Matilda blushed and tried to say something, then abruptly turned around and ran out of the room.

"You've stolen her heart." Page put her hand to her chest and fell on the bed, pretending she was Matilda, hit by Cupid's arrow.

Triumph laughed while Amador examined the room.

"I see you've been training." Amador stared at the bathtub.

"Listen, Page…" Triumph paused.

Something was off about him today. Triumph seemed unusually serious.

"What is it?" Page stared into his eyes.

"Where the fuck should I start?" He nervously picked up the book that Page had left next to the bed.

"You came to borrow a book?" She smiled.

"Look, Page, we didn't waste time in vain. I tricked my way into Emperor's library. He's collected almost all the significant works in his private collection. So…" Triumph paused again and helplessly looked at Amador. "I think I found something of use."

"Well…" Amador came to the aid of his indecisive friend. "You know that for a long time, there were only three majors—the oldest ones. They ruled over the minors by themselves."

"Yes." Page nodded.

"At that time, the Queen of Swords suddenly began to manifest fire energy." Amador waved his arms, depicting the queen with fire in her hands. "After some time, the energies of water and earth manifested in her as well."

"And so, the fourth Major Arcana appeared." Triumph could not stand still. "Empress: the energies of all four queens and their elements woven into one major."

Page sat on the windowsill, not sure where they were going with this.

Triumph got closer and took her hands in his. "Page, we think you're on your way to manifesting all four energies and becoming the next Empress." He stared into her burning eyes.

"It's been quite a while since Empress disappeared, and her dimension is empty," Amador added.

Page looked between the two of them, silent for a full minute. A million thoughts hit her at once. She felt flickering flame in her palms and moved to the middle of the room.

"I'm just a princess, not even the Queen of Wands." She looked pleadingly at the majors, holding tears back.

"Semantics." Triumph got closer but stopped, as if afraid to approach.

"But the majors are immortal. I can't be the Empress; we already have one." Page looked into Amador's eyes, searching for hope.

"She's been gone for a long time. Who knows? Maybe there's a way to incinerate a major," Amador said quietly, afraid to trigger her.

"I'm sure High Priestess is already keeping her eye on you. Nothing gets past her," Triumph said, but Page was missing half of the words.

She couldn't live a normal life because of her fire, and now she was supposed to deal with all four elements?

Page knew all too well that she was not capable of mastering the energies. Her life would be destroyed. She felt hopelessness and fear taking possession of her body.

"Plus, you need to be careful with Magician. I wouldn't be surprised if he's already found out about you. I'm serious, Page." Triumph's eyes drilled into hers. "He is dangerous."

Page's ears were ringing. She was gasping for air, almost choking. Endless waves of fire exited her body all at once without stopping. In an instant, the curtains, the bed, the books, everything caught fire. Page couldn't control what she was doing, as if watching herself from afar. Small plants and flowers in the pots on the windowsill grew at an incredible speed and climbed up the walls and ceiling, shaking the whole house.

"Page!" Triumph and Amador yelled, but their voices got lost in the noise of the destruction.

The King of Wands and the rest of the family ran into the room, stopping abruptly. The king's eyes widened in horror. "Daughter," he whispered.

Page didn't just stand in the middle of the fire; she *was* the fire. Vines covered the whole room, finally reaching her body, entwining around her legs, waist, and arms. Black water was splashing from the bathtub onto the floor.

Her manic gaze stopped at a familiar but hated face: Justice. The major entered wearing a red robe with a green mantle and a crown emblazoned with a small square, a sword in her hand. Page held her gaze and laughed hysterically. Tired of trying to fight, she was angry and exhausted. Suddenly, she saw a pair of ashen eyes that soundlessly sang a calming, wicked lullaby.

TWENTY-THREE

BAPHOMET.

Baphomet sat in his bedroom, trying to heal the serpent's bite. The poison was burning his ashen blood.

"Who did you fight?" High Priestess, as usual, appeared out of thin air.

"Why ask if you sense the energy?" Devil muttered distractedly.

"Boo." La Papesse snorted. "Let me." She came closer and put her fingers, covered in moonstones, on the bite. She cast a spell with a whisper, and the pain went away immediately.

"Thank you." Baphomet sat back, nodding his head.

High Priestess closed her eyes, and after opening them, she stared at Baphomet. "She is here?"

Devil knew she sensed the presence of the Empress. Baphomet had found her in the cave in a terrible state. All the majors, except for the elders, looked like they were in their twenties, but when he had seen Empress in the darkness, he couldn't believe his eyes. Her hair had turned white, as if she were an old woman, and wrinkles covered her pale face. When they flew to his dimension, she couldn't even open her eyes, afraid of the sun. She'd gotten used to the darkness after all these years.

"Oliver is taking care of the Empress." Baphomet rose to grab a drink. "She's different now. Magus kept her chained up in that cave like an animal."

La Papesse rose, walking from one corner of the room to another. "Magus broke the law. We can't attack fellow majors," she thought out loud. "Abyss will be furious."

"We can't actually prove it was him. The Empress never saw who took her. Plus, it seems she might have lost her mind a little." Baphomet paused. "Magus knows about Page. I'm afraid he might do something to her too. Her energy is powerful."

He locked eyes with La Papesse. Devil had never felt any fear in all his immortal life—not even when Abyss's black hole had almost consumed him during the war. But now he was scared. He had finally found Page, and even if they were not together, his heart belonged to her. He was devastated at the thought that Magus could take her from him and drain her energy, as he had done with the old Empress.

"We won't let it happen." High Priestess took his hand. "We've still got time. Even if he tries something, he'll probably wait until the last moment, when her energy reaches its potential but she's not yet immortal."

Devil hesitated for a second. The thought that something didn't add up didn't leave him. The old Empress was alive, Page's water was black, and her fire was white. It didn't resemble the normal Empress at all.

"Is there a chance that Page is something else?" he asked. "Could she be a new tarot card?"

La Papesse stood in silence for quite a while before she spoke. "The deck is complete. It can be shuffled in countless variations, but the constant has never changed."

High Priestess walked toward the door, and turning back, fixed him with her gaze. "Did you start gambling again?"

"Yes," Baphomet confessed.

At that moment, Iblis stormed into the room. "Boss, I've watched over the princess, as you've ordered." He paused.

Devil's soul left his body for a moment at the thought that something bad had happened. "Speak!" he yelled, and the sky above them darkened.

"Justice is going to take her."

Baphomet breathed heavily. *No one is taking Page anywhere. Not Magus, not Justice, not even Abyss himself.*

High Priestess teleported them to Page's house in a split second. Page stood covered in fire, like a burning goddess. Baphomet couldn't even see where her body ended and the flames began. The earth element was also raging at her command. She positively looked like a devil creature in the middle of a flaming hell.

Her eyes locked with his, silently begging for help. And he suddenly felt sick as her pain hit him. He wanted to cover Page with his ashes, shielding her from the whole world.

Baphomet moved slowly toward her, not breaking his gaze. He sent out an ocean of ashes, blocking the fire on his way.

"Page, my siren," he whispered without fully realizing what he was saying. "It's okay. I'm here. You're safe."

Devil moved closer and gently touched her hand. Page burst into tears, sobbing loudly.

"Come here." He felt a lump in his throat and could barely speak. "It's okay. I'm here."

Page's fire finally began to die. Baphomet wrapped his arms around her waist, and she powerlessly clung to his body.

"Now that the show's over, I must take you, Princess of Wands," Justice said in an icy voice, looking cold and pale, just like her dimension did. She raised her sword up, ready to deliver the swift hand of justice. Her face showed no emotion.

"You're not taking her *anywhere*!" Baphomet growled and hugged Page tighter. He couldn't let anyone hurt or imprison his siren; she'd already suffered enough. But Baphomet was mad mostly at himself. He shouldn't have listened to High Priestess. He should have been next to Page, protecting, supporting, admiring.

Triumph walked toward Devil, stopping beside him. "Not so fast, Justice." He shielded Page as well.

Silence descended on the room, and Baphomet heard Page's faint heartbeat. He took her in his arms, afraid she would fall.

"Justice, a quick word," High Priestess said, breaking the silence. "Come on." She practically pushed the major out of the room. "Baphomet, you too."

Page stared at him, and he wasn't sure what her gaze meant. Was she mad that he had touched her, or was it that she didn't want him to leave?

Suddenly, Page's eyes rolled back, and she fainted. Baphomet carefully carried his siren to her bed, ashy from the fire, before he left.

TWENTY-FOUR

PAGE.

Justice never took Page. Whatever High Priestess told her had worked. Page didn't leave the bed for almost two weeks, slowly gaining her power back. Triumph and Amador visited her every day. Aqua couldn't enter the Wands Arcana, but she sent a new letter with Amador every day. She wrote about her job, and the gossip of the Arcana, but mostly about Amador. Through her letters, Page realized that Aqua didn't just like Amador; she was in love with him, madly. Only Gaia didn't send a word, or anything at all.

Page was reading a letter from Aqua, lying down in her bed, while Triumph and Amador discussed the approaching majors' ball. They didn't talk to her about the whole Empress thing again, and she was grateful. Page didn't accept the idea yet. She was afraid to think what her life would look like with four uncontrollable energies raging inside her. Most likely, Justice would lock her up forever.

"Page, tell Amador that you feel better," Triumph begged. "We need to get you out of the house."

"Let her rest," Amador insisted.

"I'm much better." Page smiled. "Maybe on the weekend, we could go out."

"We need champagne to start a new chapter." Triumph raised an imaginary glass.

"Fine, but only because Page said so." Amador softened. "Aqua can't wait to see you. She's already talked my ear off about you."

"Ask Gaia to come too." Page looked at Triumph.

"Sure," he promised.

The King of Wands didn't talk to Page. He was angry that she had been lying about controlling her fire all this time. Her father was constantly fearing that Justice would come back.

"Dear, are you sure it's a good idea to go out?" the Queen of Wands timidly asked her daughter, but handed Page the earrings that went with her dress for the night.

"If Justice will imprison me again, I should at least have one fun, carefree night with my friends," Page insisted.

She sat at the club with her friends, sipping champagne. She'd decided not to think about anything tonight and just enjoy the moment. Page was afraid that if she continued to stay home constantly worrying, she might go crazy.

"Triumph, do you want to dance?" Gaia asked.

"Sorry, tonight I promised all the dances to Page." He stood up and gave Page his hand, inviting her to the dance floor.

"Sure," Gaia muttered.

"Triumph, go with Gaia." Page looked at her girlfriend, who was obviously upset. "I'll join you for the next song."

As they left, Page poured herself more champagne. When she looked up again, Baphomet stood in front of her.

"Can we talk?" he asked, hypnotizing her with his presence. "Please."

Page was fighting the desire to follow him immediately without any resistance. "What do you want?" She tried to sound indifferent.

"I'd prefer to speak in private." He looked at Aqua and Amador sitting in silence, as if they didn't hear or see them at all.

He did *help you,* a voice in her head insisted.

"Fine," Page agreed and got up, following him.

Baphomet stopped in a narrow, dark corridor that connected the terrace area with the club. Page clearly felt his beastly breathing. He was dangerously close.

"What do you want?" Page asked, meeting his ashen eyes. She bit her lip, corrupted by his proximity, and the major looked greedily at her mouth.

"Forbidden, seductive fruit," Baphomet growled. He stalked closer, and Page leaned away until her back rested against the wall. Baphomet moved like a predator toward cornered prey. He wrapped one arm around her waist, and Page put her hands on the wall for support, having no way to escape.

"How can I stay away from you?" Devil pressed his body into Page, almost touching her lips.

Page didn't move, and she began to melt under his touch. Baphomet squeezed her waist, and she groaned.

"I could listen to those moans forever." He moved even closer to her lips.

You shouldn't let him touch you. He chose not to be with you. The thought ran through her mind.

"You chose not to be with me," Page repeated the words out loud. "Leave me alone."

"Page…" Baphomet whispered her name like a magic spell.

"So, who's tempting the future Empress here?" Triumph's voice, as usual, sounded playful.

Devil recoiled from Page and looked curiously at the major. "How did you know?" Baphomet growled.

Page couldn't believe her ears. *He knew!* Baphomet knew that she was becoming the future Empress and hadn't even bothered to tell her, watching her suffer.

"It doesn't take a genius to put two and two together." Triumph paused. "I understand High Priestess has already shuffled her special deck for Page's future."

"Yes." Devil only glanced at Page.

"And?" Triumph tried to sound neutral, but his high pitch betrayed his worry.

"Let's go." Baphomet turned to the exit. "Ask her yourself. The insufferable woman insisted that no one could know until Page is completely reborn."

"Where are we going?" Page said, barely able to keep up with the majors as they stepped away.

"To Agatha." Devil led the way.

"It's nighttime. Everything is closed," Page said.

"Not a problem. We'll wake up both Agatha and High Priestess." Baphomet sounded determined.

"I'm quite sure I heard that High Priestess never sleeps." Triumph had to put in his two cents.

Page sat in the back seat and looked at Baphomet's face in the rearview mirror. He looked a little on edge.

Baphomet pounded loudly on Agatha's door nonstop until a couple of minutes later, the woman opened the door, a candle in her hand. She was wearing a long dressing gown. Obviously they'd woken her up.

"Majors Devil, Chariot." Agatha bowed. "Page."

Baphomet entered the shop without being invited, and the others followed him.

"How can I help you?" Agatha sounded lost.

"Call High Priestess. We need to talk to her," Devil demanded.

"I do not have such authority." The fortune teller frowned, shaking her head at the request.

"Now you have," he said, crossing his arms.

"I'm afraid—"

"Otherwise, I will not be so polite." Baphomet glared at her furiously.

"Please, Agatha," Page begged.

"I really don't understand what's going on." Agatha sounded terrified and angry. "Fine—for you, Page. Someone clearly does not have good manners."

"And what else would you expect from Devil, right?" Baphomet smirked.

The fortune teller took out a large moonstone and touched it with both hands, reciting a spell in a language Page didn't recognize. A crystal web rose around the gem. A few moments later, a familiar haze appeared, along with La Papesse.

"The deck shuffles too often when you two…" High Priestess looked at Triumph. "… *three* are together."

"Glad you could join us, La Papesse." Baphomet was clearly not in the mood.

"Did you just come out from one of your mazes? Judging by your frighteningly exhausted look." High Priestess studied the major.

"I gambled," Baphomet confessed.

"I see." High Priestess raised an eyebrow at Devil.

"This is not about me. Page knows she's the future Empress."

"I see." La Papesse was calm and unbothered.

"I'm starting to think 'you see' nothing. Didn't you assure me that Page should not know under any circumstances, until the very last moment?!" Baphomet almost screamed. "As for me…" He cleared his throat. "Can I be with Page now?"

Be with me? What the hell are they talking about? Page gave Baphomet a questioning look, but he was focused on High Priestess.

"It remains to be seen," La Papesse answered.

"How about we see it right now?" Devil pushed back the chair and gestured for High Priestess to sit down at the table for the reading.

"You need to sleep," La Papesse mumbled as she sat down at the table.

"Definitely—after we're done here," Baphomet snapped.

"Sit down," High Priestess invited everyone and took the sacred deck in her hands. "Agatha, leave us."

The woman bowed and silently withdrew.

Triumph pulled up extra chairs for himself and Devil, and Page sat down between them, directly across from La Papesse. She felt nauseated; it always happened when she was too nervous. She silently took Triumph's hand in hers. High Priestess covered the cards with her palm and said something unintelligible.

"I will draw a few cards for Empress's future." La Papesse looked at all three of them in turn.

Page took a deep breath and tightened her grip on

Triumph's hand. After all the challenges she'd been through, Page didn't believe her future was bright.

High Priestess's fingers were long and lean, strewn with moonstone rings. She pulled out five cards and began to flip them one by one.

She turned over the first card and looked at Page. "Empress." The woman looked at Baphomet. "Devil." She pulled another. "Lovers." She touched the fourth card. "Death."

No one said a word, and Page heard the crackling of the candle in the midnight silence.

"Chariot, upside down." La Papesse turned the last card. "War."

"One more card," Devil insisted.

High Priestess hesitated before taking one more card from the deck.

"Blank card. Unknown." The major folded her hands.

Triumph broke the silence. "Quite a positive reading."

"Death and war. Princess…" High Priestess looked into Page's eyes. "If you don't change completely by the arrival of the full blood moon, you will die." La Papesse looked at Devil. "Baphomet corrupts your energy."

"How?" Page didn't dare look at Baphomet. She needed to know, needed to understand why he hadn't told her, why he'd just walked away and left her there all alone. The thought tore her heart apart.

"Empress is pure and bright. She creates life. Devil will corrupt your energy with his darkness."

"Have you seen me?" Page smirked. "I'm far from pure and bright."

"Doesn't Death also mean rebirth, the withering away

of the old ways? Mort used to describe his card this way." Triumph couldn't help himself and touched the cards. "And Lovers card is a true union. Or something like that."

"Can't you tap into the energy of the real deck and sense what's going on?" Baphomet finally spoke, staring at La Papesse.

"I felt the emerging energy of the Empress, but for some reason, the deck is hiding the rest from me," High Priestess confessed.

Page was no longer paying attention though. A million thoughts raced through her mind like wind in an open field—she and Baphomet, war, death, the full blood moon.

"Page, are you okay?" Triumph held her by the shoulders.

"Yes, I'd better go." She stood up slowly. "Headache."

Page caught High Priestess's gaze.

"Don't be afraid, Princess of Wands. We are all different for a reason."

"Stop speaking in platitudes." Triumph rolled his eyes. "Come on, Page."

They had almost reached the limousine when Page saw Baphomet heading toward her.

"Page!" he called out as he crossed the road.

Triumph looked at her questioningly.

"It's okay, Triumph, could you please wait for me in the car?" She forced a smile to her face.

"Sure." The major sat inside the car and closed the door.

"Page, I've never wanted to be apart from you even for a minute. But I had to. La Papesse assured me it was the only way to keep you safe." Baphomet kept his distance. "I can't let you die."

"Oh, stop it!" Page lit up, and her voice swept loudly along the deserted street. "High Priestess told you to do it, and you humbly agreed to give up on me, despite the fact that these few months could be my last."

"Page." Devil didn't move.

"Good night, Baphomet." She got into the car and slammed the door.

Triumph looked straight into her eyes. "Page, I'll be by your side, no matter what happens. You can count on me."

"I know." Page took his hand. "I am so grateful to have you."

The major kissed her forehead.

"When exactly is the full blood moon?" Page whispered, looking out the window.

"Three months." Triumph gave her a grim look.

The words echoed in her head. She'd had her whole life to learn how to control her fire energy, and failed. Now, in three months, she had to manifest and control all four energies. It seemed impossible. Yet Page still had hope. She had no other choice.

TWENTY-FIVE

BAPHOMET.

High Priestess was forced to fill Justice in on what was happening to Page. After hours of arguing, the major had finally agreed. Maybe Justice was afraid of what Page might do to her when she transformed, or maybe she was also tired of following the laws that Abyss imposed on them all. It didn't matter to Baphomet; the important thing was that Page was not going anywhere, for now… But the realization that she might actually die stopped his heart every time he thought about it.

He'd gambled, fighting the desire to follow the soundless pull of his siren and go to her. But the more he thought about everything, the more he began to realize that High Priestess was almost as much in the dark as the rest of them, if not more so.

Fuck La Papesse's advice. I'm going to finally make her mine. The prophecy rules can go to hell. We can at least spend these last months together, Devil finally decided. *But what will I do if she dies?*

He clenched his fist, fighting further thoughts.

It wasn't difficult to find Page, considering the fact that Triumph told him they were planning to go out. All the ashes inside Baphomet quickly swirled in bliss when he saw Page in the club. He was a fool for ever thinking that he could stay away from this siren.

The day's events passed in a blur—Triumph, the fact that Page had already known about her future, Agatha, High Priestess with her reading. All this time, Baphomet had avoided looking at Page. He felt like a traitor, leaving Page on her own while Triumph had stood faithfully by her side.

After she'd left with Triumph, Baphomet had stood on the deserted street for a long time. He knew he was paying the price for not listening to his own heart. Devil thought he'd go home or maybe even go back to the gambling club, when the car stopped next to him.

"Dummy in love." Triumph smiled dazzlingly.

"Get in, Baphomet." Amador opened the door. "I didn't think that my card could be drawn for the Devil himself. I must confess, it gives me pleasure, seeing you in love."

"Shut up, Amador," Baphomet blurted out. "As you can see, I destroy everything in my path. Certainly, love and Devil don't mix well."

"Wrong answer." Triumph couldn't help but smile. "Your behavior tonight was just brilliant. Of course, you acted like an idiot—but such a sincere idiot. Even I couldn't do better. Page loved it."

"Right. She loved it so much that she ran away." Baphomet raged at the thought of how "triumphantly" he'd ruined everything.

"Don't be a fool." Amador put a hand on his shoulder. "She'll forgive you."

"You think?" Baphomet's mind screamed with hope.

"I'm going to go deaf." Triumph covered his ears. "Where to now?"

"I need a drink." Baphomet collapsed on the seat of the car, exhausted.

"Classic move." Amador smirked.

The majors sat in the lounge until the morning. Triumph and Amador patiently listened as Baphomet talked about when he first saw Page, how he couldn't stop thinking about her, and mostly, how he didn't deserve her.

"The diagnosis is easy: madly in love," Amador concluded.

"Well, it's already morning. Go to her." Triumph got up, finishing his champagne.

"In this condition?" Baphomet protested. "I look like shit."

"All the better." Triumph laughed. "Don't you dare change. Page should see all the suffering you've been through."

Triumph dropped him off at Page's house. Baphomet cursed Amador and Triumph in his mind when he saw the look on the Queen of Wands' face as she opened the door. The woman looked at the major in horror, considering his deplorable state. Page refused to come down, but Baphomet didn't plan to give up. He had to fix everything; otherwise he would simply go crazy, and the tarot universe would need to look for a new Devil.

TWENTY-SIX

PAGE.

Page sat silently in her room, watching the dance of the candle's flame in the heavy darkness, and did not fall asleep until the next morning. She woke up early with tired red eyes.

"Matilda, I'm going to rest some more. I'm not feeling well." Page turned on her side and buried herself under the blankets.

"Do you have a fever? Should I make you some tea with honey?" Her lady's maid was already touching her forehead.

"Some tea would be nice. Something for the nerves." Page tried to smile.

She heard a car stopping outside, but commanded herself not to get up or even wonder who it was. Matilda came back with the tea, looking pale.

"It's the major, Devil."

Page didn't answer. Her heart tossed like a lost boat in the deep, cursed waters of the ocean. Soon she heard footsteps, and her mother entered.

"Baphomet is asking to see you," the Queen of Wands reported calmly.

"Tell him to go to hell," Page mumbled from under the blanket.

"He looks devastated," her mother added softly.

"I don't care," Page insisted.

"Okay, let me tell him." The queen exhaled and left.

After a few minutes, her mother came back, looking more hurried than before. "He refuses to leave. He told me he's going to wait as long as necessary."

"Tell him I do not wish to speak with him, today or ever." Page sat on the bed and crossed her arms.

"Oh, Sun!" the Queen of Wands exclaimed.

She left again just to come back a few minutes later, completely on edge.

"He is not leaving! I told him you don't want to see him, but he's just not leaving. It's ridiculous!" The queen threw up her hands.

Burning with anger at how he was behaving and what liberties he was allowing himself in her house, Page got up, and without even changing, went down.

"What part of 'go away' don't you understand?" she said, her eyes flashing fire when she found him in the foyer.

"I'm not leaving until you let me explain myself." Baphomet was unshakable.

"No need. Please leave." Page pointed her finger at the door.

Devil took a step forward and pulled her shoulders closer to him. "I can't do that." His ashes touched her, and Page felt an irresistible pull. "I thought about what you said, and you're right." The major moved closer. "No matter what the cards say, or High Priestess, or destiny, I can't be away from you. My heart seeks you everywhere I go." He paused before continuing. "I will worship you, Empress or not."

Page was silent.

"All this time without you has been a living hell. I tried not to think about you, to find distractions." Baphomet eagerly sought the spark of hope in her eyes.

"Oh, I remember very well your distractions—all five of them." Page lifted her head and looked at him with a challenge in her eyes.

"Page, I didn't plan to do anything with the girls," Baphomet said gently. "I'm not interested. Not in them, or in any other girl, for that matter." He looked at her tenderly.

"Yeah, right." Page raised an eyebrow. She'd seen the way those girls had been clinging to him.

"Can't you see that I was forever smitten as soon as I saw you? Everything inside me calls to you. Yes, I've behaved like a fool, but all I want is you."

Page was torn. All this time, she'd believed he just didn't want to be with her. But why, then, did he come to rescue her, and why was he here now, begging for forgiveness? The thought that he cared for her filled her soul with happiness, because she cared for him too, despite everything.

They stood there in silence, drowning in each other.

"I was smitten too," Page whispered and threw her arms around his neck, hiding her tear-filled face in his hair.

Baphomet took her by the waist, and their lips met hungrily, as though it'd been years since they'd tasted each other. Page felt a gentle veil of love envelop their souls, pulling both of them into the depths of an unbreakable spell.

"Is your father also at home?" Baphomet cleared his throat.

"Yes," Page whispered, wondering why he was

bringing up the king right now. "They're probably having breakfast."

"I would like to talk to him." He sounded a bit nervous.

"My parents aren't your biggest fans," Page said with a frown. "Especially my father."

"Let's go. Even though I would rather face one of my demons than the King of Wands." He smiled, and Page laughed.

She took Devil's hand and led the way to the summer garden, where the whole family was already having breakfast. When she loudly cleared her throat, her father slowly emerged from behind the newspaper, and the garden fell silent. Ricardo turned white just looking at Baphomet.

The Queen of Wands was the first to come to her senses. "Page, major Devil, please join us." The queen smiled charmingly.

"Good morning." Devil tilted his head slightly. "Thank you."

Page and Baphomet sat in empty chairs, still holding hands.

"To what do we owe your visit?" The King of Wands cast an angry glance at their intertwined hands.

"I would like to formally ask your permission to date your daughter." Devil looked tenderly at Page and then back at her parents. "I perfectly understand that I am not the candidate you've dreamed of, and…" He took a sip of water. "And my reputation is not perfect."

"That is an understatement," the king muttered.

"But I want to be with your daughter, and I can't imagine myself with anyone else." Baphomet looked at Page, and her eyes welled slightly with black water.

"Oh!" The Queen of Wands clapped her hands.

"And what does my daughter want to add to this?" The King of Wands raised his brows.

"The feelings are mutual." Page lowered her eyes.

"My daughter is a lost cause. I see this now very clearly. She's always looking for more problems. Page can do whatever she wants; I give up." The King of Wands met Devil's eyes. "Anything else?"

Page saw that Baphomet was filling with rage, and she squeezed his hand slightly, hoping to calm him down.

"I'm sure you know that the majors' ball will take place this week. I would like Page to accompany me," Devil said through clenched teeth.

She was amazed at his restraint. If it had been her, little sparks of flame would already be dancing along her skin in anger.

Page's eyes widened in excitement at the mention of the ball, and dark water droplets appeared on her olive skin. The Queen of Wands smiled broadly.

"Fine." The King of Wands was about to dig into the newspaper again when Devil spoke.

"I'd like to invite Page to spend the weekend in my dimension after the ball."

The eyes of the King of Wands darkened.

"I understand that Page talked to you about her new project," the Queen of Wands said quickly. "Creating a photo of Baphomet in his dimension for her new tarot deck is a great idea. None of the scenery in the studio can compare."

Devil glanced at Page. "Yes. I'll ask Sun to give Page permission to visit," the major said, playing along.

"I'm sure he won't mind. I've heard you're on good terms," the Queen of Wands added with a charming smile.

"Amongst all the majors, we have the most understanding," Baphomet added.

"I'm tired of trying to save Page when she doesn't want to be saved. As I said, a lost cause." The King of Wands returned to his newspaper.

"I won't take up your time any longer." Devil could hardly contain himself, angry at the king. "Thank you."

Baphomet left, and Page followed him. The Queen of Wands caught up with them on the porch.

"I'm sorry for my husband's behavior. He is not himself after what happened—and might still happen—to Page. But he's not a bad man." The queen paused and then smiled. "Take good care of my precious daughter."

"I will make sure she's pleased." Baphomet sang the promise with a honeyed voice.

Page blushed. Out of his mouth, it sounded dirty.

She walked him to the car. Devil leaned on it and wrapped his hands around her waist. The sun had already risen high, its rays making her hair glow. Baphomet pushed her locks to the side and kissed her neck, inhaling her scent.

"I'm obsessed, possessed by you." Devil's tongue gently licked her neck, and Page moaned, her need for him growing. It was like this any time he touched her. She could barely control herself.

"I don't know how you can live with your father. Believe me, you're not a lost cause. You're a burning goddess."

"He's just worried." Page brushed her heavy thoughts away. "I want to be alone with you," she whispered and slipped her hands under his shirt, touching his cold skin.

"If I could, I would whisk you away to my dimension forever," he promised.

Page smiled, pressing her lips against his. When his rough hand moved from her stomach to cup her breast, Page pressed herself into his body and groaned.

The sound of a slamming door made Baphomet move back slightly.

"Have a good day!" the Prince of Wands called as he walked quickly toward his car.

"Page, the ball is on Saturday. I always wear black, but you can choose a dress of any color."

"Okay." Page smiled.

"I'm already going crazy at the thought of you waking up next to me in my bed." His half-lidded eyes drank her in, and she could almost feel the silk of his sheets against her skin.

Page bit her lip. "Hold that thought."

TWENTY-SEVEN

BAPHOMET.

"Mine forever," Baphomet sang to himself, leaving Page's house.

Before the ball, Devil had to talk to Sun. The minors couldn't travel to the majors' dimensions without special permission. Baphomet flew in his chariot, greedily inhaling the air. These days, he didn't just exist; he *lived*. Love took him on its wings, and it was the most alive feeling in the universe. Who knew?

It was hard for Devil to visit Sun in his luminous dimension. They were complete opposites, like the Fool and the Blank card. Baphomet put on his sunglasses, blinded by the penetrating light.

"Baphomet, glad to see you emerge from the shadows of your demons!" Sun hugged the major, burning his darkness with pure light.

"Indeed." Baphomet smirked.

"What brings you here?" Sun narrowed his golden eyes. "I know you're not a big fan of my dimension."

"Nothing personal. It's more of a physical condition." Devil smiled.

"I know, I know." Sun tapped him on the shoulder.

"I need permission for my..." Devil paused, knowing that the major would make a huge deal out of his request. "... for my girlfriend to visit my dimension."

Although it seemed impossible, Sun shone even brighter. He looked at Devil and laughed. "If memory serves me right, you swore to never bring a woman into your house," Sun sang, sounding smug.

"I did, but I've changed my mind, for her." Baphomet hated to be so open, but he knew Sun would not leave him alone.

"I must know everything. Do you know what this means?" The major stared at Devil. "The Wheel of Fortune is making a turn shuffling the deck, and your card has been drawn."

"Not mine—hers. She is inexplicable." Baphomet paused again. "La Papesse foretold that she is destined to be the future Empress, but I doubt it. Something in her is different from all the previous energies. She is pure and dark at the same time."

"Oh, dear Sun, you're in love," Sun concluded, glowing with happiness.

"How modest of you to name yourself." Devil smirked.

"Don't try to change the subject." Sun smiled. He never lost his temper. "Who is she?"

"The Princess of Wands, but I call her my siren. Do you think a new card could appear in our tarot universe?" Baphomet asked the question that had been spinning in his head for many days now.

"Impossible," the major assured him without even considering the possibility.

"I see," Baphomet thought out loud. "So, about permission..."

"Not a problem." Sun beamed again.

"Make sure there's no expiration date," Devil added.

"Even so!" Sun yelled, happily surprised. "Maybe she should move in with you, then."

"Hopefully soon." Baphomet stood up, trying to avoid the next comment from the major.

"By the way, I've heard that Magus is gathering support. Who knows what he plans?" Sun spoke thoughtfully. "He even asked Mort to visit him."

"Mort? I see…" Devil said quietly. "See you at the ball, Sun." He quickly walked to his chariot.

Magician had gone into hiding again, locking himself up inside his untouchable dimension. Baphomet was certain he would attempt to do something to Page, as he had with the old Empress. Or maybe Devil was just paranoid. Either way, he didn't plan to sit back and take his chances. Page was still mortal, and Magus could take away all her energy at once. Baphomet had to find a way to learn of his plans.

He shrugged as he got out of his chariot in Mort's dimension. The Devil and Death were both considered the dark cards of the deck. But the thirteenth dimension was another level of darkness. Deadly silence, freezing coldness, and hopelessness filled the air. Only the never-ending whispers of souls broke the silence.

"Devil," Death greeted him in an echoing voice without showing himself.

"Mort, you creep. Come out," Baphomet demanded.

Mort walked toward him, barely touching the ground, pale and cold. He went straight to business. "You never come here. What happened?"

"I need a favor." Baphomet still stood at the gate. No one living had ever crossed into the thirteenth dimension.

"You will take such risks, even after I betrayed you all?" Mort narrowed his eyes.

"Everyone makes mistakes." Devil spoke without judgment.

"I'm listening." Mort nodded.

Baphomet hated asking for help. But Page had changed his life, and he was changing as well. Seeing Page and Triumph and Amador together helped him realize he couldn't do everything on his own.

"I've heard Magician wanted to see you. I need you to get close to him and win his trust." Baphomet paused. "And then obviously tell me what he's planning."

Fuck. Now the love story. Baphomet cursed. He hated sharing his feelings. Actually, he'd never done it before. But here he was, talking about Page for the second time today already. He patiently filled Mort in on everything that was going on.

"Did you rehearse this speech?" Mort laughed when Baphomet finally stopped talking.

"Shut up." Devil rolled his eyes.

No wonder Triumph and Mort used to date. They're both a pain in the ass.

"What's in it for me?" Mort was clearly enjoying this situation.

"I can speak with Triumph on your behalf." Baphomet saw how Mort's dead eyes came to life. "He and Page have become very close. Practically inseparable."

"I bet you don't appreciate that," Mort teased.

"At first, I wanted to burn his hands off." Baphomet smirked. "But not anymore. Triumph is a good friend."

"Fine," Mort agreed, smiling. "But don't forget about the deal. Triumph should forgive me."

"I'll try. But it might be difficult."

Triumph and Mort had been together for a long time. No one had expected that they would ever separate, until the day Mort conspired with Abyss during the Millennium War. Triumph had cut him from his life immediately. Truth be told, Baphomet didn't even know what the major of the Blank Dimension had promised to Mort in return for his betrayal.

"I know—I screwed up big time," Mort mumbled.

TWENTY-EIGHT

PAGE.

First thing the next day, Page went to the garden, trying to move the air, or at least feel it, or … something. But she felt no connection with the Swords element whatsoever.

All four energies—all four. She was repeating the words of High Priestess in her mind. *The deck knows I can't control anything. It won't allow someone like me to become the next Empress.* She was losing hope.

Page went to her favorite dressmaker to order a dress for the ball. Hilda was a young woman from the Pentacles Arcana. Page sat at the table drinking coffee while Hilda looked for the right fabric.

"Do you want matte black?" the dressmaker yelled from far corner of the shop.

"I was thinking a translucent sparkly black dress. Classy, but sexy." Page smiled to herself, thinking about Baphomet.

"Understood. Black and sexy." Hilda showed up with a piece of cloth. "Is it true that you're dating Devil? It's all people are talking about."

"Maybe." Page blushed.

"Well, now I understand why the black dress." Hilda winked at her friend.

The door to the shop opened, and a servant came in, a young boy with ginger hair and wild eyes. He looked strange, animal-like. Behind him, his major followed: Strength. Page grew anxious and irritated at the same time, thinking about Strength and Baphomet together.

"Major Strength. It's an honor." Hilda bowed.

The major didn't answer, but gave a tiny smile of approval. She looked at Page sitting with her coffee, wearing a short green dress and walked toward her. Tiny flames started to fire from Page's skin.

"You must be Page. I saw you at the bakery." Strength studied Page haughtily.

"Princess of Wands." Page cleared her throat.

"Leo." The major looked at her servant. "Check with Lady Hilda if the dress is ready."

Leo obeyed and disappeared, following the dressmaker into another room.

"I've heard you had a little rendezvous with my Baphomet." Strength sat on a chair next to Page.

"Not sure what you mean," she answered calmly, though her insides were churning. Page and Baphomet had only just gotten back together, but this woman was already here, obviously wanting something from her, making her jealous and angry.

Can't I have at least one day of peace? Page begged.

"My dear," Strength said impatiently, "Devil is not good company, especially for an inexperienced minor like you. He will use you and not even remember your name."

"I think I'll be able to make up my own mind.

Thank you." The churning inside her quickly turned to anger, and her skin released a few more flames.

"Magus was right. So much fire," Strength muttered.

"Excuse me?" Page was starting to get tired of this conversation.

"My good friend Magician told me lots about you." Strength looked at Page omnisciently.

"He doesn't know me at all!" she snapped.

Strength laughed loudly, almost snarling. "He is one of the oldest of us. He just needs one look at minors to know them." The major reached out and carelessly touched Page's hair.

"I doubt that," Page said, jerking away from the woman's touch.

"Stubborn. This may intrigue Baphomet," she muttered. "But obviously not for long. He likes variety."

"Like he did in your open relationship?" Page blurted out.

Strength's face changed suddenly, elongating into the mouth of a lion, complete with sharp, gleaming teeth. "I could swallow you without choking, girl," the major snarled.

"Charming." Fear slithered down her spine, but Page held the major's gaze, unflinching.

"So much glibness in a simple princess." Strength stared at her as if trying to look deeper.

Fortunately, Hilda and Leo came back, interrupting their conversation.

"My lady, please look at this." Leo held an amazing matte-black dress in his hands.

"Beautiful." Strength didn't even look at him. "What dress are you looking for?" She stared at Page, demanding an answer.

Hilda quickly came to her rescue. "Page hasn't decided yet. She thought about pink."

Page almost choked on her coffee.

"What bad taste." With that, Strength left the shop without saying goodbye, Leo close behind.

Page's temper flared, and the coffee she held started to boil in her cup. Strength was gorgeous, and she felt like power. She was a match for Baphomet in every way—unlike her.

"Don't worry, Page. I have the perfect fabric for you." Hilda smiled.

"Pink?" Page giggled.

"You'll look breathtaking. Just a second," the dressmaker assured her. Hilda went to one of the aisles and came back with a beautiful black fabric. It looked like melted stars had spilled all over it. It was the perfect material, and Page couldn't wait to see the dress Hilda made for her—or the look on Baphomet's face when he saw her in it.

The day before the ball, Page met with her friends in another unsightly café. She wanted to ask Triumph and Amador to help her with the air element, if they could.

"I take it Baphomet finally came to his senses and won you back?" Triumph narrowed his eyes at Page when she sat down.

She didn't question how Triumph had guessed; she was probably glowing with happiness. "Yes," she answered shyly, telling them the short story of what had happened.

"Page, how wonderful!" Aqua hugged her friend. "As long as you're happy."

"I'm going to accompany him to the majors' ball," Page said with a thrill. She'd never dreamed of being able to go to a regular ball, let alone the majors' ball. Page tried to enjoy the moment, despite the dark shadow of possible death that hung over her.

"It makes sense, especially since you're also becoming—"

Before Amador could finish his sentence, Triumph threw a fork at him.

"I'm going too," Gaia said in a calm voice without much enthusiasm. "Star ordered a dress from my showroom and invited me to be in the audience. Not participating, but still."

"Hooray! We can stick together." Page clapped her hands.

"I think you'll be stuck to something else," Triumph said, slowly leafing through the menu.

"Triumph." Page rolled her eyes.

"Aqua will come with me too, so I can introduce her as my partner officially," Amador said proudly.

"You're moving fast," Triumph teased.

"Are you going with someone, Triumph?" Page touched his arm.

"No, I like to go alone, so I can flirt with everyone." The major winked.

"You flirt with everyone anyway." Page laughed.

"I can keep you company, as friends." Gaia looked at Triumph, hope in her eyes. "I'm going anyway."

"Perhaps. Why not?" The major sounded indifferent.

"Perfect! All together at the ball!" Page got up and pretended that she was dancing a waltz as Triumph caught her and twirled. All the customers turned around to look at them, given that there was no music playing in the café.

"Stop it, people are staring!" Gaia almost screamed.

Page looked at her with surprise. Gaia was becoming more and more rude. Even now that Page was back together with Baphomet, she still was jealous of Page's relationship with Triumph.

"I have to find a dress!" Aqua abruptly got up from the table, breaking the uncomfortable silence.

"I have several dresses in your color from the show." Gaia also stood up. "Let's go to my showroom. I want to pick something out too."

"Thanks, Gaia." Aqua took her by the arm. "'Til tomorrow!"

"I'll pick you up, my love!" Amador shouted after her.

"Thanks, my love!" The princess's watery voice filled the café.

Page smiled. Triumph was right: Aqua and Amador were moving fast.

There was a pause after the girls left the restaurant. Triumph and Amador stared at Page.

"Page." Triumph broke the silence. "How are things with your elements?"

"So far, nothing new. No signs of air." Page didn't look up, folding a napkin into a bird.

"I thought so." Triumph moved closer. "Amador and I thought that it might not be a bad thing to visit his dimension." He took Page's hand and looked into her eyes.

"What for?" Page tenderly looked at her friends.

"My card is an air card, together with Fool, Magician, Justice, and Star." Amador switched to a whisper. "We thought you might visit my dimension to be surrounded by the Swords energy. Maybe that will help to speed up the process."

"I doubt it. I'll just be sitting in the air waiting or something." Page almost laughed at this ridiculous idea.

"We've got no time at all. Let's try everything. We can't have you die," Triumph insisted.

"Fine. But do you think Sun will allow me to freely visit your dimension?" Page hesitated.

"Leave it to me." Triumph grabbed her hand.

"You guys are the best, thank you!" Page sang, and a few black tears rolled down her cheek.

"Here we go again, crybaby." Triumph wiped her face with a napkin, then looked at it in disgust. "This napkin has been used at least a few times before us. When is Aqua's charity event going to be? I'm not sure how much longer I can come to places like this." He quickly threw it away and wiped his hand on his shirt.

Page and Amador laughed, the seriousness of the moment fading. It was enough to let Page almost forget the looming deadline hanging over her head.

CHAPTER
TWENTY-NINE

PAGE.

Baphomet had been waiting downstairs for a long time. Page was late, as usual. Hilda did her absolute best for her friend and delivered the gown in the morning, a translucent, iridescent black dress, tight-fitting through the bodice, with one lowered shoulder. The second shoulder strap passed to the same side, a golden brooch in the form of a grapevine branch gathering the straps together in the front. Hilda added two long gloves made of the same material.

"She-Devil." The Queen of Wands looked at her daughter with her mouth slightly open.

"Sparkle, I have no words to describe your beauty." Matilda was combing Page's hair.

"Will you add some jewelry?" Her mother sorted through the jewelry in her box.

"I think it's perfect like this." Page rubbed peony oil into her neck.

"Agreed." The queen approached her daughter and kissed her.

"Mom." Page hugged her. "Thank you for standing

up for Baphomet and me." She paused. "I thought you didn't like him."

"Whether I like him or not, it doesn't matter. I want you to finally live, now that Justice has somehow left you alone." The queen straightened Page's hair. "I want you to be happy and to know what love is, even if you choose Devil."

All three laughed. Page hadn't told her parents about the whole Empress mess. They'd already been worrying enough about her.

Page walked out onto the porch, and the warm wind played with her hair. Under the moonlight, it took on a silver, shining hue.

Baphomet stood by the car, enchanted. "Siren." He slowly licked his lips and pulled Page toward him. Their bodies tensed like the strings of a guitar being pulled taut. Page threw back her head slightly, and Baphomet gently kissed her neck.

"You are the whole universe," he whispered. Devil pressed his lips onto her slightly parted mouth. He tasted like irresistible, poisonous hemlock, and she willingly drank it in. "I doubt that I'll be able to hold out for long time at the ball. Your closeness drives me to insanity," Baphomet sang seductively.

They were almost last to arrive, two dark souls in the night. The theater hall of the ball was enormous. Page could barely make out the ancient frescoes on the ceiling. The walls were also painted with scenes from the history of the Arcana. Page paused to look at a painting where Devil, in his raw form, was about to be consumed by the black hole. An orchestra of at least one hundred people was playing classical music nearby. Baphomet went to the bar for some champagne.

"Princess of Wands! What a pleasant surprise to see you here." Star approached her in a dazzling silver dress with a crown on her head.

"Glad to see you too." Page smiled sincerely.

"Who did you come with?" Star slowly studied Page from head to toe. "Wait… Judging by the black color and the grapevine, you came with Baphomet, and not with Triumph."

"How observant you are." Page beamed. "Triumph and I are just friends."

"Dear." Star turned to Emperor, standing not far away. "You certainly remember Princess of Wands."

Emperor joined them just as Devil returned with champagne. "Here you go, my siren." Baphomet kissed her cheek. "The queue for the bar is so long that I had to show my claws to get the bartender's attention."

Page laughed, and Devil leaned down and whispered against her ear. "Next time *you'd* better go for champagne. You're definitely impossible to miss."

Page bit her lip, feeling a lick of flame shoot through her body from his proximity.

Emperor coughed.

"Emperor! Glad to see you." Baphomet turned to the others without removing his hand from Page's waist. "Let me officially introduce you to my girlfriend, Princess of Wands."

"Is that so?" Emperor asked in surprise. "You don't waste time. Even at the show, I noticed how you were devouring her with your eyes."

"What can I say? Only a blind man wouldn't have

noticed it." Star winked at Page and moved a little closer to Emperor.

"I must go and greet the new arrivals," the cold major said, ignoring Star, and left.

"You look like a supernova, Star." Page raised her glass. "Cheers."

"It's a crime to drink champagne without me," Triumph said as he, Gaia, Amador, and Aqua approached them.

"The whole company is together." Star smiled and beamed. "Amador, you're lucky." She looked at the major mysteriously.

"You missed half the ball." Triumph looked reproachfully at Page and Devil.

"Page doesn't like to rush." Baphomet lightly kissed her again.

"And here's Sun!" Gaia shouted, looking at the entrance.

"Waltz time. Sorry." Star hurried after Emperor.

Everyone headed to the center of the hall. Page did not look at the other majors. All she could see at that moment were Baphomet's eyes, ashen in a passionate darkness. The music began to play, and Devil led Page, swirling her around without taking his eyes from her. A veil of Devil's invisible ashes swirled around them like a tornado at the speed of light. Baphomet slowly tilted his head, and their lips joined in unison in a far-from-inno-cent kiss, the ashes spinning at such a speed that they slightly lifted them off the floor. Page couldn't see anything around her. Her life moved in slow motion next to this magnificent major.

"You are mine," Baphomet whispered.

"And you are mine."

As the dance ended, Devil slowly lowered Page to

the floor. "I think we've done our duty." He met her gaze.

"Yes, we can slip away," she whispered.

"Baphomet!" Sun raised his hand on the other side of the hall. His voice was sonorous and pierced all space at once. It soared up to the ceiling, and at the same moment, echoed back into the room. He looked unearthly, his strong body glowing in a pool of gold, and his long, straight hair cast a golden shadow, his big eyes so bright that it was impossible to look into them without squinting.

"Sun!" Baphomet smiled at the major approaching them.

"Before you slip away—and don't tell me it wasn't your plan—please introduce me to your charming date." Sun turned a blinding smile to Page.

"Princess of Wands." Page bowed slightly, and the major bowed in return. "Pleasure to meet you."

"Heard lots about you." Sun turned to Devil. "What did you call her? Let me remember… Oh, 'my siren.'"

"Sun…" Baphomet intertwined his rough hand with Page's.

"If I didn't know you better, I'd think you were shy," the golden major teased.

"Or in love." Strength approached them, accompanied by Magician. She looked stunning in her matte-black dress. "Sorry, what on earth am I talking about? She's just one of your little whims, as always."

"Watch your tongue." Baphomet's voice echoed through the hall, and everyone turned to look at them.

"Or what?" Strength obviously had drunk too much and was not going to retreat.

"Page is mine, and under my protection. Even the

majors can be locked in a maze." Devil looked at Magus and then again at Strength.

"Defending your freaky little pet." Strength smiled haughtily, but Magus put himself between her and Baphomet.

"It's not the right time," he whispered. "We probably should go." He gave them a fake smile.

"Great idea." Sun was still shining. It seemed nothing could unsettle him. "I love drama. I don't remember any for a long time. The deck is really shuffling." Sun looked mysteriously at Page.

"You came alone?" Page asked charmingly.

"Not everyone is as lucky as Devil." He smiled.

"Well, Star doesn't have a dance partner either. I'm afraid Emperor is not a fan of dancing, amongst other things. You could invite her," Page added casually.

Sun glanced at Star standing alone next to the bar.

"You're lucky." The major tapped Baphomet on the shoulder. "I won't detain you." Sun bowed again.

Devil took Page's hand, and she followed him to the exit. The princess noticed that her friends were still dancing and smiled slightly.

Once they were in the car, Baphomet grabbed Page's thigh, incinerating her body. His other hand slowly rose to her center, and when he touched her core, she closed her eyes, blossoming from the heat inside.

"Fuck." Baphomet squeezed her thigh tighter. "I'm afraid I won't make it all the way." He licked his lips.

"How do we get to your dimension?" Page moaned. "Can you get there by car?"

Devil devoured her with his eyes and opened his mouth slightly, continuing to touch her. "No." He breathed heavily. "You can't get there by car. Triumph has some kind of carriage agency for the majors. Too far." Baphomet moved away and squeezed his hands on the steering wheel so hard that it crackled.

Page rose and moved toward him. She gently nibbled his ear, then licked her lips and gazed up at Baphomet with her large, pearly eyes.

Devil hissed. "Fuck." He slammed down on the gas.

Page crossed her legs, trembling with anticipation.

<hr>

Before long, they were at the end of the neutral area, in front of the closed metal gates. Baphomet knocked a few times. A little window in the door opened, and the man behind it recognized him.

"My lord. Your chariot is ready." The man bowed.

The door opened, and Page saw a few magnificent chariots parked next to one another.

"I suppose the lady has clearance for the trip?" the man asked Baphomet without meeting his gaze.

"She does." Devil gave him a piece of paper.

Permission from Sun, probably, Page thought to herself. As soon as they sat inside the carriage, decorated with grapevines and painted in black, it slowly lifted up in the air on its own, and they flew away. It was surreal. Soon everything disappeared, and they were lost inside the misty clouds.

"It's magical!" Page was looking around, still not believing that this was happening to her.

"It is. I do it so often that I don't even notice the surroundings anymore." Baphomet smiled, his hand slipping underneath her dress and touching her hips.

The clouds got thick and foggy, and the scent of wine permeated the air.

"Almost there." Baphomet glowed.

The chariot stopped in front of big gates made of hematite, Devil's gemstone. Page looked up, but couldn't see the end. It seemed that the gates were endless. Baphomet just waved his hand, and they opened by themselves.

"That's some serious security," Page said.

"I am not fond of guests ... usually." Baphomet lifted Page in his arms.

When they entered, Page saw a main plaza lit by millions of torches. Grapevines were growing everywhere, and a fountain in the form of an inverted pentagram stood in the middle. "It's beautiful," she whispered into his ear.

"The air feels different when you're here." Baphomet sounded even more magnetic inside his own dimension. His voice lulled everything around him, and it seemed even time had stopped when he spoke.

Page looked behind the fountain at the big, dark castle, which was difficult to see because it was completely covered with grapevines. "Is this where you live?" she asked curiously.

"Yes, this is home," Baphomet answered simply without taking his eyes off Page.

He went up what felt like endless stairs with Page still in his arms. Oliver was waiting for them at the entrance.

Page was surprised to see the same man here. "Do you only have one servant for all of your properties?"

"Oliver goes where I go. I don't like having many people around," Devil whispered.

"Doesn't he want to live in his court?" Page felt bad for the man. He must be lonely.

"He's dealing with his demons, walking the labyrinth, working for me," Baphomet explained. "It might take a long time before he's ready to leave."

"What do you mean, 'ready to leave'?" Page frowned.

"When you let demons to feed on your soul for too long, you get sent to my dimension." The major cleared his throat. "The only way to leave is to face your demons."

As they approached, Oliver couldn't hide his smile as he looked at the couple.

"Hello, Oliver." Page smiled back.

"Welcome, my lady, my lord." The servant bowed.

"You should put me down," she playfully insisted.

"Only after we cross the threshold," the major whispered.

"Anything I can do for you, Master?" The old man continued to smile.

"No, Oliver." Baphomet hugged Page even tighter. "Actually, yes. High Priestess must not enter the dimension under any circumstances."

Page laughed.

"Understood, Master." The servant disappeared.

The castle was scary and beautiful at the same time. The ceiling was at least ten meters high, and the walls were decorated with black paper and paintings of grape leaves. The space smelled of lust, soot, and burning wine.

"The house is hypnotic, like you are," Page breathed in Devil's ear.

Baphomet was quiet. He was studying Page as she was studying his house.

"Let me show you my bedroom." His voice was saturated with viscous anticipation.

Page took Devil's hand and followed him, remaining silent. Baphomet's bedroom took Page's breath away. The top floor had no ceiling or walls. Instead, massive columns of hematite rose up to the sky. Delicate black curtains swayed slowly in the night air, hanging from the tops of the columns, and candlelight illuminated the space. In the middle of the huge room stood a round bed covered with curtains descending from somewhere above. Page stopped at the edge and looked out at the endless torchlit fields of labyrinths.

"How beautiful," she whispered.

Baphomet came up to her from behind and hugged Page with one arm, pushing her moonlit hair to the side and gently kissing her neck. "You are the only woman I have ever invited into my dimension." His tart voice enveloped Page, and she slowly turned to him, wrapping her arms around his neck. "I've dreamed about this night from the moment I saw you coughing in my presence."

"I couldn't breathe," Page whispered lightly, touching his lips.

"I knew the second you started coughing that you'd inhaled my ashes. No one has ever breathed in the real me before." His words melted reality.

Baphomet moved Page closer, greedily grabbing her hips, and dug his lips into her soul. Their tongues intertwined, devouring each other. Devil slowly lowered the straps of her dress, and his rough hands touched her breasts. Under his fingers, her nipples tightened so much that she ached with tension and desire. The major leaned over and kissed her breast, pressing Page closer to him with one hand. When she moaned, he looked at her with drunken eyes.

"Fucking perfection." Baphomet's voice bathed her in ecstasy.

Devil lifted Page up in his arms as she wrapped her legs around his body, and he carried her to the bed. He greedily tasted her delicate skin, and she groaned, drunk with pleasure. Devouring Page with his eyes, he pulled off her dress eagerly, then took off his suit.

"I want you." Page bit her lip, feeling herself burning with desire, ready to go up in flames like a phoenix.

Baphomet sank down onto her, but held himself up on his arms. His hand trailed down until he found her center, before he dipped a finger in.

"Always so wet," Devil said, his eyes glinting with satisfaction.

Baphomet leaned slightly to one side, and their naked bodies, lips, and souls melted into one. He entered her slowly at first, looking straight into her eyes, afraid to hurt her.

"More," Page moaned, and he started to move deeper, growling, softly killing her and bringing her back to life with each thrust, blinding Page with his magic.

The river of her desire overflowed its banks, and Page wanted him to worship her body forever. Baphomet moved faster and faster, his growls beginning to sound more and more primal.

"Fuuuck." He sounded like an enchanted beast.

Page moaned. They were like two flames in a bonfire, dancing a tantric dance under the full moon surrounded by thousands of demons. The glow within her grew brighter and brighter with each stroke. She dug her nails into his muscular back, no longer holding back her moans, wanting him closer. As though he understood, Baphomet slipped his hand under her neck and pressed her body to him. Flames began dancing along her skin as the pressure built. Just when she thought she might die from the exquisite feeling, he thrust even deeper. Wave after wave of euphoria crashed over her as she came, trembling all over, unfolding the secret layers of her soul. Baphomet burst into thunder and moved harder, no longer in control of himself. As he came inside Page, she felt another orgasm deep inside, intensified by his release.

Collapsing down next to her, Devil tenderly kissed Page, glowing with melodies of pleasure. "Stay here with me forever," he whispered.

CHAPTER

THIRTY

PAGE.

The next morning, Page and Devil lay next to each other, looking at the clouds through the black curtains, their minds soaring in the sky. A knock on the door had Baphomet straightening the blanket over them.

"You can come in, Oliver," the major called loudly.

Oliver slowly opened the door and walked in, bringing Page back to reality a bit.

"Good morning, Master, Queen." The old man bowed.

Page's eyes widened and looked questioningly at Baphomet, who just smiled.

"Where would you like breakfast to be served?"

"In the main dining room. We're starving." Baphomet pulled Page closer and kissed her back.

Oliver lowered his eyes, though a smile played at his lips.

"Tea, coffee?" Oliver asked, looking inquiringly at Page.

"Coffee, please." Page glowed.

180

"May I suggest the coffee beans that grow in our dimension? They have a tart taste."

"Sounds perfect."

"Great choice." The man bowed and left.

"He likes you. He's very proud of his coffee." Devil lowered Page beside him and kissed her lips.

"Why did he call me Queen?" Page narrowed her eyes playfully.

"As I said, you're the first woman I've invited to my home. He and all the servants will probably marry us in their minds while breakfast is being prepared."

Page laughed and wrapped her legs around him. "And what would that make me? The Devil's princess?" She couldn't help but smile.

"Devil Empress. You will rule over this dimension with me, Dempress." Devil's gaze was piercing as he looked at Page.

Page fell silent. She thought that Dempress would be a much better fit for her than Empress, considering her past and her energies. But it was just a fantasy. Such a tarot card didn't exist.

"At your service." She got up on the bed and curt-sied, liking how the word sounded on his lips.

Baphomet tried to grab her, but she jumped out of the bed and ran to hide behind one of the curtains. He flew up to her and wrapped his wings around her body, only a black curtain separating them. Page was frozen in awe, her eyes glued to the huge, magnificent wings around her, shining like black diamonds under the morning sun.

"Did I scare you?" Baphomet loosened up his grip a little.

"No, I've never seen anything more beautiful in my life." She was mesmerized.

Devil gently kissed her earlobe. "Say it again," he whispered.

"I have never seen anything more beautiful in my life." Page slowly moved away and walked around him, gently touching his wings with her fingers.

"A little closer to the center." Baphomet trembled under her touch.

"Like this?" Page whispered, her fingers tracing along both wings at the same time as if touching silk fabric.

Devil roared and with one flap of his wings, approached her tightly, lifting her off the ground as if she were a feather. Page heard her own heartbeat as they flew up. All of this was a magnificent dream from which she didn't want to wake up. From this height, one could see all of the dimension.

Soon, she saw a large black throne in the middle of the clouds. Baphomet lowered Page onto it and carefully knelt at her feet, kissing them passionately, slowly rising up with each sensual touch. Page skimmed over his wings and moaned as Devil's lips pressed against her inner thigh, so close to where she wanted him. Shivers covered her body.

When she caressed the part of his wings he liked most, Devil snarled and moved up, pushing open Page's legs even wider. The major quickly pulled her close to his body and entered her fully in one movement, growling and quickening his thrusts. Page moaned, brushing his wings with her frantic breathing. She felt Baphomet's skin break out in goose bumps of pleasure.

"Tell me if it's too much. I can't control myself," Devil said abruptly, barely able to get the words out.

"More," Page groaned, running her fingers along the inside of his wings.

He ruthlessly thrust into her until they both shattered. Sounds of euphoria pierced the morning silence of the clouds like hellish chimes as they came together in each other's arms.

"You have now officially taken your throne," Baphomet whispered after a while.

"An interesting coronation procedure." Page laughed and threw her head back.

Devil took her chin in his hands, drawing her face close to him, and looked intently into her starry eyes. "I'm besotted," he said gently, kissing her lips.

"So, this is your throne?" Page looked around. The throne was made of hematite, and a large inverted pentagram adorned the back of the seat.

"The official pedestal is in the house. This one I use alone to watch people in the mazes—the ones who couldn't fight their demons on their own," the major explained, still out of breath.

"Alone," Page echoed.

"The throne is big enough for the two of us," Devil said, staring deep into her eyes.

Baphomet talked like he was sure that she would become the Empress, even though she was still missing the air element. She wanted to feel as sure as he was. But her whole life hadn't gone as she had hoped, and she was afraid that this time would be no different.

"Just very dar—"

Page didn't finish. Instead, she began to gasp for air. A big, cold wave rushed through her veins, making her shiver. She began to scratch her palms, unable to stop. They were burning with cold. She wanted this terrible feeling to end. In the next moment, ashes poured out of her palms, enveloping her. Her eyes widened, and she jumped out of the ashy fog.

"Dempress," Baphomet said with admiration.

"What just happened?! Did I do that?" She couldn't believe her eyes—or rather, her hands. Page didn't know what to think. The Empress didn't hold ashes. Only the Devil did.

"Because you are a Devil Empress," Baphomet interrupted her thoughts. "Perhaps me being inside of you helped to manifest the ashes." He narrowed his eyes, and she couldn't help but laugh.

Page still couldn't believe she'd manifested the ashes. It was simply impossible. Yet another element she would probably never be able to take control of.

"What should I do with them?"

"Oh, so many things. I'll teach you." Baphomet kissed her palms.

When breakfast was over, they went outside. The square was still lit by burning torches despite the sunlight, and forbidden magic slowly flew in the air. The mirages kept appearing and disappearing behind every corner, tempting Page to follow them. Unintelligible cries of suffering people sounded like faint background music drowned out by the rustling of the grapevines' leaves.

"Let me show you the rest of the castle. I'm afraid if we enter my bedroom again, we won't leave." The major put his hand under Page's top and moved her closer. "You fit right in. Like this dimension was made for you."

Page noticed thousands of doors in front of her. "Where do they lead?" The doors were made of hematite, each adorned with a huge lock. Page couldn't even see where maze of doors ended.

"These are entrances to labyrinths. They are endless. You can only find the exit if you are truly ready." Baphomet sounded like a formidable ruler in his dark domain.

"And this?" Page touched the only door without a lock.

"It's—"

Devil didn't finish because she had already opened the door.

A huge pedestal stood in the middle of an endless room. A few naked women with red hair, half human, half animal, were chained underneath it.

"Our lord!" they yelled in joy. "You've abandoned us for so long! Come to us. Give us your warmth and passion."

An arrow of jealousy pierced Page's heart at their words. She looked at Baphomet as he clenched his jaw. She felt like throwing up, imagining him with these creatures.

One of the women noticed Page. "The girl can't give you what you truly desire. She seems too pure to be able to go for the things you like." The creature smirked evilly at her.

"Quiet!" Devil roared, and the women clung to the ground in fear.

Anger boiled inside her, and Page ran away, not wanting to witness any more. Baphomet quickly followed her.

"Are those your … lovers?" she asked, turning on him and crossing her arms.

"No." He went to hug her, but Page stopped him with an outstretched arm.

"I don't believe you. She wouldn't speak the way she did if she wasn't close to you." She paused, gathering her will. "I thought this was real, but I really don't know you."

"Don't say that. You're the only one who can know the real me," Baphomet almost begged.

Page was silent for a while, still hearing the laughter of the creatures inside the pedestal room. She huffed in frustration. "I want the truth. Stop thinking I can't take the truth about you," she muttered.

"They are not my lovers." Devil paused, looking for words. "But they were, a very long time ago. I keep them next to my pedestal to remind me of what I used to be: a creature who didn't know true closure or true love. You hold the ashes now. If you don't believe me, you can inhale my memories. Here." He moved his hand, likely releasing the invisible ashes.

Page didn't move. She didn't need to see his thoughts and memories to believe him. She had to accept that he had a past, and probably not a pretty one. He'd accepted her past, and now it was her turn. Page stepped closer and brushed his lips with hers.

"You are mine," she whispered.

Oliver cleared his throat behind them, nervously shifting from foot to foot. "I'm sorry to interrupt, but Justice brought in a new prisoner."

"We will receive her here," Baphomet commanded and took Page's hand, leading the way.

When they entered the throne room again, Devil spread his wings, and horns appeared amidst his raven hair. Baphomet studied Page. She knew he was looking for fear in her eyes. But Page just smiled. His horns were beautiful, as if made from hematite. The chained women, half human, half animal, bowed, afraid to gaze at Devil. Baphomet invited Page to sit beside him on the pedestal.

Oliver opened the door and bowed to Justice, who entered with a sword in her hand. Page felt cold creeping down her spine. This major could take her at any moment. Justice's mouth opened slightly when she saw Page sitting on the throne next to Devil.

"The deck is really shuffling. Baphomet and a possible future Empress." Justice paused, studying Page, as if she had never seen her before. "Hello, Page. I wish I could say long time no see. An interesting wardrobe choice." Justice eyed the black shirt Devil had given her.

"Welcome, Justice." Devil raised his pinky and index fingers, evoking the horns of a demon. "Who did you bring?"

"A murderer." Justice glanced at Page.

"Bring him in, Oliver." Baphomet waved his hand.

The servant came into the hall with a young man. Baphomet flew up to him.

"Look into my eyes." Devil tilted his head, staring into the soul of the young man as he stood hypnotized. "Justice, I'm glad to accept maniacs or cold-blooded murderers, but this young man was defending himself."

"The law is the law," Justice said dryly.

"You're right." Baphomet drew out the words with a sigh.

"A law that is contrary to the nature of things and of mankind itself," Page flared up, unable to stay quiet. "Are we still going to follow the laws imposed on us out of fear?"

"She has not yet become a major, but is already eager to establish her own rules. Are you willing to take on the wrath of Abyss if we start to disregard his laws?" Justice smirked.

"If necessary." Page caught fire, and a burning ball rose from her palms. "Live and not grovel."

Justice looked at Devil, who returned to the pedestal and sat next to Page.

"Page is right," Devil concluded and took her hand in his. "The soul of this young man is pure, and I do not have a labyrinth that chains the innocent."

Page wanted to howl with happiness, unlike Justice, who raised her sword.

"You will regret this, Baphomet. Or have you forgotten the war with Abyss?" Justice's voice sliced through the room, cold and unwavering.

"I remember it very well, as well as the fact that you fought on our side." Devil arched an eyebrow, locking eyes with the adamant major.

"At least we're not consumed by the black hole," Justice said.

"These laws only exist to keep us all in line, including the great majors," Page said, meeting Justice's gaze with much more confidence this time.

"I'm afraid I have nothing to add, Justice." Baphomet bowed his head.

"Don't think it will get past Abyss unnoticed. Magus and a few of his loyal majors are keeping their eyes open."

"No doubt." Devil didn't blink. "The time will come when you have to choose a side."

Rather than answer, Justice abruptly turned around and walked out of the room. Page looked at Baphomet gratefully, and without saying a word, kissed him passionately.

"That was a bold thing to do," Devil said, his tone one of curiosity and not judgment.

"I hate all these unjust laws that we're forced to live by. Especially after they found me guilty without any trial."

"You're right." Baphomet sighed. "We've been groveling for far too long."

The rest of the day, they did not leave his quarters. Toward midnight, the major took Page home. As she was about to exit the car, he took out a small box.

"I want to give you something," he said almost shyly, handing the present to her.

Page smiled and opened it excitedly. The hematite inverted pentagram—identical to the one Devil wore, just a bit smaller—shone like a black treasure under the moon.

"It's forged from the gate of my dimension. Now you can freely visit me whenever you want." Baphomet helped her put the pendant on.

"So beautiful." Beaming, she posed for him, loving the way his eyes lit up just for her.

THIRTY-ONE

BAPHOMET.

At the ball, Page looked like a real Devil queen woven from the most seductive matter. Baphomet caught himself thinking that any demon would gladly kneel before her. After all, Devil himself, the lord of all demons, had already kneeled before her willingly.

When they were finally alone, Baphomet lost his last touch with reality. They were two souls whose cards were pulled out together by destiny in the tarot layout. He made love to Page tenderly and passionately at the same time, surrendering to her the very last ash from his veins. His siren felt like perfection. Everything and everyone before her had just been a pathetic attempt to fill the void.

Baphomet had hoped that Page would not want to leave when the time came.

Devil knew that his gambling addiction would hunt him.

He still went to the casino, but not to play. The time had come to take new lost souls into his dimension.

Baphomet sat at one of the tables, sipping his drink and looking around without blinking. He had already poured out his invisible ashes, and they filled the whole room. Iblis stood at his right hand, awaiting his orders. Baphomet closed his eyes and looked into the souls. He didn't like this part—so much suffering—but it was his role in this universe, and he was good at it. Baphomet saw it all: dreams, fears, destroyed possibilities, fighting—demons that were fed again and again. Devil signaled to Iblis, and the demon moved.

"Wait." Baphomet stopped him. "That man, no." He looked at the man sitting at the next table. "He's still trying to fight his demons on his own. Let's give him a chance."

"Understood, Boss." Iblis went to carry out the orders.

Mort came in, and Baphomet's eyes lit up. He'd been waiting for the major of the thirteenth dimension.

"So much sin and life." Mort's voice echoed as usual as he sat down next to Baphomet. "I'm not used to it."

"Found out something?" Baphomet asked, looking at the people being taken.

"Magus doesn't trust me yet with the important stuff," Mort muttered. "I can't stand his company anymore. The guy is out of his mind with his ambitions."

"This I know, even without you." Baphomet smirked. "Keep your eyes open."

"Fine." Mort exhaled and sipped his drink.

"If he doesn't share his plans, try to at least to find out where his gates are."

"You know he always uses his magic. I didn't enter his dimension through the gate even once."

"Still, look where the inhabitants are going, or the guards," Baphomet thought out loud. "Any clues would help."

"Did you…" Mort paused. "How is Triumph?"

Baphomet smiled sadly, looking at Mort. Devil knew very well what it felt like not to be with the person you loved. He felt bad for Mort. His reality was dead, in the literal sense of the word, and even more so without Triumph.

"Speaking of which…" Baphomet couldn't hide a smile, looking at the entrance.

Triumph walked in, and without yet seeing Baphomet and Mort, immediately waved to the waiter. "Champagne."

Devil noticed how Mort tensed and straightened his back. "He's coming over here," Mort squeezed through his teeth in panic.

"Stop shaking, you idiot," Baphomet cursed.

Triumph's happy face changed to shock and finally to anger when he saw Mort. He approached the majors, but remained standing.

"Triumph," Mort whispered.

"No. Hell no." Triumph was furious. "You invited him? Since when is the Devil is a matchmaker?" He stared at Baphomet.

"Triumph, hold your horses," Baphomet reasoned.

"I'm out of here." Triumph turned around. "See you never, Mort."

"He's helping Page!" Baphomet shouted after him.

At that moment, the waiter brought Triumph's champagne.

"Give it to me." Triumph grabbed the champagne,

intending to drink straight from the bottle while he looked at Baphomet. "Spill it out." He lounged in a chair.

Devil noticed how Mort's face shone with awakened life.

CHAPTER

THIRTY-TWO

PAGE.

A qua, Triumph, and Amador were already waiting in another unremarkable café when Page showed up with Star. She'd met the major at her office to discuss her taking part in the modern tarot deck. To Page's delight, Star was on board. To celebrate, she invited the major to join them for lunch.

"Star, my brightest!" Triumph sang as he got up and kissed the major's hand. "Welcome to this Sun-forgotten café."

Star smiled a bit timidly as she greeted everyone.

"Princess of Wands, you might yet unite all the majors again. I see more of them now than I've seen in the last century, now that you're around." Triumph looked approvingly at Page.

"How are things going with Emperor?" Amador asked.

"They're not going. It's been so long, yet he's never wanted to move to the next stage of our union." Star sounded frustrated—angry, even.

"Have you ever thought about expanding your gaze

194

to other candidates?" Page asked quietly, hoping she didn't offend the major.

Star laughed at the impossible idea. "What other candidates?"

"Don't tell me you didn't notice how Sun looked at you!" Page blurted out.

"You're mistaken." Star drawled the words as if thinking them over in her head.

"I'm not," Page insisted. "I hold fire inside of me, and I can sense when fire burns inside another person. And he burns when you're around. Plus, I have eyes, and it's completely obvious that he likes you."

Star smiled, clearly considering this possibility. Page had decided she didn't really like Emperor. He seemed very distant and cold with the beautiful major.

"Maybe I should expand my horizons." Star smiled and winked at Page.

"The best thought you've had in millennia. Cheers to that!" Triumph raised his champagne glass.

Only after some time did Page realize that Gaia hadn't joined them. Page felt bad for some reason. Lately, she'd noticed that her girlfriend had become somewhat cold, angry, and even detached.

"Where is Gaia?" Page asked Aqua. Surely, she would know.

"She couldn't make it. Something's off about her these days," Aqua said with a frown.

"I didn't really have a chance to speak to her during the ball. I might visit her showroom," Page decided.

"Not sure that's a good idea," Triumph said.

Page shook her head, surprised. "Why?"

"I can't talk about myself, it's not modest." Triumph pretended to lock his mouth and throw away the key.

"I don't follow." Page frowned.

"It's possible," Amador explained, "that Gaia likes Triumph. And since he doesn't feel the same way about her, she might feel awkward being around him."

"I noticed it too," Aqua muttered guiltily.

"Look, it's Sun himself!" Triumph yelled, happily and quickly rising from his seat. "This place is not Sun-forgotten after all. Amador, let's go say hi."

When the two left, Aqua moved closer to Page.

"Gaia invited Triumph up to her room after the ball, but he didn't accept the invitation. And apparently, she's also jealous of you."

"She was drunk. I'll let her know it's no big deal." Page sounded determined. "She can't ignore us because of some stupid things she said after champagne. She probably doesn't even remember it."

"You're a good friend, Page." Star looked at her with a sweet smile. "But jealousy is a demon that corrupts the core."

"All the more reason to speak to her. She's our friend," Page decided, closing the topic.

Sun, a glorious, golden sight, was coming to the table with Triumph and Amador in tow.

"Hello, everyone. Star." Sun bowed.

"Sun, I didn't know you were coming to the neutral zone for lunch," Star said playfully.

"Lately, more and more majors come down. I want to see what the buzz is about," he said with a shrug.

"Just admit that some of your spies spotted Star, and that's why you flew here. I'll never believe you would choose this cheap café willingly," Triumph said. Then, as if nothing had happened, he tried to get the waiter's attention to order more champagne.

Sun looked lost. Clearly, he didn't know what to say. He just stood there, fluttering his golden eyelashes.

"It's okay, we'll keep it a secret," Triumph teased. "Did you hear about Page's new project?"

"No, what is it?" Sun answered quickly, happy to change the topic.

"It's a modern tarot deck, and you, my dear friend, will need to pose for her completely naked, sitting on top of your white horse!" Triumph explained and triumphantly put his hand up.

Page almost choked. Sun started to laugh, the sound piercing the air with joy.

***

Some time had passed, and Page spent almost every day together with Baphomet. He would pick her up from work, and they flew either to his dimension or the summer house. Page felt that the Wheel of Fortune of her destiny was spinning faster and faster. She drove away the thoughts about the full moon and her missing air element.

Today, Page had finally gathered enough courage to visit Gaia. She stopped at the entrance of the showroom, feeling a little nervous. She hadn't done anything wrong, but somehow, she felt guilty.

Gaia was adjusting a dress on a mannequin, making some changes when Page walked in.

"Gaia!" Page smiled.

"Page?" Gaia said, sounding unpleasantly surprised.

"We missed you at lunch the other day. Star and Sun joined us," Page reported, not knowing where to start.

Gaia still hadn't looked at her. "I'm very busy with my new collection these days," she said coldly.

"I can imagine. It looks beautiful!" Page exclaimed in admiration and touched the dresses.

"Thank you, no fire dresses this time," Gaia snapped, finally raising her eyes to Page.

Page wasn't sure how to react. She hadn't expected such rage. Obviously, Gaia was mad at her.

"I realize now it was a mistake to make a fire dress for you at my first show," Gaia said.

"I don't understand. Did I do something wrong?" Page asked with a frown.

"You never do." Gaia smirked. "You just get all the attention. You're with Baphomet, and you act like you're clueless about Triumph's feelings—even though you keep him close, like a pet."

"That's not fair, Gaia. Triumph is my friend!" Page insisted, sparks firing off her skin. She didn't care about the sparks right now. Gaia didn't have the right to judge her like this. Page truly believed she hadn't done anything wrong. She shouldn't have to defend herself or feel guilty for being friends with Triumph.

"You know he likes you, and you let him believe something between you two would be possible one day!" Gaia yelled.

"We're just friends. He knows very well it's not possible. What do you suggest? That I cut him off because he likes me?!" Page yelled back, losing her patience.

"But then who will worship you?" Gaia smirked, hatred in her eyes. "Page this, Page that. Don't tell me you don't like his attention."

Page felt her fire burning within her. "Gaia, I came here as your friend. But you're crossing the line. If Triumph wasn't okay with how things are between us, he would tell me."

"Fine, but I'm not watching this twisted game of yours," Gaia said, sounding resolute.

"What twisted game? There's no game."

"He still likes you, and he hopes you'll like him back one day. You're just leading him on," Gaia challenged.

"Even if that's true, that's his business, not yours." Page sighed, tired of these accusations. They weren't getting anywhere.

"You're right. It's not my business. None of you are my business. Amador and Aqua, you and Triumph. I don't see where I fit into that group anymore. I'm done."

"Are you serious? Just because Triumph liked me?" Page couldn't believe her ears.

"No, because I'm in love with him. Seeing how he looks at you is torture." Gaia became quiet.

Page felt bad. She wanted to hug her friend, but when she tried, Gaia put a hand out.

"Don't. You will not fool me as you do the rest. Who knows what deal you made to get the energies? Even though you pretend that your powers are a curse. Sooner or later, everyone will see what I see." Gaia turned away.

Without meaning to, Page felt a ball of fire and black water appeared in her palm. She hurried to exit the shop before she might destroy it.

"And don't count on me for your art project!" Gaia shouted after her.

"I figured that much myself!" Page shouted back, slamming the door.

THIRTY-THREE

PAGE.

Page came back home before dinner and locked herself in her room. She sat in the open window, watching the moon. She thought about her life and how much she'd come to love it. She had her friends, Baphomet, a job she loved. Even the energies didn't scare her as much as before, because she wasn't alone in this fight. But would it be enough for the deck to accept her? Tears rolled down her face. She didn't want to die—not now, when she had finally just started to live.

Page went downstairs, a little nervous and afraid of her father's mood. Lately, she had been avoiding him as much as possible.

The Queen of Wands was pouring wine into glasses. She noticed Page and studied her daughter, dressed in a short blue dress, her curly moonlit hair half up, half down.

"Here's my beautiful daughter." The Queen of Wands smiled. "You skip breakfasts, you avoid me at work, and you're rarely home even at night. I didn't even have a chance to ask how your visit to Baphomet's dimension was!"

"Sorry, Mom. The visit…" Page paused. "The visits were amazing."

"Happy to hear at least something. Yesterday, we published the first card in the magazine and people loved it!" The queen beamed. "I got so many letters. Everyone wants to know if we will continue with the series."

"That's amazing news!"

"So, what do you think about Devil's dimension?" her mother whispered, checking whether the hall was empty.

"It's beautiful, and … scary. It feels like it's a part of him. By the way, what is it about Devil and grapes? I mean, there are grapes everywhere!" Page sat casually and sipped the wine, happy that her father was absent.

"Pleasure, lust, and obsession, my dear. I could go on and on. But hopefully he's found balance between his human and animal desires. That is the ideal position for Dev—"

The Queen of Wands silenced herself abruptly as her husband walked in.

"Should we expect hooves in addition to your uncontrollable energies?" the King of Wands attacked.

Page tried to fight the desire to defend herself. Her time spent with Baphomet had helped her realize that she wasn't an outcast and that there was beauty in her otherness. Devil believed in her so sincerely that gradually Page also began to love all her "shortcomings."

"Some people think I'm just the way I should be, that my otherness is beautiful," she said, trembling. "Even though my own father can't accept me."

"Is that so?" The King of Wands rushed towards her furiously, but her mother put herself between them.

"Dear, please," the Queen of Wands begged.

"Did you hear it?" the king fired back. "I'm the only one who is desperately trying to keep you out of trouble! What other ideas did he put in your head?" He grabbed Page by the arm, demanding an answer.

"Page, please. Just apologize." The Queen of Wands looked at her pleadingly.

"No!" Page shouted in a shaking voice, unable to take it any longer. "I was trying to fit in, as Father insisted. But I can't change who I am. I only wish for him to accept me."

"Get out of my house!" the king screamed with anger Page had never seen in him before.

Without saying a word, she ran upstairs crying, her face stained in dark lines from the tears. Not thinking twice, she immediately started packing her suitcase. Matilda entered without saying a word and silently helped Page collect her things. She waited until everyone in the house was asleep before leaving for a hotel in the neutral zone.

Page had never been to Triumph's office before. It took some time to find it. He didn't rent an office in the high buildings, like the rest of the majors. Apparently, Triumph owned a racing club. As Page entered the huge premises, she saw a group of workers cheering for two cars.

"Do you know where I can find Triumph?" Page asked the workers.

One of them pointed to the speeding cars. They

were moving so fast, Page couldn't decide if they were driving or flying.

"Who is he racing?" Page joined the group.

"Devil," the man answered casually.

Page hadn't expected to find Baphomet here racing with Triumph in the middle of the day. The cars were getting close to the finish, and the workers started yelling. One of the cars came first, winning by a few seconds. Triumph got out of his car and went to Baphomet.

"Not bad, not bad at all … considering I'm the fastest man in this universe." Triumph patted Devil on the shoulder.

"You definitely are." Baphomet smiled.

"Well, done, Boss!" the workers cheered for the winner.

The majors turned to the group and saw Page. Somehow, she felt uncomfortable and just waved, a little put out. Both majors started to walk toward her.

"Page, my darling. I didn't expect Baphomet to find out about us like this." Triumph kissed her playfully.

"Stop it, or he'll believe we're secretly seeing each other at your workplace." Page rolled her eyes and pretended to hit him.

Devil smiled and put his hands around her waist, enveloping her with his alluring magic. "It's a lovely surprise, my siren," Baphomet sang magnetically, putting her under his spell fully.

"Get a room." Triumph smirked.

"I didn't know you liked racing." Page looked at Baphomet, who still didn't let her out of his embrace.

"Triumph offered his racetrack to help me with…" Devil paused. "… my gambling problem. To get out the adrenaline."

"Excellent idea." Page looked at Triumph and smiled. He was a good friend. No, he was one of a kind.

"What are you doing here?" Baphomet moved her hair from her face and breathed in her fragrance.

"Not having an affair, if you were wondering," Page assured Devil, and he laughed. "It's something I need to discuss with Triumph … in private."

"Say no more." Baphomet kissed her. Page desperately wanted to leave together with him and feel his harsh, tempting hands on her body. "I will see you soon, siren."

Devil shook Triumph's hand. "Thank you, my friend."

"Any time. Come here." Triumph decided that shaking hands was not enough and hugged Baphomet tightly.

Page and Triumph gazed after Devil as he disappeared behind the building.

"Is everything okay, Page?" Triumph seemed a bit concerned.

"It might sound stupid, but I have to get this out." Page took a deep breath, steeling herself.

"Okay." The major tilted his celestial head.

"I went to see Gaia yesterday."

"Oh boy." He rolled his eyes theatrically.

"Yes. And she was very upset and rude. She accused me of toying with you, giving you hope…" Page paused, looking for the right words. "That one day we might be together … romantically."

"Page." Triumph took her hand.

"No, listen, she got me thinking. I just really love you, and I want to talk about this, because I don't want to lose you." Her voice broke as she thought about the possibility. Triumph had become dear to her. She couldn't stand the thought of losing him.

"Page, it's not a secret that I liked you from the first time I met you at Gaia's show. But after all the time we've spent together, I have come to love you as my friend. I've lived long enough to know if someone likes me, and you have your eyes on Baphomet. And that's okay." Triumph took her shoulders in his strong hands and looked Page straight in the eyes. "I chose to let it go and be your friend. And I really value our friendship."

"I do too," Page whispered and hugged him, relieved.

"And a piece of advice: don't let other people enter your head and make you doubt yourself."

"I'll try." Page smiled just as Aqua and Amador approached them. "So, apparently everyone hangs out at the racing club except for me?" Page narrowed her eyes.

Aqua laughed. "Everything okay?"

Page nodded and told them about her chat with Gaia. When she was done, she found herself blurting out everything that had happened with her father the night before, too.

Aqua listened with horror in her eyes. "Page, my angel, I am sorry." She embraced Page in her soothing arms. "Forget the hotel. You can live with me."

"What? No!" Page shook her head.

"Don't look at me like that. You hold water, so you can enter my Arcana without breaking the rules. And I have always wanted a sister. Plus, my house is too big just for me and my father," Aqua insisted.

"Aqua, I can't," Page protested. She didn't want to be a burden to anyone anymore. Living with Aqua was not safe, for starters; Page could destroy everything with her fire or other energies. But she couldn't deny that part of her wanted to move in with her friend. Aqua had become like the sister she'd never had, who accepted and supported her unconditionally.

"I won't take no for an answer," Aqua decided.

"But I might burn your house down." Page hesitated.

"At the Cups Arcana, which is literally made of water?" Aqua narrowed her eyes.

"Right. All right, then!" Page lit up. "I'll get my stuff and move in tonight."

"Living together with my bestie!" Aqua jumped in excitement, and they danced in the middle of the racing club.

"You two are something." Triumph smiled tenderly. "But I think Page will be moving in with Baphomet soon."

"Shut up, Triumph. That's ridiculous." Page rolled her eyes.

"It's not. I don't think you understand what a step this is for him. Literally no woman ever has gone to his dimension, unless they were sentenced to go there." The major smirked. "I don't want to bring her up, but he's never invited Strength. She used to ask him all the time to show her his home, but Baphomet would always find excuses."

"Yes, thank you, Triumph, for bringing up his half-his-lifetime lover, it really makes me feel better." Page pretended that she was mad.

"You're missing the point, Page. He treats you differently. He loves you," Triumph concluded.

"I can't believe my ears," Amador teased. "What happened to Triumph, who doesn't believe in love? I thought after Mort, you stopped believing."

“Don’t exaggerate,” Triumph answered defensively. “I’m only starting to consider that it’s possible, that’s all.”

“Maybe you can meet someone at Aqua’s charity event tomorrow,” Amador sang.

“Thank you, Sun. You’ve heard my prayers! We can go back to the restaurants with clean napkins!” Triumph raised his hands in prayer.

Everyone laughed.

THIRTY-FOUR

PAGE.

P age sat at her desk, looking out the open window. The cars passing by merged into the grey mass. She didn't move, drowning in her own thoughts. Time passed inexorably, and she clearly felt that the new energies were becoming stronger and stronger in her body. But the Swords element still had not manifested, and Page was afraid to admit even to herself that terror was gradually creeping up on her.

She was brought back to reality by a knock on her open door. Her mother's secretary, a short young girl, stood hesitantly in the doorway.

"Princess of Wands. You have a package," the secretary said, her eyes lowered as though she were afraid to look at Page.

The rumor about her relationship with Baphomet had spread with the speed of the Eight of Wands, and Page more and more often caught strange looks being thrown her way.

"Bring it here." Frowning, Page wondered what it could be. She wasn't expecting anything.

"I'm afraid the package is too heavy."

Page got up and went out into the lobby. A sea of peonies filled the entire space, and she breathed in the gentle, enveloping scent of her favorite flowers.

"Here's the card." The secretary held out a small envelope to Page. She quickly opened it.

I miss you, my siren. Triumph mentioned that you're going to Amador's dimension to train. I'd like to accompany you, if you don't mind. Yours, Baphomet.

Page couldn't help but smile. When she looked up, her mother had joined her in the lobby.

"Holy Sun. What a gorgeous bouquet! And it's not even peony season!" The Queen of Wands threw up her hands. "Page, come to my office, please."

Page hadn't spoken to her mother since the day she'd left the house to live with Aqua. She tried to gather her strength to tell the Queen of Wands about everything that was happening to her, but for some reason, every time, she postponed the conversation for later. When Page entered the office, her mother locked the door.

"Page, talk to me. I've heard you're living with Aqua. I am so worried. Rumors reach me." She cleared her throat. "I must admit, I didn't believe them, but…" The Queen looked into her daughter's eyes. "You *are* changing…"

"I've already changed, Mom." Page was trying to hold back the tears. She felt like a little girl who just needed her mother's hug, believing that everything would be all right after that. Page was tired of being strong, of having to fight for everything, including her life.

"So, it's true, then. You *are* the future Empress." The Queen of Wands hesitated.

"Either that, or according to High Priestess, if all

four energies don't manifest in me by the full blood moon…" Page's voice trembled, and her eyes filled with onyx tears. "Then I'll die."

When Page began to cry, her mother approached slowly and held her tightly in her warm embrace. "Everything will be fine, my love." The Queen of Wands gently touched her hair, as she had always done when Page was a child. "The majors can't help you?"

"They're trying. I'm going to Lovers' dimension today, to train."

"I'm happy that you have such good friends." The queen smiled softly. "And I'm here if you need anything at all."

Page hugged her mother once more, then went back to the lobby to wait for Triumph, Amador, and Aqua. They'd agreed to pick her up and go to the end of the neutral zone together. When they arrived, Triumph's chariot was already waiting for its owner. The carriage looked exactly as it was depicted on the card in La Papesse's tarot deck. Page looked with admiration at the two sphinxes standing next to it.

As the chariot smoothly went up into the sky, Page studied Triumph. He looked so different now in his natural element. He stood while riding, wearing armor decorated with crescent moons, a laurel star crown on his head. He looked magnificent. Page could clearly see the two sphinxes driving the carriage, one was black, and one was white. Aqua could not stop talking. It was her first time flying, and Amador tenderly held her hand.

"I hope you'll like my house, Aqua." Amador shone with happiness.

"Of course she will," Triumph answered for the

princess. "I can't imagine a better dimension for a date. It's paradise in the truest sense of the word."

"How do they know where to go? There are no reins," Page asked, looking at the magical sphinxes.

"I control them with my mind. We were created together." Triumph sped up.

<hr>

Baphomet was already waiting for them at the entrance of the sixth dimension, and Page's heart raced excitedly when she saw him. As soon as the carriage stopped, she hopped out and ran straight to him. Devil grabbed her in his arms and whirled her around.

"My little devil." Baphomet took a deep breath that sounded almost like a growl. "I missed you."

"I gave you your usual room, Baphomet. Please stay *discreet*." Amador emphasized the last word. "The population of my dimension is already scared to death that Devil is visiting our paradise."

"We'll behave like two angels in the flesh," Page promised, smoothing her dress.

"I doubt that." Triumph smirked. "More like the Devil and she-Devil that you are." He clapped Baphomet on the shoulder.

Amador gazed at Aqua, who was impatiently waiting to see the inside. He had only to wave his hand in the air and a huge wall of pink smoke disappeared. An incredible picture opened up before them: pale pink clouds were floating everywhere, even right at ground level. They slowly poured from one form to another. An unbelievably large, lush tree woven from flowers and clouds grew straight into the sky and could be seen from any corner of the dimension. In the distance, between the clouds, a huge castle sat dreamily in a gentle pink haze.

"Welcome!" Amador smiled, and his eyes shone like two sapphires, his fingers entwined with Aqua's hand.

"So beautiful." Aqua admired her surroundings and tried to touch the small cloud right next to her, but it seemed to be running away.

"I suggest we go straight to the castle. Dinner is scheduled in thirty minutes. By the way, I invited Sun and Star."

"They're together?" Page enquired of Baphomet excitedly.

"Sun is trying," Devil said, scooping up Page in his arms and nodding to everyone else. "See you at dinner!" He rose up without warning, spreading his dark wings the color of a moonless night.

"Is this your idea of discreet?" Amador shouted after them.

They soon arrived at the balcony of one of the chambers almost at the top of the castle.

"Do you know this dimension well?" Page straightened her dress and looked around.

"During the war, we often met here to discuss our plan of action. Amador has always given me this room."

"You…" Page paused. "… spent time here with Strength?"

Devil was silent for a moment, studying her face. "Let's not talk about her. That page of my life has been turned forever. Come here," Baphomet said gently, moving closer to her.

Page didn't move at all. She was standing and staring at her shoes, avoiding his gaze. She was jealous, even though she'd decided to accept his past. The image of Strength with Baphomet woke up a demon inside.

Strength was a gorgeous, powerful major, and Page… Well, she didn't even know who she was.

"I need to get ready," she said dryly.

"Page, there's no need to be jealous. You're the only one for me," Baphomet reassured her, slowly approaching. "Since the moment I saw you, I've had to force myself to keep from jumping you any time we're in the same room."

His words made her heart quicken. Baphomet definitely was the only one for her, from the very beginning, and despite everything. She wanted to say it, but decided to find a better time, when Strength had not been mentioned in the conversation at all.

"You are too poetic to be the Devil," Page teased and wrapped her arms around his neck.

"I can be very romantic, my siren," he said, folding her into his embrace.

"I hope dinner won't take too long." Page slightly bit his lip and looked into his eyes with an inviting challenge.

"We can always skip dessert—and the main dish, probably," Devil tempted her, and Page was instantly captured in the depths of his cosmic eyes.

"I need to change first." Page laughed.

She chose a red dress made of delicate tulle and a choker with a red flower of the same material. Her body resembled the silhouette of a rose in this formfitting dress. When she came out of the bathroom, Baphomet was sitting on a chair, reading a newspaper. He quickly raised his gaze to Page, licking his lips as he devoured her curves with his eyes.

"I'm afraid we can only stay for an aperitif." Devil dug his fingers into her hips, slowly lifting the dress and bringing his lips closer to her center. She held on to his shoulders and threw back her head at Devil's thirsty lips on her core.

"I think it's okay if we're a bit late," Baphomet growled and abruptly rose, lifting Page and carrying her to the edge of the balcony.

She grabbed the railing with her hands. With a quick movement, Devil parted her legs so widely that Page thought she would fall. She dug her long nails into his back.

"You are mine," he growled and slammed into her.

Page almost screamed with pleasure, only now realizing how much she'd missed his body and his intoxicating touch. Her body reacted instantly, bursting into flames like a torch. She ran her nails down his back, and the fire came out of her fingers, leaving small cuts on his skin from which dusty smoke began to come out. Baphomet didn't even notice. He seemed to let go of the reins, pounding into her so hard that Page could feel the deepest cells inside burn with the blossoming agony of pleasure.

"Be mine forever," Baphomet whispered, his body trembling.

"I'm yours." Page wrapped her arms around his neck, and Devil groaned, his movements speeding up.

When the euphoria hit them at the same time, Page lost all control. Her body exploded, and waves erupted from her skin. Black rain poured down from the sky like liquid tar from hell. In the next second, the balcony began to shake, and a tree emerged from the ground, reaching up to the sky like a shooting star. She opened her mouth when she noticed that the leaves on the tree were woven from black matter and white fire. Page stood under the rain, looking at her creation. It was frightening, but so perfectly beautiful in its dark uniqueness.

"You will be the most powerful major that has ever existed," Devil predicted with admiration, kissing her gently.

Page didn't answer, just buried her face in his tousled hair. She finally realized that her magic could be beautiful, even if it was beautiful only to her and Baphomet.

But suddenly, a gust of wind rushed over the balcony and reminded Page that she was still missing one energy.

When they finally went down to the ballroom, Page was amazed at the magnitude of the castle. The walls were painted with love murals, and magical trees made of pink clouds grew right in the middle of the castle. The waiters, dressed in pale pink tailcoats, served champagne in crystal glasses. All the guests were already standing in the middle of the hall.

"Page!" Amador narrowed his eyes. "Discreet. I said *discreet*. Are you trying to redecorate my dimension as a doomed paradise?"

"Sorry." Page lowered her eyes.

Everyone present laughed.

"She's sorry." Amador waved his hand, giving up.

"The future Empress is full of surprises." Sun shone, as always.

"Let's drink to Empress's success during the blood moon." Star raised her glass.

Page tensed at the mention of the deadline. As if noticing, Baphomet wrapped his hand around her waist and brought her closer to him.

"We can do it," he whispered. "Together."

"How is the Swords energy?" High Priestess's voice sounded like a spell, intertwined with the music escaping from the gramophone.

"We're working on it," Baphomet blurted out.

"And by 'working,' you mean fucking to death every

time she's next to you," High Priestess said, raising one eyebrow in a high arch.

Devil almost roared, and his wings flew open, filling the space around him. Silence again reigned in the hall, but was soon interrupted by the piercing laughter of Page. Triumph joined her, unable to stop.

"You could use some fun too, High Priestess. I'm afraid your abstinence is turning you into a bore." Triumph put his hand on La Papesse's shoulder.

"You are insufferable, youth," High Priestess replied, much softer now.

Amador invited everyone to the next hall, and the guests followed their host. In the middle of the salon stood a huge table with all sorts of delicacies. The servants stood by the wall, waiting for the majors. As the guests approached the table, they pulled back the chairs in unison.

"I want to raise my glass to friendship." Triumph got up from his chair and looked at the guests one by one.

"To friendship." Everyone raised their glasses.

High Priestess was sitting next to Page, and she tried not to turn to La Papesse, avoiding conversation and squeezing Devil's hand under the table instead.

"Baphomet, I forgot my deck at the entrance. Will you bring it to me?" High Priestess asked in an almost commanding tone.

"How can I refuse you?" Devil answered sarcastically and looked at Page, who pleadingly held his hand.

As soon as Baphomet got up from the table, La Papesse turned to Page. "Empress is life. Her energy is so strong that it fires from her body into the world. Does it remind you of someone?" High Priestess looked deep into her eyes.

"I guess," Page answered doubtfully. "But I'm not sure I have what it takes, that I have such a power."

"Did it ever occur to you why Baphomet fell in love with you so passionately? With all the energy Empress holds, she is also pure sexual pleasure—something Devil can feel and relate to. He sensed it in you before any one of us could see what you are. You hold it all. Don't doubt yourself. *That* is the biggest enemy."

"I hold all but air," Page muttered.

"I hope you get the energy of the Swords too." High Priestess moved closer to her. "Do you feel darkness in you?"

"Why do you ask?" Page tensed.

She thinks someone like me can't be the Empress. I'm far from pure and blissful. The thoughts rushed in her head.

"Empress has always been associated with harmony and purity. But you'll be different, because you chose Baphomet. He envelops you with his ever-dancing dark ashes… It will corrupt or save you, depending on what the outcome will be."

"Is that bad?" Page whispered, biting her lip in worry.

"Perhaps, perhaps not. Maybe it's time for a brand-new Empress. We should not be afraid of the dark. After all, it's the only way to the light."

Devil returned holding the box containing the sacred tarot deck and handed it to High Priestess.

"Please, let's skip the reading tonight," Triumph said pleadingly. "No offense, but your layouts are always a mood killer."

The rest of the evening felt blissfully light. They all went to the hall and danced like they hadn't danced in years. Triumph paired up with High Priestess, and it was impossible not to watch them. It looked like Triumph had decided to show her some fun, lifting High Priestess up and down, then lowering the woman straight to the floor. At some point, La Papesse even went to the end of the hall and ran fast at Triumph, jumping into his arms. The majors could hardly keep a straight face.

"Fuck, I'm going to explode." Baphomet laughed out loud as soon as the dance finished, and Triumph froze with La Papesse in his arms.

The friends laughed hysterically, High Priestess along with them.

THIRTY-FIVE

PAGE.

Page and Baphomet woke up the next morning to birds chirping outside the window. They left the castle and headed toward the huge clearing strewn with blue flowers, where Aqua and Amador already waited for them. The sun had not yet risen high, and the dew on the grass had not yet dried. The air was fresh and full of tender harmony.

Star and Sun had left yesterday after the party, and so had High Priestess. It was just the five of them.

"Good morning." Triumph was the last to join, buttoning his shirt on the go. "Did I miss anything?"

"Miss what?" Page raised her eyebrow. "How I breathe in the air of the seventh dimension?"

"Yeah, we didn't think it through, Amador." Triumph laughed.

"Actually, you could help Page train the ashes." Baphomet's arms gently wrapped around her waist.

"Okay, what should we do?" Aqua quickly agreed.

"Ashes can block other elements, reveal memories, and squeeze into the soul, bringing tempting demons along—"

"Reveal memories?! What do we need to do?" Aqua screamed.

"Nothing, just sit there."

Baphomet moved and hugged Page's waist from behind, his lips lightly touching her ear. "Pour out your ashes, make them approach the person, and try to pick up their memories."

"Okay." Page gently kissed him before turning her palms up.

"Don't doubt yourself," Devil whispered and squeezed her waist a little tighter.

Page closed her eyes, concentrating, and soon felt tickling in her palms. A few ashes left her body.

"Holy shit, that's amazing!" Triumph blurted out.

"You can see them?" Page widened her eyes.

"Yes, right here." Aqua pointed.

"Fucking amazing … and a bit creepy," Triumph added.

"I thought I could see them because I hold the same element, but apparently yours are visible to everyone," Baphomet muttered, clearly as surprised as Page was.

Page didn't know what to think. Her ashes were different. She wondered what it meant. Could she do the same things that Devil did?

Page turned to Baphomet, feeling a bit lost, but he smiled broadly as he blotted out the sun.

"Let's see what they can do," he suggested excitedly. "Send the ashes again."

More ashes poured from Page's palms, approaching Aqua, Amador, and Triumph. When it touched their skin, all three began to cough.

"Stop it, fucking hell!" Triumph begged, coughing even more.

Page stopped immediately. She looked at Baphomet, searching for the answer he didn't have.

"You really are the Devil Empress." He gently kissed her. "Your ashes are visible, and that's why people can inhale them."

Page felt that nothing could scare her when Devil, with all his glorious darkness, was next to her.

"Should we try memories?" Page turned to her friends.

"Fucking no." Triumph got up. "I refuse to be a lab rat."

Page and Baphomet laughed.

"You can try on me," Baphomet sang and tilted his head closer to her, inhaling her ashes.

Page closed her eyes, but no matter how hard she tried, she didn't get any images.

"Nothing." Page pouted her lips.

"Let's go see the lagoon." Triumph slyly looked at Amador.

"What kind of lagoon?" Aqua lit up.

"Amador has a lagoon that makes a person admit his greatest desires."

"Or his biggest fears." Amador turned to his friend with displeasure.

"Please, that sounds so mysterious!" Aqua pleaded.

"Don't be a bore," Triumph said, pretending that he didn't notice his friend's hint.

"Okay, if that's what everyone wants. But don't say I didn't warn you."

The majors walked ahead. Page took Aqua by the arm, and they followed the men, remaining a little behind.

"How is the loving couple?" Page narrowed her eyes slightly.

"Page, I'm in seventh heaven. These are the best days of my life." Aqua lowered her voice slightly. "And nights."

"Of course! He is the Lovers." Page winked. "I'm happy for you."

"Have you spoken to your brother?" Aqua sounded a bit worried.

"No, he's a little aloof these days. Plus, now that I live with you, I barely see him. Why?"

"I heard a rumor that he's been seen with Gaia." Aqua paused.

"Seriously?" Page's eyes widened. "Are you jealous?"

"Of course not. But tell him to be careful. If the rumors got to me, they could easily reach unfriendly majors as well. Gaia is from a different court."

A frisson of worry snaked down Page's spine. "I'll talk to him, thank you."

"Even though we're not together, I still care about him," Aqua added.

"I know."

As they walked, Page picked wildflowers and handed them to Aqua, who wove them into a wreath. She made one for herself and one for her girlfriend. They walked contentedly for a long time, and just before arriving at the lagoon, Aqua put a beautiful wreath of flowers on Page's head. Baphomet turned to them, studying Page with a tender look in his eyes.

"How do you like my crown?" Page rose on her toes to reach his lips.

"It's perfect." Devil squeezed her, and Page bit his lip. "Perhaps it's time for me to order you a real one."

"Hmm." She looked into his eyes and smiled broadly.

"Here we are." Amador stood near a small lagoon with a waterfall that shimmered in all shades of the rainbow. "Veritas. Do you still want to drink the water of truth?"

"I'll pass." Triumph sat down on a big stone near the water.

"I'll probably pass too." Baphomet smiled and joined him.

"But that's not fair," Aqua protested. "Why did we walk all this way?" She blushed slightly. "Here, I'll start."

Amador went to a small well near the lagoon and drew water into a beautiful transparent vessel, which began to glow like the northern lights.

"Just one sip." Amador gave the vessel to Aqua. "*Verum dico.*"

As soon as she sipped the water, Aqua's eyes changed color slightly, switching to dark blue. She took a deep breath, as if fighting herself. "I would like to…" Her voice sounded distant, like in a dream. "I want to get married!" Aqua blurted out and looked at Amador, embarrassed.

Page giggled, and Aqua quickly passed the vessel to her without giving anyone a chance to comment on her confession.

"Your turn, Page."

"I'm not so sure anymore." Page smiled awkwardly, but took a sip of the water. After a second, the words poured out of her, slightly slurred. "I'm afraid that I'm not worthy to become the Empress of our tarot universe. Soon, I'll die, and I'll never see Baphomet or all of you again."

Frowning, Devil approached Page and hugged her tightly. "I won't allow it." He paused. "If you die, I will follow you, incinerating the gates of Death's dimension on my way."

He grabbed the vessel and took a small sip. "One day, I want to have children with Page—little she-Devils with hair the color of the full moon."

"It's against the rules," Page whispered, but she couldn't help but smile at the thought.

"Fuck the rules." Baphomet pressed his forehead to hers.

"Fuck the rules." She repeated his words like an echo.

"Your turn?" Aqua looked at Amador.

"I don't need water to tell you what I want more than anything." Amador got down on one knee and took out a ring made of Iceland spar, sparkling in the sun. "Will you marry me?"

In surprise, Aqua covered her mouth with her hands, her eyes wide, several tears rolling down her cheeks. "Yes!" She jumped up and down, and Amador carefully put the ring on her finger, then passionately kissed her.

"Congratulations!" Page shouted even more joyfully than the bride herself.

"An incorrigible romantic." Triumph got up from the stone and hugged his friend. "Good timing though."

"Congratulations." Baphomet did the same.

"Page, we'll make the wedding after the full blood moon, of course," Aqua said.

Page knew that her friends believed she would become the next Empress. But she wasn't so sure.

"Please, no. Please, let's celebrate before the blood moon. I want to see my best friend as a bride. I'll not take a chance."

"Okay!" Aqua agreed immediately and jumped in excitement.

When they returned to the castle, a servant met them with a letter on a small tray. "A message for major Devil." He bowed and held it out.

When Devil took the letter, Page noticed that it was sealed with the emblem of a lion.

"Sorry." Baphomet stepped aside slightly and opened the letter, quickly skimming through its contents.

"Everything okay?" Page asked, sitting on the couch next to Aqua and examining her ring.

"I'm afraid I need to leave." He turned to Page. "Do you mind if Triumph takes you home?"

"Of course not." She wanted to smile, but a small shadow ran through Devil's eyes, and it made her heart stop for a second. "Are you sure everything's all right?"

"Yes, just need to…" Baphomet faltered. "… check something out."

"Be careful." Page kissed him, but couldn't help the worry she felt. It surged in her heart like water at high tide.

CHAPTER
THIRTY-SIX

PAGE.

A few days passed, but Page still hadn't heard from Baphomet. She decided to distract herself with work. She was sitting alone in a cozy little café, chewing on her pen and trying to write down ideas, but the pages of the notebook remained blank. She didn't know why it was so difficult for her to decide how she saw Triumph's card. The major embodied so many things, it felt like she was always missing something.

"Here you are." Triumph sat down at the table with a charming smile. "I stopped by the house, and Aqua said you might be here."

"Actually, I'm trying to plan your photo shoot, but so far without success," Page said, frustration lacing her voice as she continued to bite the pen.

"That's full of germs." The major snatched the pen from her mouth. "It would be better to occupy your mouth with something else."

"Triumph." Page blushed. "You, you…" Not knowing what to say, she grabbed the pen back.

"I meant ice cream or a lollipop," Triumph said, unable to restrain his laughter.

226

Page hit him playfully on the shoulder.

"Ow, that hurts!" The major rubbed his arm and looked carefully at Page. "I see you're becoming stronger by the day. In any case, I came to give you something," Triumph whispered, looking around the place, making sure no one was listening.

"Why the secrecy?" she whispered back.

The major took out a small vial from his pocket and placed it on the table, covering it with his palm. "Here, drink it," he whispered almost silently.

"Is it blood?" Page asked with a frown, noting the dark red color in the vial.

"It doesn't matter. It's important that you drink every last drop of it," Triumph insisted.

"No way. I'm about to throw up just looking at it." Page crossed her arms and looked away.

Triumph stared at her without blinking and whispered seriously, pronouncing every word. "Do you trust me? If yes, then I beg you to drink without asking any questions. Do you trust me or not?" With the last words, he moved the vial closer to her, still covering the contents with his palm.

"Of course I trust you," Page replied. She looked down at his palm, wrinkling her nose. Even though he loved to joke around, she knew Triumph wouldn't be cruel. Whatever this was, he was telling the truth: it was important. With a sigh, she took the vial and tipped it into her mouth.

"It's disgusting."

"Good girl." Triumph smiled. "I suggest washing it down with champagne. I mean, it's really gross." The major winked.

"You think? What was it?" She grimaced.

"I'd love to tell you, but I can't give you any explanations. Sorry," Triumph said with a shrug.

"Well, this time I fully support your idea about champagne," Page decided and waved to the waiter.

"To trust!" The major raised his glass and smiled.

"Have you heard from Baphomet?" Page blushed. "I haven't seen him for days. I'm starting to worry."

"He's okay. I saw him." Triumph stopped himself, weighing his words. "Well, I saw him today."

"Thank Sun." Page exhaled. "That means nothing has happened to him."

"Should I pick you up in this evening?" Triumph added champagne to his glass.

"Why?" she asked, a bit lost. With all her worrying, she'd spent most of her time either working, at home with Aqua, or training. She had no idea what was going on in the world.

"Tonight is the majors' new year. Emperor arranges a magnificent ball every year." Triumph sounded excited.

"Strange that Baphomet didn't tell me anything about it," Page said quietly, feeling as if the shadow of crow's wings hung over her.

"Sun asked for your presence as the future Empress. He wants to make an official statement in front of all the majors."

"That's a fucking joke," Page cursed. "First no one could know about me, and now everyone should be informed?"

"Page, rumors spread. Magus and some other majors are against you. They're afraid, because you're something new entirely. Sun wants to show them that you're one of us," Triumph said.

By that evening, Baphomet still hadn't shown up, and Page couldn't help feeling that something bad was going to happen. Pushing the feeling aside, she stepped out of the limousine and entered the ball with Triumph. She'd gone to Hilda earlier, hoping her favorite dressmaker would have something worthy of the event, and she wasn't disappointed. Page's body resembled a candle in a white silk dress, her open back and arms decorated with pearls glued directly to the skin like drops of melted wax.

"Triumph, future Empress," Emperor personally greeted the arrivals while sitting on a throne located right in the middle of the hall.

"Someone's got an ego gone wild," Triumph leaned over to Page and whispered, making her laugh.

Aqua stood in a dazzling blue dress holding Amador by the hand and talking to the shining couple, Star and Sun. Page furtively glanced at the arriving major, Death. She had never seen him before. He was dressed in a black suit with a long tunic over it, and his fingers were studded with skull rings. His already bloodcurdling eyes were accentuated with black eyeliner. Death bowed slightly to Emperor and walked toward the bar, settling down not far from Page. Cold sweat ran down her back. Triumph turned away, pretending he didn't notice him.

"Where is Baphomet?" Amador looked inquiringly at Page.

"I have no idea. I haven't heard from him since he left your dimension," Page admitted.

"He'll come. Sun insisted that all the majors should be present this year. Big changes, big news." Amador tried to calm the princess down.

"What the actual fuck?!" Triumph practically yelled, looking at the entrance.

Baphomet slowly entered the hall—holding Strength by the arm. She was dressed in a long black dress to match her companion. Page couldn't believe her eyes, looking at her beloved with another woman, hoping deep inside that this was one of Devil's mirages that would evaporate. But it was reality—a reality that tore her soul into burning fragments, like the body of a sinner destroyed forever in the dimension of the Judgment tarot card. The princess had so selflessly blazed for Devil all this time that finally, her heart burned to ashes, leaving an emptiness inside. Feeling as though she were in a nightmare, she only distantly felt Triumph squeeze her hand. Aqua grew pale as she looked at Devil and then turned to her friend.

"Do you want to go to the ladies' room?" The Princess of Cups looked pleadingly at Page.

"Later, Aqua," Page whispered. She felt broken, empty. "I have to see this."

"He went crazy, I swear," Sun mumbled under his breath.

"I don't want to watch this." Star took a new champagne glass from a passing waiter and headed to the balcony.

"I'm sorry, Empress," Sun said, confused, and followed his date.

"Seriously, what the fuck?" Triumph was visibly angry, downing his champagne in one gulp, still not taking his eyes off Baphomet and Strength as they approached the bar on the opposite side of the hall. "Page, I'm sure there is an explanation. Maybe she used some kind of magic on him."

"Look, one more surprise," Amador interrupted, staring at the entrance and the incoming major: Fool.

"I'm surprised he showed up," Triumph thought out loud. "I don't even remember when we last saw him."

"He came because of Page. Everything starts with him—infinite potential." Amador gently looked at Page, pale as death.

Everyone present was staring at Fool. To put it mildly, the major was not dressed for the ball. He wore ordinary trousers and a tunic, with a white rose in his pocket. Devil also turned to look at Fool, and his gaze met with Page's for a split second. She wanted to cry; she wanted to turn him into ashes right here in front of everyone. She abruptly turned away and hurried to the balcony, afraid she might do something crazy.

Aqua quickly caught up with her friend. "Page, I don't know what to say. This is some kind of nonsense."

"I'm not going to make a scene, Aqua," Page said nervously.

"I don't care—burn this place to hell if you want. I just don't want to leave you alone," the Princess of Cups said faithfully.

Page walked over to her friend and intertwined her fingers with hers. "I'm sorry. I don't want to go back inside. How can I escape from here?" She looked around as the majors withdrew inside.

"After Sun's speech and the first dance, you can leave. Unlikely before; most of the majors came just to see you."

"I'll ask Triumph not to leave my side," Page decided and took a deep breath before heading back inside.

"You don't need to ask. I won't leave you for a second." Triumph appeared and offered his hand, escorting Page into the hall.

"And here she is." Sun had already begun his speech, standing in the middle of the hall. "As I said, the Princess of Wands is on her way to immortality as the future Empress!"

There was a slight noise in the hall.

"I've heard that the energy of the Swords Arcana has not manifested yet, not to mention she's summoning ashes and black water," Magus said arrogantly. "Let's be honest and admit why we're all here: she is a threat to our tarot universe. She is a threat to us all. She needs to be held and observed in a safe place, until we know for sure."

Silence reigned in the hall. Page gulped down her champagne and stepped forward.

"I don't care what you think. If I exist, then the deck wants me to. And I've been imprisoned before. Never again."

Page released a flame so big that it touched the chandelier on the ceiling. Magus angrily looked at Page and was about to add something else, but before he did, Fool, who had been sitting right on the steps all this time, got up, staring intently at Page.

"Let me look into your eyes, child." Page slowly raised her eyes, and Fool stared at her, coming very close. "Hmmm." He turned his head to the right, then to the left. Finally, he turned around and walked slowly toward the exit.

"The deck hasn't been shuffled for so long that your Arcana has turned into a rotting swamp. I hope the princess will be able to bring some cleansing energy, but maybe not... Do not forget that the deck is not shuffled by itself, but we shuffle it, winding the Wheel of Fortune with our actions." With this, Fool evaporated into the air, and a whispering was heard in the hall.

"Magus, keep your stupid thoughts to yourself."

Triumph approached him in anger. "Believe me, you don't want to be Page's enemy. She has much more support from the majors than you do."

"We'll see about that," Magus whispered. "Until the blood moon." He disappeared too.

"Orchestra music!" Emperor waved to the conductor.

The music literally roared, and Triumph slowly led Page to the center of the hall.

"It's almost over," he whispered as they began to dance.

Out of the corner of her eye, Page saw two black silhouettes circling not far from them, and her heart exploded again, as if the Tower card had overtaken her.

"Change partners!" Emperor announced, and everyone exchanged partners with the couple next to them.

Page saw a pair of black eyes staring at her.

"Princess." Mort bowed.

"Death," Page whispered coldly.

"So, I can count on your visit no later than the full blood moon." His voice echoed as if woven from several voices at the same time. "I will personally meet you in my dimension," he said smugly.

"Over my dead body!" Page blurted out.

"That's exactly how it works." He laughed and added a little rhythm as they spun along the hall.

"Change partners!" Emperor announced again.

"We're just in time." Mort bowed and looked at Star and Devil as they stopped right next to them.

Page struggled to contain the energies rising in her body. Her world collapsed, and she faintheartedly thought that Death's dimension would not be so bad after all.

"Devil." Page bowed slightly, as was customary.

"Page." Baphomet's voice sounded like the voice of a ghost. "This is temporary." The major looked pleadingly into her eyes.

Page was quiet.

"Just trust me. That's all I can say." Devil paused. "Soon everything will be as before," he said, clearly not believing his own words.

"No," Page answered so loudly that all the couples turned in their direction.

"It was necessary. It was…" Baphomet closed his eyes as if his whole body suddenly ached.

"Okay, necessary for what?" Page stopped dancing and looked into his eyes.

"I can't tell you anything except that you need to trust me," Devil whispered. "Please, inhale my memories. At least try."

Page did, but there was nothing. She still couldn't master this element, or maybe he sent empty ashes because he couldn't show her anything to justify his behavior.

"I see nothing. Enjoy your night with Strength." Page tore off the hematite pendant from her neck and placed it in his palm.

"This was a gift." Baphomet seemed disarmed.

"I don't want it anymore, just like I don't want you in my life anymore." She burst into tears.

Page turned around, and before the music ended, she quickly headed for the exit, ready to burn everything and everyone.

The energies left her body with an explosion like she had never felt before. They were burning like a bonfire, reaching almost to the ceiling. Black peonies trudged around the curtains, floor, chairs, and ceiling, covering everything like darkness covered the earth on a moonless night. When Page had almost reached the exit, resinous rain covered the majors.

"That was quite an exit." Triumph quickly ran down the stairs, catching up with Page.

"I didn't plan to make a scene, but it hurts so much." She stopped almost at the end of the long stairs and sat down on the steps, exhausted. "I can't believe he did that. Why is he so cruel…?"

"I'm sorry, Page." Triumph hugged her tightly.

THIRTY-SEVEN

BAPHOMET.

Baphomet opened the letter, quickly skimming through the contents.

Devil, I came across the information that your little pet is in danger. I could help, under one small condition. Come to my dimension to discuss the deal if you want her to live. — *Strength.*

A looming shadow hung over Baphomet as he headed toward the hated dimension. Leo led him straight to Strength's study, where the woman sat languidly on the sofa in a bright orange exciting negligee, her fiery hair tied up in a messy bun. Devil looked at her quickly and made a stern face, making it clear that he was here only to talk about Page.

"I'm listening." Baphomet cut to the chase. Her letter had said she had information that Page was in danger, and he was in no mood for games.

"I see since you met your beloved, you have become a bore," the major murmured and moved closer to Devil. "I remember you greedily taking this nightgown off me many times. Maybe we should first remember the old days."

Strength approached Baphomet, wrapping her arms around his body and leaning in so that their lips almost touched. "I want you," the fiery major whispered.

Strength's smell and embrace had become foreign to him, even alien. Her touch felt like shackles, not caresses. Devil did not feel the slightest desire to possess this woman, not now or ever.

"I came here to talk about Page," Baphomet insisted and stepped back.

Strength's expression changed suddenly, slightly exposing her animal teeth. Devil knew that she was hurt, but their relationship had fizzled out long before he'd met Page.

"Before I tell you anything, we need to enact a tied deal," Strength insisted.

"Never heard of a tied deal." Baphomet narrowed his eyes. Obviously, Strength wanted to use this to her advantage somehow.

"Because you don't hang out with Magus. He's a master of spells." Strength smirked. "It's a deal that can't be mentioned to anyone until the end of time. Anyone who breaks it will be consumed by the black hole. You can't *tell* anyone." The woman smiled wickedly.

"And in return, what do you want from me?" Baphomet questioned, losing his patience.

"Nothing extraordinary. I need to clear my reputation. News that you left me for a freak princess is not good for my image. You will be with me for the next month. And I will save her from Magus."

"I don't want to make any tied deal with you," Devil said, crossing his arms.

"Suit yourself, but I know for sure that without my help, your princess will die." Strength paused. "Bound by a tied deal, I will have to fulfill my part of the bargain too. It's a win-win."

Baphomet stood in silence. He didn't believe Strength would help Page just to spend a month with him.

He released his ashes, and they passed through Strength's armor with no difficulty at all. He saw her desire to control him, how she hoped to win him back after he'd break up with his siren. But Strength *did* plan to help Page, afraid that if she helped Magus, she would lose Devil forever.

Strength doesn't know me at all. It's all about her and her power, Devil thought sadly to himself.

He didn't see anything else. Magus had probably erased her memories somehow. Baphomet had to protect Page or at least try to.

"Fine, I agree," he announced in a cold voice.

"Wonderful!" The major clapped her hands in excitement. "Give me your hand."

Strength took his hand and whispered a spell. Smoke enveloped their hands, creating gray shackles between the two majors.

"I will help to save the Princess of Wands from Magus one time, and in return, Devil will once again be mine for the next month, which includes public appearances together, dates, and sex," Strength announced triumphantly.

"What exactly do you mean by 'sex'?" Baphomet questioned, his eyes narrowed.

"It means bringing me pleasure," she teased.

"Deal," Devil answered calmly, careful not to give his thoughts away.

"Deal." Strength beamed.

The smoke squeezed from their hands in a thin, tight whisp before it dissolved completely.

"How do I save Page?" Baphomet demanded.

"Kiss first?" Strength gave him a victory smile.

"I will not break the deal: public appearances, dates, and bringing you pleasure. No one mentioned kisses," Baphomet announced.

"Fine." Strength snorted. "Magus is planning a ritual, a blood transfer to take possession of her energy. Right before the full blood moon. But if she drinks his blood first, the transfer would be impossible."

"So, you will get me his blood," Devil concluded.

"I will have it in a few days, so we can make our first public appearance at the majors' new year. Should we go to my chamber?" Strength sang invitingly.

"Only after I get the blood. I'll be waiting to hear from you," Baphomet said dryly and left.

Fucking Magus, Devil cursed in his mind. *I'll break her heart, again... But Magician will not have Page and her power.*

With such thoughts, Baphomet returned to his dimension and didn't leave it for a few days until he had finally received a long-awaited letter from Strength. Devil did not visit Page. He was afraid he might say something, let some detail slip before he was able to help her.

Finally, the treasured vial of blood was in his hands. Baphomet headed to the racing club; he needed Triumph's help. After all this time, Baphomet realized that the warrior major was a devoted friend to both Page and him. When Baphomet found him, Triumph was sitting on the terrace watching the race, and of course, drinking champagne.

"Baphomet! What a surprise. Came to race?" Triumph smiled charmingly.

"I wish, Triumph. I need your help." Devil looked around, making sure no one was watching them, and took out the vial.

"I know you're thirsty, but walking around with someone's blood is a bit creepy," Triumph complained, looking at the vial. "Or did you come to ask for my blood as well? I'm afraid it won't give you any pleasure. At most, you'll be able to get drunk from the amount of champagne in my veins."

"You're an idiot." Baphomet smirked, rolling his eyes. "You need to find Page immediately and make sure she drinks it 'til the very last drop."

"Why not do it yourself?" Devil could tell Triumph was suspicious.

"I can't…" Devil stumbled. "Can't explain. Can you do it?"

"No problem," Triumph assured him, taking the vial.

"Send me a note when it's done. It's important," Baphomet insisted.

"Don't worry, will do," Triumph promised.

Devil was sitting on his throne, watching the labyrinths, when he received the letter from Triumph that it was done. Baphomet took a deep breath, knowing that at least for now, Page was not in danger. But at the same time, a heavy stone was pulling his heart to the bottom of hell's pit. Tonight, his contract with Strength would begin. Devil took a sip of his drink and went to get ready for the stupid ball.

His date was waiting for him at the stairs, dressed, of course, in a black dress to match him. Baphomet's heart grew numb with pain when they entered the hall, and he inhaled the familiar, intoxicating aroma of his siren. Page looked like a supernova exploding and illuminating the darkness around her in her white silk dress. Devil hardly controlled his desire to leave Strength and tell Page everything. Strength was victoriously smiling the whole time.

Baphomet was quietly watching his siren when their eyes met. She did not appear to be breathing, and her face blanched whiter than the pearls on her flawless body. He couldn't approach her; he had nothing to say. Instead, Baphomet was pouring himself one glass after another. When Page defended herself to Magus, Devil realized she was no longer just a princess who had been struggling with her powers. Now before him stood a Dempress who finally owned who she was. He admired her.

When her magic left her magnificently wicked body, Baphomet whispered, "Fucking perfection."

The deal was done. Devil slowly entered Strength's chambers and looked around. Everything was as he remembered, except for the fact that the room was scented to the point of suffocation with some kind of incense. Strength clearly wanted to please him, knowing how sensitive he was to her smell.

"I'll quickly take a shower," Strength sang, unable to hide her triumph.

He slowly poured himself a drink and sat in a large chair, looking at the night sky. Baphomet tried not to think about Page and how she must be feeling right now. He just needed to survive this month somehow, and then one day, the deck would be shuffled, hopefully drawing their cards together again.

Strength came out of the bathroom in a long,

translucent fire-colored dress, her hair loose and fluffy. She looked intently at Baphomet, waiting for his reaction. Of course she was beautiful, but Devil's soul irrevocably belonged to another woman. Page's love was a gift the deck had given him after thousands of years of loneliness. He would never have crossed the threshold of this bedroom if his siren had not been in danger.

Baphomet didn't want to talk. He approached Strength, slowly lowering the gentle fabric from her shoulder. She closed her eyes in pleasure. Devil wrapped his body around her, and in a matter of moments, they were on the bed. She wriggled like a lioness under his every touch and kiss. During the night, Strength burst into euphoria from his hard flesh, lips, and fingers countless times. Finally, exhausted but happy, she opened her eyes. Her face changed dramatically.

She found Baphomet still sitting in the chair, as at the very beginning of the evening, slowly sipping his drink, fully dressed and calmly looking at the woman.

"Deceiver! Devil in the flesh!" Strength raged.

"Nothing new there," Baphomet said quite calmly. "The agreement didn't mention anything about me actually touching you. My mirage ability is one of my favorites."

"Don't think that you've won. You still will spend this month with me. I deeply doubt that your beloved will accept you after that," she hissed slyly.

"What will happen between me and Page is not your business. Good night." Devil stood up sharply and immediately left the eighth dimension.

THIRTY-EIGHT

PAGE.

L ife had entered its usual course for Page, but without Baphomet. She tried to skip every possible event to avoid seeing him, but still managed to spot him once when he'd been leaving an expensive restaurant, holding Strength by the arm. Tears rolled down Page's face. He'd pierced her heart through and through, like the blades from the Three of Swords card.

Several times a week, Page and Triumph flew to Amador's dimension. Page was getting better at separating one energy from another, but the energy of air was still dormant.

Page hurried down the stairs of the office in a soft purple satin skirt and a matching bra.

"Daughter, why are you leaving so early?" the Queen of Wands called out to Page.

"Aqua is preparing her wedding party. She asked me to help her choose a dress and all sorts of small details, like flowers for the event."

"Do you still live in her Arcana?" The queen lowered her voice.

"Yes," Page answered defensively.

"But this is against the rules," her mother muttered.

"I don't care anymore about the stupid rules, Mom. Love you. I'm late." Page kissed the woman and left.

For the past week, Aqua had been completely absorbed by preparations for the wedding.

"Page, you're so late!" she said a little nervously and went to the table, grabbing a huge album.

"Page, thank Sun you're here." Triumph kissed her and lifted her slightly off the floor. "Save me," he whispered to make sure Aqua didn't hear. "What is this three-volume essay?" He turned to the bride.

"It's a wedding album! So many decisions to make… Here are the tablecloths. Which color suits us best: cornflower blue, or electric blue?" Aqua said with enthusiasm, examining the pieces of fabric.

"I'll go look for champagne in the kitchen." Triumph escaped.

"In the big fridge!" the Princess of Cups shouted after him.

"Aqua, I only know dark and light blue. You lost me with the corn thing. Let's start with the flowers. What did you choose?" Page looked at her happy friend, absorbed in anticipation of the upcoming wedding.

"I want blue orchids." Aqua quickly turned the page and jabbed her finger at the photo of the flower.

"Beautiful and gentle, just like you. Then maybe white or powder-colored tablecloths will suit better? In order not to dazzle your guests with too much blue." Page barely suppressed a smile. "Plus, the energy of the groom: air, white color."

"You're right! It's his wedding too."

The girls laughed.

"Page, you are a savior." Triumph returned from the

kitchen with a bottle of champagne. "Before you arrived, I was planning an escape in order not to drown in the influx of all this blue. By the way, Aqua, your father is back. I met him and his companion in the corridor."

"I don't want to hear." Aqua blushed slightly. "Sun protect me from having such a marriage as my poor mother and father had."

"I'm sorry, Aqua. It must be hard not having your mother around. You've never heard from her again?" Page gently pushed her friend's hair out of her face.

"No, from the moment she left with my older brother, we've heard nothing at all. I was only five years old. Of course, I understand that my father is a womanizer and not an ideal husband. But it was possible to live somewhere not so far away. I doubt she'll return."

Triumph broke the silence. "I'm sorry, Aqua."

"Okay, on a positive note, Hilda made sketches of a few dresses." Page handed the bride a small sketchbook.

Triumph approached Page as she stood, looking at a picture on the wall of a sinking ship in the depths of a rough sea.

"What's up, Empress?" Triumph whispered.

"I'm afraid I'm sinking like this ship." Page didn't take her eyes off the picture.

"I'll pick you up." Triumph took Page's hand in his. "Did you hear that the next day after the blood moon, a council will be held about you? Magus insisted."

"What's his problem with me?" Page looked at her friend. "If I don't die, he plans to imprison me?"

"I wanted to say that…" Triumph drank his glass in one gulp. "No matter what, I will fight together with you."

Page turned and hugged him so tightly that he could barely breathe. She'd become incredibly strong.

"Page, I think I like this puffy dress with lace!" Aqua shone with happiness.

"You will be the most beautiful bride!" Page held out her hands to Aqua, and they began to dance.

"I see the preparations are going well." Amador entered looking at the dancing girlfriends and at Triumph pouring himself champagne, also dancing to the rhythm of the music.

Aqua ran up to the groom, and he gently kissed her.

"Page, I hope you have some warm clothes?" Triumph enquired.

"Why?" She looked at her friends, surprised.

"We decided to get married in the mountains!" Aqua reported with a dazzling smile. "Triumph has a house there. We'll have a ceremony at the local temple. At the same time, guests can go skiing, breathe in the fresh mountain air, or just lounge in the spa."

"Great idea. But I'm really bad at skiing. I did it only once, and it was a disaster." Page frowned, remembering her skiing experience.

"Come on, I'm sure it's not that bad," Triumph protested.

"Seriously, I'm very clumsy." Page fell on the sofa.

"You just didn't have a good teacher. I'll take on this mission." Triumph bowed slightly.

"I'm afraid you'll regret it." Page laughed.

Time flew by quickly, until only a week was left until the blood moon. Page had to stop at her parents' house to pick up warm clothes. As she carefully packed her suit-case for the trip to the mountains, someone knocked on the door.

"Come in," Page said uncertainly, fearing that it was her father.

"Sister." The Prince of Wands stepped inside and closed the door behind him. "Are you going to Aqua's wedding?" He raised his eyes to Page.

"Yes, it's this weekend. We're going early to prepare everything and ski a bit." Page looked at her brother. "Are you okay?"

"Yes, yes, all is well. If you can, give my congratulations to Aqua. Wish her happiness from me." The prince seemed nervous.

"Will do." She left the suitcase and approached her brother. "Is it true that you're dating Gaia?"

"Who told you?" he asked, surprised.

"Be careful, rumors can reach Justice as well." Page touched his hand. "Believe me, you don't want to go to her dimension."

"Stupid rules," he said angrily.

"I get it, believe me." Page looked at him gently. "But still, be careful."

"You know, I miss the time when you lived here, and all the attention was on you." He smiled sadly. "Let me help you close the bag." The Prince of Wands pressed down on the overflowing suitcase with his whole body, but couldn't manage to close it. "Holy Sun, what did you put in there?"

"Only the essentials." Page giggled, and lightly pressing on the suitcase, closed it without much effort. "Can you tell me if it's safe for me to go down?"

"He's not home." The prince gently looked at his

sister. "You know, he told me he has no daughter anymore."

"I see." Page lowered her eyes.

She pushed the thoughts about her dad away. He would never accept her. It was Aqua's weekend, and Page planned to be there for her.

THIRTY-NINE

BAPHOMET.

Strength was not going to give up on their deal. She invited Baphomet to events and dates, specifically selecting the most crowded and popular places. But at least after the experience of their first night, she no longer proposed spending nights together.

Devil avoided his friends, constantly hanging out in the gambling club. He disappeared into his addiction, drowning out all thoughts. A month had now passed, and he headed to the casino to finally celebrate his freedom. Baphomet knew that he looked terrible. He'd hardly slept and only came out into the world to accompany Strength to her stupid events. He was sitting at his usual table when he heard Capio's frightened voice.

"This place belongs to major Devil. You have no power here," the manager insisted hesitantly.

"Move away, before I turn this place into sun dust," Sun commanded.

"And I won't mind cursing you." High Priestess couldn't resist threatening poor Capio.

"La Papesse, Sun, I didn't expect to see you here." Devil smiled.

"Baphomet, you need to leave this place," Sun begged.

"Just doing my job. This is where I belong. Did you know that all the demons that I unleash into the world—addiction, cruelty, greed—were first tested on me? The soul raises only through darkness." Devil slowly continued to sip his drink.

"Is this what you're doing now? Sitting here definitely won't help you get Page back." High Priestess deliberately touched on the most painful topic.

"I know she won't forgive me. She made it clear at the new year's ball," Devil mumbled.

"You didn't see or talk to Page for a month, but it's clear to you that she won't forgive you? Idiot!" La Papesse cursed.

"Baphomet, I honestly don't understand why you did this to her," Sun said. "You've let too many demons into yourself, believing that you can cope with them all and become a master of even the most hidden corners of your soul... But I'm afraid you went crazy instead. It's the only explanation." He stared at Devil, hoping for some kind of clarification.

"I can't say anything," Baphomet insisted.

"We need to get you in order. The Princess of Cups has a wedding soon, which you are invited to." La Papesse looked at him pointedly.

"Didn't expect that Amador would invite me," Devil said thoughtfully.

"Because *you're* the only one who actually gave up on you." High Priestess pricked him with her words. "Let's go. It's time to get out of this pit of self-destruction."

La Papesse moved in with Devil, and Sun also came to visit almost every day. Baphomet spent most of his time in the maze, replaying different scenarios with his addiction over and over again. He was slowly getting better. But all his heart yearned for was to be with Page. The major often thought that it was a paradox that a petrified heart could still hurt.

"Tomorrow we're going to the mountains for the wedding. It wouldn't hurt you to get some fresh air," Sun reported, sitting next to the fire on the grape terrace.

"Page will never agree to even talk to me. Plus, I won't be able to tell her anything new," Baphomet concluded.

"We'll rely on the deck. No one can predict how the cards will be shuffled," High Priestess insisted.

CHAPTER
FORTY

PAGE.

During the flight to the mountains, Triumph raised a glass as usual. "Let's drink to true love. It was love at first sight as soon as my friend saw Aqua. I wish you happiness, my beloved friends. You three are my family."

"For us!" Page already had her camera at the ready.

The flight lasted several hours.

"Amador!" Triumph shouted to his sleeping friend.

"I'm sleeping!" Amador muttered.

"One question." Triumph ignored his comment. "Which majors did you invite?"

"Everyone who's on Page's side. Or those who have doubts, but are still our friends." Amador looked at his friend, slightly bewildered.

"So, Baphomet is invited?" Triumph's voice sounded casual.

"Well, yes." Amador blushed and looked at Page.

"Drop it, Amador. I won't ruin the wedding," Page assured him with a smile.

"That would be lovely." Triumph laughed.

"Did you invite Strength too?" Page blushed from head to toe.

"What, am I crazy?" Amador asked, surprised.

"Well, they *are* together." Page lowered her eyes.

"They were together for a month, I think. Now Strength is by herself, same as Baphomet," the groom explained. "They're not together."

"I see." Page turned to the window, watching the passing clouds.

Triumph's house was located at the very top of the mountain. The car zigzagged gently up through the snow-covered trees. Everything around looked like a wintry fairy tale. Hypnotic calmness filled the air, every snowflake and icicle.

"Welcome to my humble lair." Triumph opened the door wide.

"More like a humble palace!" Page slowly examined the house with its wooden trim, cozy woolen carpets, beige sofas, and oak table.

"And a bar in the center of the hall. How convenient." Aqua examined Triumph.

"I have one architect for all of my properties. I'm afraid he ran out of new ideas."

The girls giggled.

"I suggest not wasting any time and hitting the slopes." Aqua was already climbing the stairs.

"Your room is second on the left." Triumph opened a chest of drawers with ski suits and went through the contents.

"Meet downstairs in half an hour." Amador lifted Aqua in his arms and carried her to the room.

When everyone had unpacked, they met downstairs to go to the slopes. Page wore a one-piece ski suit with a black belt and a big white fur hat, her hair falling all the way down to her waist.

"Page, you look like an ice queen." Aqua smiled, ready to leave with Amador to ski off piste.

"Are you sure you don't want to hit the hard slopes with everyone?" Page turned to Triumph.

"Not even for a second. Come on, we'll start with blue slopes." He adjusted her hat. "You can't be that bad."

Triumph and Page took the lift up the slope, which was deserted. Everyone usually came to ski on the weekend, so there were almost no people in the middle of the week.

"Okay, let's see what you can do." Triumph seemed determined. "I'll go down a little and look at your technique."

"Triumph, my technique is zero," Page protested.

"Don't be sour." He touched her freezing nose.

She waited until Triumph gracefully descended, then turned and waved to her. Taking a deep breath, Page quickly flew down, balancing on her skis with difficulty, ready to fall at every turn.

"Slow down!" Triumph shouted to Page as she flew right at him.

"I can't!" Page shouted back, then began to laugh loudly from the fear and adrenaline shooting through her.

"Page, slow down!" Triumph shouted again, putting his hands forward and trying to grab her.

Page tried to stop, but all in vain. She shot past him down the slope at great speed. Two skiers stood in the middle of the piste, shouting and gesticulating at each other.

"Step aside!" Page tried to warn them, but they

didn't hear her screams, too busy with their argument. She was flying straight at one of them dressed in a black suit.

"Move!" she screamed as she flew straight at them and ran into the man with such speed that they flew head over heels down the slope.

The first thing Page felt was pain all over her body. Her skis flipped into an unthinkable position, and her left leg began to whine. When the slope came to an end, they finally stopped, and the skier landed right on top of Page.

"Lady, what the fuck?!" The man lifted his head.

Ashen eyes stared at her. Page could hardly breathe, either from his weight or from the blows … or from Baphomet's proximity.

"Are you trying to kill me?" Devil's eyes lit up, and Page breathed in his honeyed aroma.

"I lost control a little," she said with a pout.

"A little?" Baphomet laughed sarcastically. "You're a terrible skier."

"I wasn't the one standing in the middle of the slope and irresponsibly ignoring everything around me," Page flared up.

"Of course. This is my fault completely."

"Yes." As she tried to move, Page groaned slightly, her leg aching terribly.

"What's the matter?" Baphomet said, suddenly sounding worried. "Does it hurt somewhere?"

"Everything is fine," Page said, but her face twisted in pain.

"Let me see." Devil carefully removed a strand of snow-covered hair from her face. "Where does it hurt?"

Page put her hand on her knee.

"Here?" Baphomet gently touched her leg, and even lying on the snow, she felt his chilling touch.

"Yes." Page closed her eyes in pain.

"It'll be okay." Baphomet whispered an unintelligible spell in his language.

The pain started to go away. At that moment, Triumph and Sun literally flew up to them and stopped abruptly.

"Page, are you okay?!" Triumph shouted, clearly in horror.

"She hurt her knee, but I fixed it." Devil kept looking at Page, still lying motionless in the snow. "Does it hurt anywhere else?" He devoured her eyes.

Page tried not to look at him. She was mad. He'd broken her heart. She wouldn't let his hypnotic eyes deceive her once again.

"It hurts, but it's most likely just bruises." She tried to sit up, groaning in pain.

Sun began to laugh so loudly that snow from the tops of the mountains began to fall under the vibration of his voice. All three looked at him.

"Sorry," Sun said more seriously. "It was an epic fall." When he continued to laugh sincerely, Page couldn't help but laugh with him.

"Ow," she groaned, her entire body throbbing with pain.

"Probably enough skiing for today. I'll get a sled to take the victim home." Triumph quickly disappeared around the corner.

"You should start at the playground," Baphomet lectured.

"Didn't ask you." Page angrily looked at him.

"Don't say you're still going to ski!" Devil got up and shook the snow from his hair.

"Maybe I will. None of your business," Page said, crossing her arms in front of her.

"It's my business if you're going to hurt yourself and those around you," he insisted.

"You'd better watch how and where Strength skis." Page looked at Baphomet with a challenge.

"Don't be silly. I don't care about her." Devil approached Page a little closer, but Sun stopped him with one hand.

"Let's not argue on a sunny day like this." He looked at both of them intently. "Star will be glad if you visit us. Say, tomorrow after skiing?"

"With pleasure. By the way, I thought that the mountains might be the perfect location for a photo shoot of her card." Page began to shake the snow from her hair.

"Great! And here comes Triumph on the sled." Sun laughed again, looking at the impromptu coachman.

Triumph returned with a large sleigh covered with an animal fur blanket. Devil immediately bent down to carry her.

"Nonsense, I can walk myself," Page said, leaning away from him.

"Stop being so stubborn," Baphomet snapped before picking her up in his arms.

Knowing she could barely move, she sighed and obediently laced her arms around his neck. Her face was so close to Devil's skin that she involuntarily held her breath. It seemed to her that Baphomet was not breathing either. Ashes danced in his eyes.

"See you at the wedding," Triumph said with a broad smile once she was settled in the sleigh. They rushed away, leaving Devil and Sun looking after them.

It was decided that they would have dinner at home. Page's entire body was covered with bruises.

"Holy Sun, Page." Aqua neatly rubbed cream into Page's legs. "Good thing you didn't break your neck!"

"Given the speed with which she rushed down, I'm surprised that we got off with bruises only." Triumph stood at the window with a glass of champagne, looking for a suitable record.

"And what were the chances of crashing into Baphomet?" The Princess of Cups gazed at Page.

"The deck has a bad sense of humor." Page raised her eyebrows. "I think I've had enough skiing for this season."

"I'm afraid I must agree." Triumph laughed. "While we're skiing, you can go to the majors' spa. Wonderful place. Perfect to relax your muscles."

"Never heard of any spa for the majors before." Page took a glass of champagne from his hand.

"Because you weren't Empress before. I'll ask the driver to take you. You won't find it yourself."

FORTY-ONE

PAGE.

Page woke up the next morning, surprised to find that the bruises had completely disappeared. The frosty winter sun shone outside the window. She put on a blue oversized sweater and white leggings and went downstairs. Everyone was already awake and ready to ski.

"You'll like the spa, Page. My driver is already waiting." Triumph deftly buckled his ski boots.

"Thanks, Triumph. Do I need a swimsuit?" Page asked, impatiently pressing the buttons on the coffee machine. She desperately needed her caffeine.

"No, it's a small, cozy spa. No one will be there right now. Everything you need will be provided."

"Then I'll have my coffee and go right away. Have a nice ski day."

"Are you sure you don't want to join us for lunch? We'll be off piste, but we can ski down to see you." Aqua sounded a little guilty.

"Don't worry about me, Aqua. I promised to meet Star for lunch. Enjoy, and be careful."

Page kissed each one in turn and sat at the window

slowly drinking coffee, watching her distant friends. An hour later, she was standing at the entrance to the spa.

"Elevator is to the right, floor minus one." A handsome concierge smiled at Page, slightly lowering his eyes.

As soon as she got off the elevator, Page smelled the relaxing aroma of lavender and ylang-ylang in the air. A small fountain at the entrance created an atmosphere of bliss.

"Lady Page. Major Chariot told me that you were coming," the spa manager, Pablo, said, brushing a lock of curly blond hair from his face. "Inside, you will find everything you need: sauna sheets, towels, shampoos, creams, and aromatic oils. I recommend a dip in the spring with icy mountain water after the steam room. Ideal for the skin. Behind the pool is a lounge with a small library."

"Thanks a lot, Pablo." Page smiled peacefully.

"There's only one visitor in the spa besides you, so everything is at your personal disposal."

Page took an orange from a fruit plate and headed to the shower. Then she wrapped herself in a small linen sheet, entering the sauna, and poured water on the hot stones with a wooden ladle. Her skin, still cool from the shower, gently touched the sheet, slowly warming up from the hot air. Page peeled the orange, and savoring the taste, ate a juicy slice.

The door to the sauna opened, letting in the cool air from the outside. Page almost choked when she saw Baphomet enter, drops of water slowly rolling down his abs, only a small towel covering his body. His eyes shot to her, and she saw the hungry look in them. Her chest was only slightly covered with a cloth, and her hips were completely bare. Baphomet barely audibly growled and tightly closed the door before sitting next to her.

After a few seconds of silence, Page took a soundless breath. "You're not skiing today?" she whispered, avoiding his burning gaze.

"No, my muscles hurt. I fell yesterday." He slowly touched the wet hair stuck to her skin.

"Don't," Page whispered again, but couldn't make herself leave. "Not after you touched her."

"Will you please stop it!" Baphomet almost screamed. "I explained everything I could. Why do you always have to be so stubborn?"

"So, now it's *my* fault?" Page moved away a little, and the sheet fell down, exposing her breasts.

Devil looked at her body and growled.

"Better run away now," he hissed like a beast ready to pounce. "A few more seconds, and I'll lose all self-control."

Page knew she should leave, but she didn't move. In a few days, during the full blood moon, she would probably die. The air element had never manifested. She just wanted to feel him one more time, one last time.

"I want you. I won't be able to resist." Baphomet put his hand on her hip, slightly lifting the sheet.

Page froze for a second and said nothing, holding back her moans of pleasure from his intoxicating touch. She moved to the wall and opened her legs a little wider. Devil watched her every move and growled, deftly slipping his hand under the sheet. His burning lips brushed Page's hot skin.

"I would go crazy if you left." He pressed his lips against her neck, and Page moaned, wanting more of him. She quickly pulled off the towel and touched his hard flesh with her fingers. Baphomet moved closer, burning her body with kisses and whispering to her in his own language. Strained with desire, Page arched her back, pressing her lips against his.

"I can't wait any longer," she whispered breathlessly and wrapped her legs around him, pulling his body closer.

Devil entered her with a snarl as if mad, and Page screamed from the exquisite feeling of him inside her.

"Always fucking perfection." Baphomet worshiped her as he entered.

One thrust after another, deeper and deeper, faster and faster. Their bodies intertwined like a dark spell and its sorcerer.

"Don't stop." Page was on the edge, writhing like a snake under his strong body.

"I want you to be mine again," he begged.

Page bit his lip, and Baphomet snarled in pleasure.

"I will rip off the head of anyone who dares touch you," he growled, his eyes crazed.

"I am not your property," Page moaned to the rhythm of his thrusts.

As Devil pushed harder into her, Page's energy shattered into chips scattered into all corners of the room. He watched her hungrily, then yelled with his own release.

They lay wet and hot in silence. Baphomet slowly ran his fingers over her face. After some time, Page gathered her strength.

"I have to go," she whispered.

"I see." Devil did not move, still squeezing her in his arms.

"I'm afraid I can't forgive you." Page took a deep breath. "You broke my heart."

"Just trust me," Baphomet whispered hopefully and waved his hand. "Here are my ashes. Please try again."

"You know very well I'm not capable of reading memories."

"Just inhale. Keep them, please. Maybe one day."

Page hesitated for a moment, but took a deep breath, inhaling the ashes. Then she hurriedly got up and walked out. Her whole body was on fire.

She went to the spring and plunged headlong into the icy water, still thinking about Devil. She knew she had shown weakness, but it had felt so good, she couldn't do otherwise.

There was only one street in town with local boutiques and restaurants. Page saw Star sitting by the window in a small, cozy café and waved to her through the glass. Star smiled.

"Major Star." Page bowed as she approached the table.

"How formal," the major teased, looking like a full eclipse in the sky in a black fur coat with long, loose silver hair. "I've heard you don't ski."

"Ah." Page made an embarrassed face. "According to Baphomet, I pose a threat to the local community."

"He misses you." Star looked at Page knowingly.

"He ruined everything," Page said with a huff as she made herself comfortable by the window. "I don't understand what's going on in his twisted mind."

"Not everything is as it seems," the major muttered.

"Did he tell you anything?" Page blushed.

"Nothing. It's the same answer every time: 'I can't talk about it.'" Star shrugged. "But I assure you, he doesn't care about Strength, doesn't want to hear even a word about her."

Page was silent. She didn't want to talk about him anymore. After all, her life wasn't only about Baphomet.

She changed the topic. "Magus will fight me if I stay alive."

"From the moment you came into our lives, the Wheel of Fortune has been wound up again. The new energy is waking up, but changes are never peaceful."

"I guess not." Page smiled.

"You know, I've always admired Empress. You cleanse everything around like water. You ignite like fire. You ground like earth. You flow like air. All four Arcana in harmony."

"Star, I am far from that image," Page whispered.

"You're closer than you think." The major smiled gently.

FORTY-TWO

PAGE.

The next morning was a flurry of happy activity as they prepared for Aqua and Amador's wedding that afternoon.

When the time finally came, Page put on a dark blue velvet dress that hugged her figure so tightly, she could barely walk. Instead of a top, Hilda had sewn a corset made with pearls, starting from the throat as a choker and descending down in the shape of a peony flower, covering her chest and tightly fitting at the waist. Page wore several pearl rings over long velvet gloves.

"A dream comes true," Triumph said as she came down the steps. He stood dazzlingly handsome in a black tuxedo and gave her his hand.

"Thank you." Page blushed. "You're not bad yourself."

"Blue suits you." Triumph smiled.

"How dare you! According to Aqua, this color is called midnight." Page laughed.

The Temple of Cosmic Tarot Energy was located at the edge of the town. Today was a perfect sunny, frosty day for the wedding. As Page and Triumph got out of the car, bells were ringing. The workers were already arranging the benches for the guests, the florist carefully checking each orchid. High Priestess had personally offered to perform the union ceremony. Page studied the temple carefully. Stained-glass windows under strong sunlight created a mysterious atmosphere and reflected on the floor of the temple in different colors. Each window was dedicated to a different major. The majesty and beauty of the place took her breath away.

Page closed her eyes, inhaling sacred energy. She felt Baphomet's ashes move inside her. Suddenly, his memories flew in front of her eyes, but they were chaotic, and she couldn't catch anything—too fast, too many. For a second, she saw Strength's face and stopped the picture. She could see Baphomet holding Strength's hand as the smoke wrapped around them. Page breathed heavily, trying to see more, but the image was gone. She didn't have enough time to see the full picture. She stood in the silence for a while, trying to make sense of what she's seen before she finally came back to reality.

She shook her head. Today was Aqua's day.

She slowly walked to the altar to check if everything was in place. A huge book half the size of Page's body lay on a stand. Judging by the binding, it was at least several thousand years old. She carefully opened the manuscript, slowly turning page after page. It was the history of the tarot universe. Fool appeared first, then High Priestess, portrayed as a young girl. Page continued flipping through the manuscript. She paused carefully at the page where Fool was helping Abyss come out of a black hole, smoke curling around their clasped hands. Page's ears were ringing. It was the same smoke, the same hand gesture she'd just seen in Baphomet's memories. There was an inscription right at the bottom, but Page couldn't read the majors' language.

"Triumph, come here!" Her voice echoed through the temple.

A few minutes later, Triumph entered the hall, adjusting the bow tie around his neck and wiping red lipstick from his face.

"Some things never change. I see you've met the florist." Page laughed out loud. "If Aqua discovers a withered orchid, I will blame it on you without a twinge of conscience!"

"You wouldn't!" Triumph narrowed his eyes.

"Come here. What does this say?"

"Hmm…" The major bent slightly, trying to make out the words. "Tied deal."

"What does that mean?"

"I have no idea. I've never seen this image before." The major carefully examined the drawing. "I guess this is High Priestess's book. She's not famous for sharing of information with other majors. If you don't mind, I'll go back to the florist. Haven't finished yet." He smiled.

"But of course." Page burst out laughing, still smiling when she found herself alone again, aside from the workers carrying a huge blue bouquet.

"Future Empress, I see you are interested in my book," High Priestess said, suddenly standing behind Page.

Page jumped slightly, startled. "Sorry, I couldn't resist. This is the first time I've seen such an ancient thing."

"This book is as old as our tarot universe."

"What does 'tied deal' mean?" Page stammered, afraid of what she might hear next.

High Priestess stepped forward and looked at the

book. "It is interesting that you opened to this page." La Papesse was obviously trying to have a vision, because she rolled her eyes, and they turned black like a night sky enveloped in a purple sunset.

"What were Fool and Abyss doing?" Page insisted.

"Performing a tied deal." The major closed the manuscript. "It's an agreement that no one can know about. If one of the participants even indirectly vocalizes that a tied deal has been made, or relays some detail of it, even an insignificant one, they will be consumed by the black hole immediately."

Page no longer heard what High Priestess was saying. She remembered the dance with Baphomet and his words. *Just trust me. That's all I can say.*

Page began to hyperventilate, wondering what Baphomet could have made a deal about. It was important, and he wanted Page to see that memory. If what High Priestess was saying was true, though, she could never ask him.

"And here are the guests." Page heard the words of La Papesse as if from afar.

"I'm in charge of the guest book!" Page shook herself, remembering that it was Aqua's big day, and quickly ran down the stairs to the entrance. There was no use in worrying about Baphomet now.

Sun and Star arrived first.

"Empress! What a lovely day, isn't it?" Sun stood holding Star by the waist.

"It is! Would you like to write a few words for the newlyweds?" Page held out a pen to him.

"Of course." Sun was clearly enjoying the moment. "I haven't been to a wedding since…" He thought for a moment. "It was so long ago, I can't even remember."

"Where is Triumph?" Star looked around, waving softly to High Priestess.

"He's working with the florist." Page giggled.

"Typical Triumph." Star winked at her.

Aqua's father, the King of Cups, arrived next.

"Are you without a companion today?" Page smiled at him gently.

"Today, all my attention is for my Aqua." His eyes watered, and the king hurriedly took out a handkerchief.

The guests began to arrive all at once, and Page couldn't keep up by herself.

"What did I miss?" Triumph asked, clinging to her from behind.

"You took too long," she complained.

"You can't rush passion." He winked.

"Help me look for names on the guest list." Page handed the piece of paper to him.

"Say no more." Triumph pretended to take his responsibility seriously.

The hall quickly filled with guests. Amador entered through another entrance and took his place to the right of High Priestess.

"I'm afraid a friend is calling." Triumph quickly went to the groom.

Page put a check mark next to the guests' names. Almost everyone was already here.

"I'm surprised you're on time." Baphomet stood in the entrance, slowly studying Page.

"Devil." She raised an eyebrow at him. "I need to check if your name is on the list. Maybe you just decided to crash the wedding." The princess scanned the names. "No, no Devil on the list."

Baphomet burst into laughter. "Try 'Baphomet.'" He moved closer and inhaled the scent of her hair.

"Yes, Baphomet. Check." Page froze as he leaned toward her, unable to help being mesmerized by his all-consuming presence.

When he didn't move, instead looking at her curiously as if there were something inside her worth studying, she spoke. "Go, go. Aqua is almost here. Or do you wish to go down the aisle with her?" Page lightly touched his shoulder, and Baphomet dared to move closer.

"I would love to walk down the aisle with *you*." He sang the words like a mystical spell.

Page got lost in his bottomless eyes. Against all caution, she wanted to throw herself into his arms at that very moment. Maybe he hadn't betrayed her after all. The thought brought her heart back from the land of damned souls.

"The bride is here!" Triumph yelled from the other end of the temple.

Everyone present was staring at Page and Baphomet. Devil spread his wings, and in a split second, he was in his seat.

Aqua entered slowly. Black tears of happiness welled in Page's eyes at the sight of her friend. Aqua looked beautiful in a soft white silk dress with a barely noticeable tint of blue. A floor-length translucent veil studded with diamonds covered her delicate face.

"You look breathtaking," Page whispered as she walked around the bride, and bending over with difficulty, took the veil in her hands.

They walked slowly toward the altar. The bride took her place across from the groom, and Page stood just behind her, across from Triumph.

High Priestess slowly raised her hands and began to utter the words. "The deck has intertwined the paths of

Princess of Cups and Amador. By the power of the all-pervading and all-enveloping energy given to me, I bless this union."

High Priestess enveloped them from head to toe in smoke and laced their arms together. La Papesse then opened the page of her ancient book and slowly recited another spell.

"I pronounce you husband and wife. The groom may kiss the bride."

The guests clapped loudly, and Triumph began to whistle. Amador kissed his wife greedily and tenderly.

"Rings." High Priestess looked at Triumph.

"Oh, yes." Triumph quickly began to check the pockets of his jacket. "Found them." He pretended to wipe the sweat from his face and gave the rings to High Priestess.

They were two simple rings made from rose quartz: Lovers' gemstone. Aqua carefully put the ring on her husband's finger, and Amador in turn kissed her hand before putting on hers.

"Congratulations!" The guests rose from their chairs and threw petals of creamy orchids over the newlyweds.

While the guests took turns congratulating the couple, the workers quickly removed the chairs and set up tables for the upcoming banquet.

***

It was time for the first dance of Mr. and Mrs. Lovers. To Page's surprise, Baphomet got up from his table and went to the piano. Aqua and Amador went to the center of the hall and whirled to the gentle melody. All eyes were fixed on them, except for Page's; she couldn't tear her eyes away from Devil. He looked magnetic as hell in his matte-black tuxedo, his hair pulled back into a bun, his prehensile fingers playing chord after chord gently and beautifully. The way they glided over the keys reminded Page of how he touched her body, as if *she* were his instrument. When the dance ended and everyone clapped, Page caught his scorching gaze on her. Devil walked confidently over to the newlyweds' table.

"Princess of Cups, Amador, congratulations again. I am truly happy for you."

"Thank you, Baphomet. Sit down with us." Amador pushed back a chair. "Aqua, who did the seating arrangements for the guests? Having Devil at the same table with your father and the Queen of Wands is a very strange decision."

"Someone clearly has a grudge against you." Triumph laughed and looked at Page.

"I had nothing to do with it," Page answered defensively and blushed.

"What are your honeymoon plans?" Baphomet asked while Triumph poured champagne and handed him a glass.

"We're thinking of staying here a little longer after the guests leave." Aqua, full of happy euphoria, squeezed her husband's hand.

Seeing how happy her friend was, Page couldn't help but look at Baphomet. She noticed that next to his inverted pentagram, he wore her pendant, which she had returned to him. Devil caught her eye and involuntarily touched both pentagrams. At that moment, Triumph got up from his seat and asked for the attention of everyone present.

"Beloved friend and beautiful Princess of Cups, please accept my congratulations again. May your life be full of happiness, passion, and in the future, children's laughter." Triumph raised his glass.

A pause hung in the air for a moment. It was a direct challenge to the rules Abyss had put in place: the majors couldn't have children.

When the awkwardness stretched on, Page raised her glass, hoping to break the uncomfortable silence. "To Aqua and Amador!"

"Triumph, you stunned everyone present," Aqua scolded him.

"I was just speaking from the heart. By the way, who invited my ex?" Triumph stared intently at the far table.

"Amador asked me to give him an invitation." Baphomet slowly put a small spoon of caviar into his mouth, and Page riveted her gaze to his sensual lips.

"Which ex? You have many." Aqua demanded an explanation.

"Mort. Truth to be told, we parted with a huge scandal," Triumph explained, undressing the pale major with his eyes.

"Triumph, Mort's changed. I've told you. He really has," Baphomet insisted, looking at Triumph.

"He keeps looking at you, Triumph," Page whispered through her teeth, as if Mort could hear her.

"Maybe I should go say hello." Triumph took a sip of his champagne and went to another table.

After dinner, the newlyweds and guests went to the dance floor. Page continued to sit, looking around.

"You're not dancing today?" Baphomet approached her, wrapping her in the hypnotic notes of his baritone voice.

"I can barely move in this dress." She turned to him and smiled a little. "Either Hilda took my measurements incorrectly, or I've really gained weight."

"I assure you, it's the first option." Devil studied Page hungrily, and she flushed. "Come with me. We'll solve your problem."

"I hope your solution to the problem is not to undress me completely." Page looked playfully into his ashen eyes.

"I had a slightly different idea, but just say the words…" Baphomet's eyes lit up, and Page laughed.

He took her by the hand, helping her pass the entire hall. They went into a small room, where the remains of the flowers and all kinds of tools were stacked. There was too little space in the room, and Page clearly felt the heat of Baphomet's energy. Their bodies and souls reached out to each other like magnets.

"What are we looking for?" Page tried to look calm, though shivers went down her spine.

Baphomet did not answer immediately, staring at her lips for too long.

"They should have scissors in here somewhere… Ah, here they are! Don't move… The official part of the event is over, so now you can show up in a mini."

He sank down and slowly began to cut off her dress. Devil gently probed her round hips so as not to injure her. Page blushed, her breathing becoming even more erratic as Baphomet's rough palms inflamed her skin. When the major finished, he didn't rise. Instead, he pressed his head against her body and looked up at her hungrily. When she made a barely intelligible groan, Baphomet squeezed her delicate body.

"I miss you so much," he whispered, as if speaking the words to himself.

There was a knock on the door. Page jumped away from him, as far as the tiny room allowed. Hilda stuck her head inside.

"I'm sorry to interrupt. The bride's about to throw the bouquet." The woman glanced at Page's dress. "An interesting solution." She smiled slightly and closed the door.

Page headed outside, afraid that if she were left alone with Baphomet even a second longer, she would not come out of that room for a long time. She stopped at the very back of the room, still adjusting her dress, as Aqua readied herself to toss her bountiful bouquet of blue orchids. The bride threw the bouquet with such force that it flew high and sloshed right into Page's hands. As soon as Aqua turned around and saw it in her girlfriend's hands, she squealed in excitement, as if this really meant that Page would also get married soon.

"Let's dance, Page!" The Princess of Cups pulled her to the dance floor.

They danced holding hands, gradually forgetting everything, not even looking at the other guests. Page felt free and happy for the first time in a long time. The guests, as if infected by their carefree nature, all joined them on the dance floor.

"May I steal my wife?" Amador said, smiling at Page. Aqua's eyes brightened, and she gently clung to him.

Page walked over to her table. It was empty, and she grabbed a glass of champagne, looking around. Triumph and Baphomet were sitting with Mort, gesticulating as they discussed something heatedly. When slow music started playing, Devil came straight to Page.

"May I invite the beautiful Dempress to this dance?" The major gave Page his hand.

"Yes." She lowered her dress that was now obviously too short.

When they stood on the dance floor opposite each

other, Baphomet pulled her waist to him with a strong hand, as if wanting to feel all her fire. Page lifted her eyes and looked at him unashamedly.

"Isn't this too close? I'm afraid we won't be able to breathe." Her voice sounded low and inviting, even to her.

"I desperately need you even closer." Devil brushed her lips.

"I learned about a tied deal today. I'm guessing that's what's going on here," Page said softly after a silence. "I understand that you can't explain anything to me. But I need to know if you've been faithful to me."

"Page." Baphomet pulled her even closer. "You know me. Deep down, you should know if you can trust me."

Page looked into his eyes—hypnotic eyes that had bewitched her as soon as she dove into them for the first time at Gaia's fashion show. She remembered everything that she and Baphomet had been through during these months. And he always looked at her this way, with true devotion. Deep down, she knew he wouldn't hurt her—not on purpose.

Before the guests began to go home, it was time for the gifts. Sun and Devil dragged a huge round structure into the temple.

"Dear newlyweds, a small gift from Devil and me." Sun looked at Baphomet. "It is a portal through which the Princess of Cups can move from her husband's dimension to her own Arcana in a matter of a second, and of course, I have already signed, giving permission for Mrs. Lovers to freely move into the sixth dimension without hindrance."

Aqua threw herself on their necks, kissing Sun and Devil in turn. The couple opened the rest of their gifts, and after a while, the guests began to leave.

"Aqua, don't worry. I'll sort out the presents and close up everything here." Page literally pushed the bride out of the temple.

"Are you sure?" Aqua hesitated.

"Of course, it's your day and your night. I will not let you fill your head with the details or logistics. See you tomorrow."

The girlfriends hugged once again, and Page waved after her friends.

The empty temple under the moonlight looked mystical and a little frightening. In the deep silence, Page heard only the sound of her own high heels on the floor, as if she were the only one person left in the world. Suddenly, she heard footsteps behind her. She turned abruptly and held her breath.

"I thought you might need help." Baphomet slowly approached her.

"Didn't you leave with Sun and Star?"

"Sun advised me to give you more time. But I couldn't help myself. I want to be with you." He stared at Page as if waiting for the verdict in Judgment's dimension.

"Play me something while I organize the presents," Page whispered as Devil stopped beside her.

The major, without uttering a word, sat down at the piano, and the music, viscous like melted caramel, spilled into all the cracks of the temple.

Page slowly stacked the presents in a small room as Devil played the tune of his soul. Then she silently approached and stood next to him. Baphomet continued to play with one hand, and his left hand only slightly touched Page.

"I do know you," she whispered, as if singing along to the music.

Devil growled, grabbing her by the waist and lifting her on top of him. He deftly unzipped her dress and pulled the bodice down, hungrily circling her nipples with his tongue. She arched her back immediately, the sensation tugging at her center. Her hands went to the keys behind her to brace herself against his delicious torment, breaking the night's silence with incoherent chords.

Without warning, he pulled away from her and sat her on top of the piano.

"Your body drives me crazy," he said, his hands running down her until he found her clit. She cried out as he circled it with his fingers. His ashen eyes danced as he watched her. With a growl, he bent down, replacing his fingers with his mouth. His tongue swirled around her, and she grabbed his head, anchoring him to her as the flames built up inside her. She heated the space without even trying to hold back her moans and fire.

"I need you inside me," she whispered on a moan.

Devil's eyes burned as he rose and slowly entered her to the hilt. They both groaned at the feeling. Then Devil squeezed her hips as he thrust, hard and deep, into her. He kissed the soft skin of her neck, and Page again found herself in Devil's paradise, surrendering to him her energy without reserve. Baphomet lowered her to the floor and turned her back to him.

"Mine," he growled, his hands coming to either side of her hips before pounding into her again and again. In a fit of passion, he gathered her hair in his hands and pulled, arching her back. "Fucking perfection," he growled, and she could hear he was on the edge.

Devil took Page in his hands, spreading his wings wide, and flew up onto the piano, this time covering her completely. Page gently slid her fingers over his wings without even feeling that her whole body was mercilessly beating against the instrument's hard surface.

"Take your raw form," Page said, needing to be as close to him as possible.

The major did not argue. In an instant, horns and tail appeared, and she gazed at him in desire, moaning even harder. The half human, half creature slammed into her repeatedly, and Page felt her body about to burst with passion. In his raw form, Baphomet was even stronger. She was sure he would tear her apart, but it would be worth it if he did. She was on the verge.

"I want to taste you," Devil whispered, and Page noticed two fangs protruding from his mouth, like a vampire bat.

Baphomet lowered his mouth to her neck and growled so raw that for the first time, Page actually thought he might be the most dangerous creature in the world. Still, she had no fear of him, only intense desire. The second he tasted her blood, she screamed with pleasure as her entire body broke into a million exquisitely delicious pieces. She trembled all over, every inch of her bursting with euphoria.

"Fucking perfection," Page groaned.

Devil was trembling too. It seemed to Page that he had entered a trance. Only after a couple of minutes did he pull his fangs slowly out of her neck and look at her with bloodred eyes.

"I'm madly in love with you."

FORTY-THREE

BAPHOMET.

On the wedding day, Baphomet was deliberately late. He wanted to see Page alone, without Sun and Star. Her silhouette in a dark blue tight dress mesmerized him like whispers of the stars in the midnight sky.

Page playfully looked for his name on the list, and Devil inhaled a promise of forgiveness. *Did she see my memories?* Baphomet thought with hope. Her bottomless eyes again tenderly cleansed his ashes, and her voice, like a nymph's lullaby, lulled him into the realm of happiness.

Baphomet tried to act at ease during the banquet and give Page time, as Sun had advised him, but he felt her enticing gaze on him at all times. He was literally burning, filling the hall with his invisible ashes, wanting her, dreaming about her. When the guests left, he returned to the temple.

His siren stood next to the altar, sparkling and illuminating the deserted temple with her awakening immortal flame.

"I do know you," Page whispered, as if singing along to the music.

Their passion was all-consuming, capable of creating a new universe in a moment of euphoric explosion. When her sacred blood rushed through his veins like a stream and filled his heart, blossoming like peonies in spring, Devil entered a blissful trance.

Baphomet studied Page peacefully sleeping in the most impossible position across the bed and smiled tenderly. After everything—or rather, after thousands of years—the deck had finally created a new card just for him.

The frosty morning air penetrated the room, and Baphomet carefully covered Page with a soft down blanket. He went down to the kitchen, still savoring the magical blood of his siren on his lips.

"Baphomet, I think it's time for me to withdraw payment for the nights spent in my house—but of course, only if Page wakes up unsatisfied," Triumph teased, taking food out of the refrigerator.

Devil playfully raised an eyebrow.

"Right, then you can live here for free." Triumph tapped his friend on the shoulder.

"Who made a sacrifice? I woke up choking on the smell of blood." Mort frowned, and as if floating above the ground as he descended the stairs.

"Did he pay *his* rent?" Baphomet teased Triumph in return.

"He also stays for free." Triumph laughed.

"Ooh, Baphomet, I get it. The vampire bat finally had dinner." Mort stopped near Devil and inhaled the air.

"Turns out you're knowledgeable about blood. Surprising, considering the reality of your dimension." Baphomet smirked. "I hope everything is going according to plan regarding Magus."

"Yes." Mort rolled his eyes. "I gained the trust of this crazy guy. I hope you understand what a sacrifice this is for me. The evenings in his medieval castle in the company of his terrifying snakes are a whole different torture."

"I will make it up to you." Triumph smiled and placed an omelet in front of his date.

Devil felt a wicked, familiar aroma filling the air, and he turned to the stairs. His Dempress stood there, still sleepy and so inviting. Page was finally his. Baphomet had a feeling that the Wheel of Fortune had made its circle, connecting the beginning with the end, like the sun and moon connected during an eclipse.

FORTY-FOUR

PAGE.

Page woke up to the laughter of Triumph from the kitchen. She put on her silk robe and went downstairs without even combing her hair.

"And here is my she-Devil," Baphomet sang, giving her a tender kiss.

Only now did Page notice that Mort was sitting in the corner of the room while Triumph was preparing breakfast.

"Good morning," she muttered, with a glance at Death, wondering what he was doing here. Something about him unsettled her.

"Good morning," Mort echoed and moved to sit closer to Page. "It looks like the wedding night went off with a bang." He paused and looked at Page's neck. "For all of us."

Triumph laughed and put two plates of omelets on the table.

"Coffee and peanut butter toast coming right up!" Baphomet sang.

Page smiled at the thought that he remembered what she had always eaten for breakfast.

Someone knocked on the door.

"High Priestess, just in time for breakfast," Devil said with a blissful smile on his face. He was so radiant when he opened the door that La Papesse looked at him with surprise, and even a hint of condemnation.

"It is not fitting for Devil to be so happy," she said, her tone serious, though she winked at Page.

"Today, I'm the chef," Triumph reported playfully. "What does High Priestess eat for breakfast?"

"And why are you so fussy?" La Papesse was clearly disarmed by the atmosphere in the dining room. "Ah, hello again, Mort."

"Hello, elder." Mort's voice always sounded gloomy and intimidatingly calm.

"How are the newlyweds?" High Priestess looked at Page.

"They're still sleeping," she mumbled, her mouth full of peanut butter.

"I'm not talking about Aqua and Amador." La Papesse paused, glancing between her and Baphomet. "I'm talking about you and Devil."

"What do you mean?" Page stared at High Priestess in bewilderment.

"Oh, having sex in raw form with a blood sacrifice in the temple is the oldest marriage ritual in the universe. Didn't you know?"

Triumph began to laugh hysterically.

"What?!" Page's mouth dropped open in shock, and her eyes shot to Devil, who had frozen as he made coffee.

"Yes, yes, congratulations," High Priestess teased.

"I've never heard of this ritual," Page said, frowning at La Papesse.

"Such a marriage has been conducted only once

during the existence of our universe. You are the second."

"And who was the first?" Triumph was still laughing.

"Me," High Priestess said calmly. Everyone looked at her in surprise, clearly speechless.

"To whom?" Triumph asked in surprise.

"Everyone has their secrets. Plus, that was centuries ago. My husband and I have become too different." Her voice went out a little.

Shaking his head, Triumph walked over to Page. "Congratulations." He kissed her, and then patted Devil on the shoulder. "Well done."

Baphomet approached Page, then lifted her up in his arms. "I didn't know, but I'm over the moon," he whispered in her ear and looked into her eyes. "Do you regret it?"

"No," Page whispered back. "But I do expect a wedding ring."

Devil laughed and kissed her passionately. "My little devil and I accept your congratulations," he informed his friends officially.

"Are you engaged?!" Aqua shouted while standing on the steps, holding Amador by the hand.

"They got married yesterday," Triumph said casually, as if it were no big deal.

"What?!" Aqua and Amador asked in unison, to everyone's amusement.

Baphomet went to the gramophone and put on a record, then raised Page in his arms again as she wrapped her legs tightly around his waist.

"Newlywed dance," Devil whispered to Page with jubilation in his eyes and spun around the kitchen.

Triumph quickly took out champagne from the refrigerator, shook the bottle, and sprinkled them until the champagne ran out. Page burst into laughter. Mort chuckled as he chewed on his omelet, playfully looking at High Priestess, who rolled her eyes.

"Page, congratulations!" Aqua said, finally getting over her shock. "But I'm gonna need more details."

"We could go to my dimension right away and have a coronation with our small company present," Baphomet suggested and looked at High Priestess.

"I understand that transfer is on me." La Papesse raised an eyebrow. "Well, on such an occasion, I can break the rules a little."

"Let me at least put shoes on!" Aqua yelled in excitement.

Familiar smoke enveloped their bodies, and everyone present found themselves standing in Devil's throne room in a matter of seconds. Page got up on the pedestal in her long, half-open black silk robe, with disheveled hair and bare feet.

Baphomet, without taking his eyes off her, slowly knelt down on one knee. "My Dempress." He lowered his head like a knight swearing allegiance to his queen.

The ubiquitous Oliver quickly entered the hall, holding a crown on a small black pillow with an embroidered peony pattern. The guests stood behind Devil without saying a word. When Baphomet got up and took the crown in his hands, Page was able to see the details. It was made of hematite and was decorated with a set of twelve star-shaped stones of emerald and jade. The body of the crown was engraved with intertwining grapes and peonies. Spreading his wings, Devil flew up and slowly lowered the crown onto her head. When he returned to the floor, he knelt down again.

"The Wheel of Fortune has turned," High Priestess intoned, breaking the silence of the throne room.

Page quickly went down to the floor and threw herself into Baphomet's arms. "When did you make a crown for me?" she whispered.

"I ordered it the same day I saw you wearing a wreath of flowers in Amador's dimension."

"I love it … husband," Page whispered tenderly.

"Live here with me, as my wife, and as the mistress of all the damned souls and all the demons," Devil almost pleaded.

"Okay," Page answered immediately.

<hr>

The next morning, while Baphomet was still sleeping, Page received a letter. To be precise, she just found it on the pillow next to her head. Opening it with trembling hands, she immediately recognized her father's handwriting.

Daughter, your brother is missing. I received an anonymous letter saying that he is in danger. I was told to wait for further instructions and not to involve the majors. Otherwise, they will kill our prince. I'll be waiting for you in your mother's office. We have to save him.

For a moment, Page couldn't think straight. Something didn't add up… Nothing added up. Who could need something from her brother? Most likely, they needed something from her.

Page got dressed quickly and quietly, afraid to wake up Baphomet. He would never let her go there alone. She understood that she was probably going straight into a trap, but it didn't matter. Page had to save her brother. It wasn't his fight.

But she had to get past Iblis first. Baphomet had assigned him to guard her. Page put on a robe over her clothes, and opening the door, stuck her head out. The demon stood next to the entrance, blocking it like a stone wall.

"Iblis." Page pretended to yawn. "Please tell Oliver to make some coffee, I'll be down soon."

"I'm not a lady's maid," Iblis growled in displeasure.

"Please." Page folded her hands, begging.

"Fine." He snorted. "But don't go anywhere, Queen. Otherwise, the boss will kill me."

Without wasting a second, Page snuck outside, and taking Baphomet's chariot, flew away.

The door to the queen's office was open, and Page immediately saw her father. He looked devastated, walking from one corner of the room to another.

"Daughter, thank Sun you're here!" The King of Wands sounded on edge. "What should we do?"

Cold sweat ran down Page's body, and her mind raced.

"I think I know where we should start. Come." She tried to keep calm in front of her already worried father, but she could hear her own nerves making her voice tremble.

They went straight to Gaia's atelier. Page took a deep breath before opening the door. She didn't know what to expect.

"Gaia?" Page slowly entered. To her surprise, there was not a single living soul in the studio.

A rustle behind a curtain caught her attention, and Page slowly opened one of the fitting rooms. Gaia sat on the floor, a little disheveled, her whole body shaking like wet cloth in the wind. A new rush of worry filled Page, and she quickly knelt beside her friend and hugged her tightly.

"Gaia, are you okay? What's happened?" Horror gripped Page.

"Page…" Gaia struggled to talk.

"Yes, I'm here. Everything will be fine. What's happened?" Page carefully lifted Gaia in her arms and put her on a chair. To her surprise, it took no effort at all. She figured the Empress powers were coming into play, almost at full strength as the blood moon drew closer.

"You're strong," Gaia said, still trembling.

"What happened? Please, Gaia, tell us. I can help. Did Magus take him?"

"Justice." Gaia trembled again.

Page couldn't believe it. She'd thought her issues with the major of the eleventh dimension had been solved long ago.

"Justice? Are you sure?" Page asked again.

"I think she wants to get even with you." Gaia dove into Page's eyes with her gaze. "After all, she didn't get a chance to imprison you."

Page hadn't expected this from Justice. She thought she'd seen a desire for change in her. Apparently, she had been wrong.

"Can I have some water, for my nerves?" Gaia said, interrupting Page's thoughts.

The King of Wands quickly poured water from a decanter and gave a glass to Gaia.

"You should also drink, my daughter. You're so pale," her father insisted, handing Page a glass as well.

She nodded and drank her glass in one gulp while Gaia and her father just gazed at her.

"Did she say something? What exactly does she want?" Page asked impatiently, putting the glass down.

Before Gaia could answer, the room began to blur,

and Page struggled to keep from falling. She threw an inquiring glance at Gaia and then at her father. Gaia slowly stood over her as Page lost all feeling in her body and fell to the floor, her vision darkening at the edges.

"That's better." Page heard a cold voice above her as if in a befuddled fog.

"You'll finally be cured, my troubled daughter." The King of Wands' words were the last she heard before a dark nothingness took over.

FORTY-FIVE

PAGE.

Before opening her eyes, Page felt pain all over her body. Her cheek lay on something hard and cold. Chills coursed through her veins. She struggled to move. She noticed the brick floor and the thick bars, as if she were in a prison. Terror gripped her at the thought. Slowly, she pushed up to a seated position on the floor, leaning her back against the wall. Judging by the darkness, she was in some kind of damp dungeon, dimly lit by a single burning torch on the wall and a tiny window. She could hear the heavy breathing of an animal and saw two pairs of red eyes looking at her from the darkness. Page barely suppressed a scream of horror when the creatures moved closer to the bars. Two enormous demons, looking like they were made of volcanic lava, stared at her.

Just then, distant footsteps sounded from down the hall, and the demons stepped back.

"Princess of Wands, future Empress, Devil's lover. Welcome to my dimension." Magus smiled wryly, studying Page from head to toe, a thick snake wrapped around his neck.

"You won't get away with this!" Page blurted out, trying to stand. Her limbs felt like jelly.

"You should rethink your attitude. After all, you're at my mercy here. Your whole life is."

"You're more arrogant than I thought," she spat, looking at him with disdain.

"Quiet!" Magus clearly was not used to being disrespected.

"What do you want from me?"

"You're something of an unexplored phenomenon. Few people understand that Empress and Magician are actually very similar. Both majors are able to control all four elements. And even if you don't hold air, somehow, you subjugated the ashes."

"So, it's about power," she muttered.

"Clever girl." Magus tried to touch her hair, but Page moved back.

"What exactly do you want from me?" She met his gaze.

"Not much. To take your power while you're still mortal." Magician laughed sarcastically. "I'll be invincible. The primary major, like the good old days."

Page didn't really care about his motives now. She had to escape. She had to protect her family.

"And my brother? Did you hurt him?" The idea of this snake touching her brother had little flames dancing along her skin. She approached the bars, forcing the major to step back from her fire.

"I could care less about your insignificant brother. He played his part, thanks to your dear friend Gaia, and now he's useless. Same as your pathetic father."

"Don't you dare hurt them!" Page grabbed the bars, wishing they were Magus. They burned at her touch.

Hissing laughter pierced the space again, and Page's head started to hurt even more from the sound.

"They are safe and sound in a cell. I won't touch them— if you behave yourself." He gave her a considering look. "I need your blood, but you must give it to me willingly. If you don't, your father and your brother will meet … unfortunate ends."

Page felt the fire in her ice over. She might not be on the best terms with her father, but she couldn't let him and her brother die because of her.

"You can have it," Page whispered, barely audible.

"Nice doing business with you, Princess of Wands. I'll be back tomorrow. I'm afraid we need a little time to clear your blood of the potion. Your girlfriend insisted on a huge dose, just to be sure." With those words, Magus disappeared.

Several hours had passed before Page heard light footsteps approach her cell again.

"Page," Gaia said coldly, staying a safe distance away.

"Why, Gaia?" Page asked.

Anger seized her soul, and she tried to control herself in order not to frighten off the princess. She hoped to find out some information that might be helpful—something she could use to get out of here or get help.

"Was it really just because you were jealous?"

"Don't overestimate yourself." Gaia snorted. "The stakes are much higher."

Page shook her head. "Then what?"

"Try to watch your whole family die and stand by

helplessly with no powers whatsoever. The minors are nobody, insignificant. Magus promised me immortality, which I deserve. I'm pretty sure there was some mistake when the deck decided to manifest energies in you." Gaia smirked.

Page slowly moved closer, touching the cold iron grate with her face. "He's using you. Even High Priestess doesn't have that kind of power, let alone Magician."

"Not him, but his master does."

Page stumbled back in surprise. Gaia was knowingly working with Abyss too. "Do you think immortality is worth your soul?"

"Funny *you* should ask that. In a day, you could be reborn. And I would sooner or later die, like all the minors. But thanks to you, a much happier fate awaits me."

"Where are my brother and father?"

"Don't worry, they won't be touched. Magus doesn't need them, he assured me. He just used your father's obsession with changing you to his advantage, same as we used your brother."

"I wouldn't trust Magus blindly."

"Spare me your sermons," Gaia said dismissively and walked away.

Page slowly sank to the floor. The demons still guarded her. There was no chance she could get past them, even if she managed to break the bars.

"Magus said she must eat." The monster slipped a bowl of porridge into the cell, speaking to his partner in a language that she'd heard Devil speak before. To her surprise, she somehow understood it.

"Atal, did you see her fire?" The second demon stared at Page. "Not exactly the right energy for a future Empress."

"Shut up, Brutus. They might hear us," Atal warned him.

Page stayed up all night hoping her guards would fall sleep, but the red eyes looked at her without breaking away or even blinking. In the morning, one of the demons opened her cell.

"Magus is waiting for her at the top," Atal reported to his partner and grabbed Page by the hand.

"Careful," Page said in their language, and the demons looked at her as if she were from an undiscovered dimension.

"How do you know our language?"

"Devil will tear you apart." She hoped her words would scare them, but was disappointed when Atal answered without fear.

"He can try. We didn't bend the knee to Baphomet, or to anyone."

Brutus flung Page onto a huge wooden chair and chained her to it before Magician appeared in the room, followed by his entourage. She wasn't surprised to see Strength and Gaia, nor her chained father and brother, led by Emperor. But her heart sank when she saw black eyes lined with pencil. Mort, who had breakfasted with them only yesterday, followed Magician with his head bowed.

"Mort, Emperor, you are cowards." Page spat on the floor.

"Silence!" Magus's voice shook the space, but she only raised her head higher.

Magician walked over to his desk, opening a manuscript.

"I bet you don't give a damn about Triumph, and even less so about me." Page tried to look Mort in the eyes, but he avoided her gaze.

"Mort can be very convincing." Magus laughed without looking up from the manuscript, quickly collecting what he needed for the ritual.

"What about you, Emperor? Too afraid of Magus?" Anger took possession of her, and she wanted to burn the heads off each of those present.

"Nothing personal, Princess of Wands. I love order, laws. Your charade with Baphomet never pleased me." Emperor, as usual, remained calm and cool-headed.

"I might have expected this from Gaia, and you, Strength." Page looked at them disdainfully.

"I always get what I want. Baphomet will be mine in due time." Strength flared up and came close to Page.

"Not everything should be about him," Page answered calmly, and closing her eyes, she directed a strong stream of ash into the major's face.

Strength coughed, and in anger, released a wave of fire at Page's face. The flame washed over her, not leaving a mark.

"I *am* fire!" Page challenged the major.

"Stop it!" Magus threw a menacing look at Strength. "Almost done." He raised a small knife and cut his palm. Drops of blood slowly trickled down his hand into a sizzling vessel. He approached Page and whispered some kind of incantation in unison with the group.

"Drink." He put the vessel directly to Page's lips, and she smelled an iron swamp.

"Page, please drink. He's going to change you back to normal. You'll finally be one of us," the King of Wands begged.

"Don't you understand, Father? I'm tired of trying to fit in. I *like* who I am."

I like being different, she thought and looked at her father with pity.

"Drink," Magus commanded.

"Not before I know that my brother and father are safe," Page insisted.

"Mort, untie them." Magus waved at the major without even looking.

Mort obeyed silently.

"Brother…" Tears rolled down Page's face when she saw the bloody smudges and bruises on his hands.

"I'm fine, Page. I didn't know anything. I wasn't part of it." He looked at his chained sister, then at Gaia, and again at Page. "I'm sorry."

"You didn't do anything wrong." Page slurred the words, choking on tears. "Send him home. And my father."

"Only after the ritual. Your beloved is probably looking for you. We don't want uninvited guests," Magus hissed through his teeth.

"No." Page defiantly squeezed her lips, refusing to drink.

"Fine. Emperor will take them to his dimension for a few days before returning them home!" Magus almost yelled impatiently. "This will give us time."

"I will deliver them safe and sound, I give you my word." Emperor dragged both men along with him.

"How do I know you're not lying?" Page begged.

"Oh, Emperor never lies. His word is the law." Magus curved his lips ironically.

"It is true." Emperor bowed and walked away.

"Come on." The major of the first dimension

brought the cup with the potion to Page's lips again, resuming the spell.

Trying not to gag, she slowly drank sip after sip, emptying it all. As she swallowed the last drop, something began to move in her veins. Unbearable pain tore at her from the inside out, and she screamed, unable to endure it. Finally, a huge snake woven from water, fire, earth, and ashes crawled out of her body and swam smoothly toward Magician. Page hung in her chair weakly, bloody smudges covering her from the ordeal.

"Finally. Now her energy will be transferred to me." Magus raised his head high, looking at the snake with anticipation. It slowly approached him, and releasing its tongue, touched his skin, tasting and studying. As if drinking poison, the snake hissed, and in one second it returned to Page, entering back into her body. She screamed again, feeling as though it were going to tear her apart all over again. Red and hot with anger, Magus ran up to her and began to beat her face with all his strength. Hot pain burst through her, and blood ran down her cheeks.

"Did you drink my blood?" Distraught, Magus shouted, whipping her harder and harder. "Speak!"

Page laughed hysterically, almost fainting.

Let it all burn to ashes. I'd rather die than give him my power.

"Stop!" Mort yelled, and Magus turned to him, ready to kill.

"There must be another spell, another way to transfer the energy," Mort explained. "You need her alive."

Magician, without saying a word, ran up to a wall containing books and in a hurry began to mumble something to himself. "You're right. Where…?" The major hysterically pulled out one book after another and then threw them on the floor.

"Take her back to the cell," he said to the demons, looking at them with disgust. "And don't take your ugly eyes off her."

Atal tossed Page onto the icy floor and locked the cell. Even though she was exhausted, she rose to her feet, knowing this might be her last chance.

"Is serving such a major as Magician better than bending the knee to Devil?" Page tried to make eye contact with the more talkative of the two demons, Brutus.

"You're trying in vain, Empress. We were born from nothing in Abyss's dimension and became something after the war was won. Only nothingness can exist in a Blank Dimension, and we needed a home. Devil doesn't hold the energy we bow to," Atal said angrily.

"If you won't help me, then be prepared. Baphomet will find me, and when he does, there will be no mercy for anyone here," Page said, sincerely hoping it was true.

FORTY-SIX

PAGE.

Toward the evening, Atal pulled her out of the cell again.

"Come on, they're waiting for you. Dinnertime." He pushed Page forward, grabbing her with his hand.

A fire ignited where he touched her, and ashes poured out. The demon backed away coughing, staring at her in amazement.

"Don't you ever touch me," Page said in a commanding voice.

"I thought Empress was flowers and nectar, not ashes and weird fire." Atal exchanged a glance with his partner, but didn't dare touch her again.

Page was led into a large dining room. Magus had clearly remained in a previous century. His whole house and its decor resembled a medieval castle, as if Page had been transported a couple thousand years back. Wooden chandeliers with candles and thick curtains adorned the space, while the servants wore starched wigs. Page froze in place, looking at the round table. Magus sat at the head, pouring bloodred wine into a cut glass.

"Failed Empress! It's so nice of you to join us." Magician, as always, smiled unnaturally, and his snake, having slipped from his neck, crawled to Page's feet.

Afraid to move, she watched the snake warily. "Get your nasty pet away from me," Page demanded through gritted teeth.

"Indeed, Magus. Even I don't like to dine in its presence," Mort said casually, chewing on a huge piece of meat.

"How gentle you are." Magus snorted with displeasure, but waved his hand, and his pet disappeared into the next room. "Eat. We don't want you to starve to death ahead of time."

Page sat down in an empty chair near Mort and once again looked around at everyone present. "Do you think I can eat with my hands tied?" she said, glaring at her enemy, but he only smiled.

"Either that, or you'll be left without your last supper." Magus slowly poured himself more wine, studying her. "I need to complete the transfer before the full moon. Luckily, I found a new spell. I'm just waiting for the last ingredient. It should be here any minute," Magus said triumphantly. "Your beloved is probably trying in vain to find the gate of my dimension." He laughed.

"What a disgusting person you are," Page said, her anger flaring. The piece of meat in her hands caught fire. She quickly put the flame out with a few drops of black water.

"You've learned how to manage the energies quite well." Magus looked at Page with a little admiration. "Under different circumstances, you would be much more useful to me as an ally." He cast a dismissive glance at Strength and Gaia.

"Our dear Empress, as I understand it, you are ready to forgive Devil for anything, even cheating." Silent until now, Strength smiled angrily as she looked at Page, having emptied her glass of wine.

"Save your energy. I don't believe a word you say," Page answered calmly.

"And no wonder. Baphomet is the embodiment of deception." Strength laughed, a little hysterically.

"It's really pathetic how obsessed you are with him." Page was burning inside, but with all her might, she tried to stay confident—arrogant, even. "I've heard Gaia was promised immortality?" she asked and then looked at her girlfriend. Something in her had changed beyond recognition.

"You can't even keep your mouth shut!" Magus threw an angry look at the Princess of Pentacles as she lowered her eyes guiltily.

"You promised," she whispered, a little scared. "I can't die like my family did."

Magus rose from his chair, and waving his hand, looked slyly at Gaia. His snake slithered into the room and struck her. In a split second, it had left fangs marks on the body of the now lifeless girl. Page screamed in horror as black tears covered her entire face.

Gaia didn't deserve this! She was just confused! Page thought, and anger woke up in her like a dragon.

"I'll kill you!" she screamed.

At that moment, a young servant ran into the room, barely managing to breathe. "Master!" His voice was filled with dread. "We are under attack!"

"Baphomet?" Magus squeezed the glass of wine in his hand, and it shattered into pieces, bloody streams of merlot slowly flowing to the floor.

Page couldn't help but smile. Baphomet had come

for her, like she knew he would. She had to manifest the air. She had to face Magus. There was no other alternative.

"Mort, check where the hell the last ingredient is!" Magus screamed. "We only have an hour left before the full moon and before the gates will fall." Magician ran his fingers over his beard, obviously deep in thought. "Keep your lions at the ready, Strength."

"Devilish light soon will shine through your darkened dimension!" Page blurted out.

"Shut up!" Magus got up, slamming his hands on the table. He turned to the demons standing at the door. "If the gates start to fall, kill her." He looked again at Page. "I need your energy, but if I can't take it, you won't get it either."

FORTY-SEVEN

PAGE.

The demons approached Page, but did not dare to touch her. She slowly got up from the table and voluntarily followed them into her cell. She heard banging on the gates more and more clearly now as the smell of devilish smoke penetrated even into her almost windowless dungeon. She thought about Magus, who chose to act on his darkness. Devil was full of sins and addictions, yet he'd found his way to the light, even if it had taken him a long time. Why was she always so afraid of the darkness inside of her? If she wanted to be a true master of her soul, she must make her darkness fully dance with her light…

Page eyed the demons, knowing she had to do something. Baphomet was fighting for her; she couldn't just die in this swampy dungeon. Night was almost upon them, and she could see a vague full moon appearing in the smoky sky. The blood moon had a red glow of dusk and haze, just like her magic did. If Magus didn't kill her, this moon would. Page thought once again that she was a mistake in the deck, that she wasn't worthy.

Then, as if in a dream, she noticed a sharp knife in Atal's hand. He was about to open the door.

But someone was running down the stairs, and Atal stopped, waiting to see who it was.

When Mort appeared, he screamed out to the demons. "I command you not to harm her!"

Mort opened his palm to reveal a dark, sparkling powder, which he blew on Brutus and Atal.

"Fuck, it doesn't work on them!" Mort cursed, confused. "I'll have to fight!"

While Mort was buying her time, Page, with her last hope, climbed up the wall, trying to see the moon fully. She managed to catch one faint ray on her bloody face. It hit, blinding her completely. Her insides were being pulled, breaking all the bones and emptying the veins. She screamed at the unearthly pain. It grew to the point that she thought death would be a salvation. For a brief moment, it finally stopped, just to begin all over again. Now Page felt like she was being put back together. She collapsed to the floor, unable to endure the pain any longer.

Suddenly, peaceful silence covered her being. Raw, pure powers were surging through her empty veins in a way she had never felt before. Page felt connected to each element as if they were part of her. The air began to dance under her breath, under her command. She felt reborn.

Page calmly looked at the demons fighting Mort. She was connected to them too; she could hear their thoughts. She got up and felt something burst from her back. She turned slightly to see a pair of black wings open behind her, barely fitting in the space of the cell.

With one stroke of her wings, Page knocked out the portcullis and Mort, along with the demons, who were thrown back. They looked at her in horror and stupefaction. Ashes began to pour from her burning palms, enveloping the demons. Her wings wrapped around Atal's neck so tightly, he couldn't breathe. Page heard his thoughts: he planned to cut her wings with a knife.

"Your knife can't cut into my wings," she declared and saw shock on his face. "Kneel to your Dempress, and be spared." Her voice sounded low, shrouded in soot, tar, and darkness. She barely recognized it.

The demons, as if hypnotized, slowly lowered their heads. "Devil Empress," they said on a breath as they dropped to a knee.

With an admiring smile on his lips, and almost crazy with happiness, Mort stepped toward Page and hugged her. "Devil Empress. Finally!"

"Mort." Page narrowed her eyes. "You're a scamp!" She laughed, relieved that he was not a traitor after all.

Page stepped forward, ordering Brutus to gather the rest and bring them outside. Atal accompanied her upstairs.

As she beat her wings, destroying everything in her path, they silently entered the hall. Magus was standing ready for the battle next to his monstrous snake. Strength had also changed into her armor. Everyone turned to Page at the same time, frozen in surprise.

"Take Strength," Page said in Devil's language to Atal, knowing that no one else understood her.

The demon obeyed and headed toward Strength. She quickly took her raw form—a true lioness, powerful and magnificent, ready to fight.

"Mort, help him!" Page commanded.

The major of the first dimension was hers.

Magus walked to the door, and Page followed him. They entered a huge ballroom.

"Let's begin," Magician said, raising his hands.

With a gesture of his arms, a huge wave of air filled with fire, earth, and frozen water rushed toward Page. She quickly raised her hands too, throwing out the same wave, the color of a demon's soul. She spread her wings, rising up. Magus hissed, and his snake appeared, revealing its poisonous fangs. Page flapped her wings with all the immortal power she had. The snake was thrown back, hitting the wall with such a speed that it died in an instant.

Magus took advantage of the moment and conjured a tree branch. It wrapped around Page's leg, and she crashed to the floor. He ran up to her and grabbed her throat. He couldn't kill her, but he could strangle her until she lost her consciousness. She tried to break free. His long claws scratched her face, leaving burning scars. Page's body was burning with white flame, and she filled the room with black ashes. Magus started coughing, as if he were about to cough out all his organs. Seeing this, she released another wave, completely plunging the ballroom into an ashen fog. Magician looked at her with hatred.

"So be it," he said barely intelligibly, coughing. "The major born during the full blood moon can't have children," he said as smoke enveloped his body, and he disappeared.

Page sat in the empty room for a while. She couldn't help but remember Baphomet's wish about having children while in Amador's dimension. She didn't want to believe Magus, but tears of helplessness covered her face.

Mort ran into the room, bringing her back to reality. A happy smile shone on his pale face when he saw Page. "Thank Sun!" he yelled.

"Let's go home." She got up, touching the burning scars on her face.

Mort took her by the arm, returning to the other room, where Strength lay motionless on the floor.

"Take her with us," Page commanded Atal, flapping her wings.

When they exited the castle, Page saw an endless army of demons from the Blank Dimension. She could feel them, could hear their thoughts.

"Bow to the Dempress!" Brutus yelled.

Page rose a little above the ground and saluted her army, and the endless ocean of demons kneeled before her in unison.

She'd done it. She was worthy. All that had happened in her life had led her to this very moment. She was reborn not only as a major, but as a new tarot card in the deck: Dempress.

The iron gates, hot to the limit, melted and flowed down. The first dimension fell. Page immediately saw Devil hovering above the ground in his raw form, a flaming torch in his hand. Triumph, in his full armor, drove a chariot with sphinxes whose eyes burned like lasers. Page flapped her wings and flew toward Baphomet. He looked at her with relief, and without uttering a word, dug into her lips with a passionate kiss.

"My little devil. You have never been more beautiful," Baphomet whispered, overwhelmed with happiness.

"I'm not scared to be the Devil Empress, because I saw in you how graceful darkness can be."

"You are fucking perfection." Baphomet paused. "Magicians's territory is unexplored, and everything is shrouded in a tricky magic. It took me a long time to find the real gate from the thousands of constantly disappearing illusory ones. But the clues Mort had given me were enough. However I see you didn't waste any time getting a whole army yourself."

"They seem nice." Page smiled and looked at the demons still kneeling on one knee. "Let's go home," she said, wrapping her arms around him.

"Home," he repeated like an echo and ran his fingers over the scars on her face, which began to disappear instantly.

"Home!" Triumph commanded. "We deserve champagne!"

FORTY-EIGHT

PAGE.

igh Priestess was already standing at the gate of the fifteenth dimension, pacing back and forth and muttering something under her breath, when the chariot sank to the ground. She looked at the arrivals, dumbfounded, a smile touching her mysterious face. Page turned to Atal, who was holding Strength.

"Take her to the maze. And after, all of you deserve a feast." She smiled slightly at the huge creatures.

"Will do, Dempress." Atal bowed and hurried inside.

"You're a natural." Baphomet picked Page up and twirled her around.

"Welcome back," High Priestess said, studying Page carefully. "I will need to write the whole tale in my manuscript about Dempress rising." She looked at Page with a smile, and for the first time since they'd known each other, she hugged Page tightly. "After all, Baphomet's energy did change you by adding an extra element: ashes. Choosing him changed your fate forever."

"Who knows? Maybe I've had ashes in me since the beginning," she playfully suggested.

"Let's go inside. All this deception has made me hungry." Mort, without waiting for the rest of the group, quickly climbed the steps of the castle.

They gathered in the throne room, where Triumph was helping Oliver open a bottle of champagne.

"Think, Oliver. All the grapes go to waste," he tried to convince the servant. "You could supply me with grapes, and I would set up wine production. I am generously prepared to share the profits thirty-seventy. Seventy for me, of course."

"Our grapes are not for sale," Oliver said dryly.

"Leave poor Oliver alone." Page laughed, entering the hall after a quick shower, a tender smile touching her face as she looked at her friends.

"It's so nice to have you back, our Empress." Oliver beamed.

When she spread her wings, the servant knelt down on one knee, admiration in his eyes. "Devil Empress," he corrected.

Baphomet pulled Page toward him. "Can't wait to shower these wings with kisses," he whispered seductively, and Page was instantly covered with shivers of desire. "All of me is calling to taste you."

Page decided not to tell Baphomet about not being able to have children. Not today, at least.

"Thank Sun you're okay!" Aqua shouted as she and Amador entered the hall. "Page—wings?" She froze in place.

"Full of surprises, as always." Amador smiled.

"We also have news." Aqua mysteriously lowered her eyes.

"The Princess of Cups is pregnant." High Priestess

stepped forward a little. "Abyss won't allow it. I'm afraid a war is coming."

A pause hung in the air, like the silence on a battlefield before the signal to attack.

"Aqua, Amador, congratulations!" Page spun her girlfriend. "We won't let my nephew or niece get hurt."

"Both. It's twins, a boy and a girl." High Priestess gently placed her hand on the princess's belly, and Aqua shone with happiness. "Dempress is born, and the new flow of energy has begun. A new era awaits." La Papesse sounded ominous.

"I hope Aqua is not bearing demons?" Amador looked enquiringly at La Papesse.

"Maybe just little horns here, a little tail there," High Priestess teased, a smile playing at her lips.

"To the future!" Triumph raised his glass.

"Hopefully we have one," High Priestess whispered.

"As long as we're together." Triumph turned to La Papesse. "High Priestess, this celebration calls for a dance."

Everyone laughed.

ABOUT THE AUTHOR

Anastasiya Serada is an indie author publishing her debut novel, *Dempress*.

She writes immersive fantasy romance, pierced with lustful desires and eternal devotion.

For more information, please visit:
https://anastasiyaserada.com/

www.ingramcontent.com/pod-product-compliance
Lightning Source LLC
Chambersburg PA
CBHW022023310726